HEADED FOR HOME

USA TODAY BESTSELLING AUTHOR

HARLOE RAE

Headed for Home
Copyright © 2024 by Harloe Rae, LLC

Editor: Infinite Well
Cover designer: Harloe Rae
Cover model photographer: Wander Aguiar
Interior design: Champagne Book Design

NOVELS BY HARLOE RAE

Reclusive Standalones

Redefining Us

Forget You Not

#BitterSweetHeat Standalones

Gent

Miss

Lass

Silo Springs Standalones

Breaker

Keeper

Loner

Quad Pod Babe Squad Standalones

Leave Him Loved

Something Like Hate

There's Always Someday

Doing It Right

I'd Tap That (Knox Creek Standalones)

Wrong for You

Yours to Catch

Score on You

Headed for Home

Complete Standalones

Watch Me Follow

Ask Me Why

Left for Wild

Lost in Him

Mine For Yours

Screwed Up (part of the Bayside Heroes standalones)

This one is for my fellow cowgirls. We can stay on for a lot longer than eight seconds, but that doesn't mean we will. Unless the stud resembles Drake Granger. Giddy up!

To Pago and Leita—my horses, past and present. I finally found the courage to tell a bit of our story. Here's to riding off into the sunset.

PLAYLiST

"I Will Wait" | Mumford & Sons
"Wrong Ones" | Post Malone & Tim McGraw
"I Remember Everything" | Zach Bryan & Kacey Musgraves
"Rise Up" | Andrea Day
"Fix You" | Coldplay
"Cowgirls" | Morgan Wallen
"I'm Gonna Love You" | Cody Johnson & Carrie Underwood
"Worst Way" | Riley Green
"In the Stars" | Benson Boone
"All I Want" | Lauren Spencer Smith
"Fallin' In Love" | Post Malone
"Save a Horse" | Big & Rich
"Dream Big" | Ryan Shupe & The Rubberband

Listen on Spotify!

"Don't lose sight of the direction your heart is headed.
Mine is racing straight for home."
—Drake Granger

HEADED FOR HOME

PROLOGUE

Drake

Seventeen years ago…

STAY COOL, MAN. STAY. COOL.

The reminder has little to do with the stuffy temperature in this basement. Excitement spreads through me in a fiery rush. My gut clenches in an attempt to smother the blaze. I'm sweating like a… well, like a thirteen-year-old about to get his first kiss.

Plenty of seventh graders in my school have already achieved this milestone. Ten of us who haven't made a pact to get it done, which explains why I'm crouched on this cement floor waiting for my moment.

Boys occupy half the circle while the girls are arranged on the other. We considered a simple game of Spin the Bottle but determined that might lead to an uneven score. Instead, each girl is going to take a turn drawing a name from Steve's hat. It's a quick elimination process to pair us up. Or it will be once the girls start picking. They exchange glances, silently deciding who will do the honors.

"I'll go." The brave voice belongs to Cassidy Brooks.

Her tone is warmer than melted honey. A shiver traces the length of my spine as she scoots forward and puts her hand in the hat. She gives the folded scraps a stir before plucking one between her thumb and forefinger.

We watch as a collective whole while Cassidy sinks back onto her heels in our circle.

It's quiet enough to hear the paper crinkle in her grip. Our rowdy bunch hasn't been this focused since the day Principal Shaw announced the year-end field trip to Valley Fair. My pulse sprints into a gallop as she unfolds the square to reveal the lucky boy. I silently plead to anyone listening above that it's me.

Cassidy's green eyes widen and she lifts that shocked stare to my face. She licks her lips, gnawing on the bottom one. "I got Drake."

Our peers erupt into a chorus of gasps and whoops. I barely hear them over the rush of waves crashing in my ears. This is a dream come true. A blush blooms on Cassidy's face as if she agrees with me. The freckles spanning her cheeks and nose are highlighted by the burst of color. My mouth goes dry while I admire her beauty that's way out of my league.

Billy slaps my back, knocking me from the stupor. "What're you waiting for? Kiss her!"

A chant begins after that. While our friends repeatedly tell me to kiss her, I shuffle on my knees toward the middle. Cassidy follows my lead, and then puts her hands flat on the floor to bring us closer. Sunlight from the only window in this room streaks across her hair to turn the shade into rose gold. It complements the red flush staining her complexion. I have the urge to thread those strands through my fingers.

Damn, I need to get a grip or I'll never get my first kiss. Our audience is still urging me on in a relentless loop. Nerves clog my throat and I gulp at the restrictive force.

As if hearing my concern, Steve veers off script to hassle me. "Think you can last ten seconds, Granger?"

My gaze doesn't stray from Cassidy when I reply to him. "Only one way to find out."

I square my shoulders and mirror her table pose. Our lips are inches apart. That's my cue to take initiative and seal the deal.

Cassidy's mouth is soft and warm against mine. The slight contact is a surge of fire in my veins. It's hot but soothing. I almost groan, which would be mortifying. Instead, I swallow her gasp.

The previous chant is replaced with a countdown. My pulse thunders faster with each number they tick off to reach zero. I fight the instinct screaming at me to taste her. This is meant to be chaste and fast. On cue, the time is done.

Cassidy lingers for an extra second, but still pulls away too soon. I chase her retreat until awareness peels my eyelids open. My breathing is labored like I sprinted a mile in Mr. Owen's gym class. Warmth like a burst of sunshine bathes me when she smiles. My lopsided grin reflects her glee. But then our moment is swept aside by loud cheering from those eager for their turn.

Uncertainty pinches her expression as if she doubts my satisfaction. That couldn't be further from the truth. After our lip lock, one thing is certain.

I'm going to marry Cassidy Brooks someday.

CHAPTER ONE

Cassidy

Heat engulfs me as Dixon strips off his boxers to reveal a cock larger than anatomically correct. That bad boy is better suited as a baseball bat to wreck house, especially a flooded basement like mine. As if his massive girth isn't impressive enough, the man has several piercings studding his shaft. I've always wondered what that would feel like inside of me. Saliva pools in my mouth while nerves clench muscles that fear the approaching stretch.

I gulp and continue to stare shamelessly. "My vagina won't survive your dicking."

He smirks, revealing the pair of dimples that got me into this predicament. "Don't worry, my beauty. You'll take every inch and beg for more."

"I seriously doubt that." My intimate bits clamp in agreement.

"Spread wide and let me in." Dixon settles himself between my thighs.

His tip nudges my entrance. I suck in a stilted breath. It does little to prepare me as his pierced thickness invades—

Someone knocks into my shoulder, sending my phone flying into the air. The thrill of my saucy read fades with my terror at the unknown fate of my beloved device. But the person who rammed into me snatches the soaring object out of midair.

"Caught it." The masculine voice beams with pride.

I launch to my feet and whirl around to confront him, but immediately freeze. He seems just as shocked to be facing the distant past. Memories resurface while we continue our staring contest. The boy from my teenage fantasies has grown into a man so far out of my league I can't believe he's standing in this crowded coffee shop with me.

Our reunion was bound to happen eventually. It's just probability. There's a few thousand people in this community but it's still small compared to most. Thanks to the very active rumor mill, it's common knowledge that the former professional baseball player resides in Knox Creek. Drake Granger is a name frequently spouted around town, especially by beautiful bombshells in their early twenties with the freedom to dream big. Me on the other hand? I didn't dare to hope that our paths would cross again. Yet here we are.

"Cassidy Brooks," Drake breathes. His expression sobers suddenly. "Is it still Brooks?"

Whatever he says doesn't register. I'm too busy sipping on the erotic elixir of his voice. The gravelly tone is a promise to provide endless pleasure. A whimper trickles from my parted lips. I blame the lingering effects of the scene I was reading. Or maybe it's his eyes.

Their bottomless shade is the type of blue I could swim in until I forgot my own name Staring feels mandatory—and is most likely encouraged—which leads me to his full lips surrounded by dark stubble. I lower my gaze to his sculpted muscles barely concealed by a t-shirt, and immediately regret it. Now my fingers practically beg to stroke over those defined edges. And don't even get me started on the colorful tattoos that decorate both of his arms.

Drake looks like he just stepped off the set of a photo shoot advertising seduction while I'm not certain I combed my hair this morning. The wild mane could stop traffic. It's not like I anticipated him literally bumping into me. I inhale deeply, which is another mistake. He smells like the sex I've always dreamed of having.

Holy horse shit, hornball. Get ahold of yourself. He's just a guy.

My reaction is purely based on the fact that I spend most of my days surrounded by farm animals and children. Not to mention the few men I interact with regularly are more weathered than an antique saddle. It's humbling to admit I haven't kept the company of an attractive male since... I can't even remember when I stopped counting.

Drake clears his throat to knock me from that lost cause. An awkward minute has undoubtedly ticked by while I shamefully ogled him. Based on the curve of his smirk, he doesn't seem to mind the attention.

It's only then I recall he had said something that resembled a question. Maybe. One fact sticks out in the lustful fog my brain has become.

"You remember me?"

The notion is more presumptuous than I'd ever give myself credit for. I haven't seen Drake since we were teenagers. Not only that but he went on to become a famous athlete who's undoubtedly met more people than I can count.

His gaze heats on mine. "As if I'd ever forget my first kiss."

I feel my eyes bulge. "We were just kids."

"Doesn't make it any less meaningful." Drake's blatant interest roves over me. "So?"

"Buttons," I reply automatically.

"What?" His laugh is rich and bolder than the coffee aroma wafting around the cafe.

My cheeks get warm while fellow Bean Me Up patrons send us curious glances. "It's just this silly retort my grandma used to toss out whenever someone used 'so' as a full sentence." I chew on my bottom lip at his look of confusion. "Because you sew buttons on stuff..."

"Ah." He nods.

My face flames hotter. "Told you it was silly."

"I like it." Drake's shrug is carefree. "But what I'd like more is to know if your last name is still Brooks."

"Is that your not-so-subtle way of asking if I'm married?"

"Can you blame me? You look..." His throat works hard to finish the statement. "Better than faded memories."

"Should I take that as a compliment?"

His eyes remain glued on my curvy waist. "Definitely. Why didn't we ever date?"

I squint at him. "Probably because you transferred to Edina before ninth grade."

"Great decision for baseball," he muses. "Not so great for us."

"As if you have any regrets."

He's quiet for a pregnant pause. "Would you believe me if I said I think about you often?"

Flutters erupt in my stomach, but I can't allow myself to get swept away in a long-lost fantasy. "Probably not."

"It's true, Cassidy..."

"Brooks," I relent. "Never been married."

"Me either." Drake's voice is smoother than churned butter. "What brings you to Knox Creek?"

"I live here."

His jaw drops. "No shit? Since when?"

"A few years now." The reminder of what brought me here tightens my chest. I rub at the sore spot that will never fully heal.

Another curse comes from Drake to break apart the emotional turbulence. "And this is the first I'm seeing of you?"

His upset mirrors my wonder from earlier. We grew up not too far from Knox Creek but it's quite a coincidence we both relocated to this exact neck of the woods.

"I don't come to Main Street often. Greener Pastures keeps me very occupied."

"Your grandma's place?" His memory is impressive.

"Mimi left the stable to me after she..." A spiky lump forms in my throat. "My mom never loved horses the way her mother did. Dad couldn't care less. The property is mine now."

"Damn, I had no idea she passed." He scrubs the back of his neck. "I'm sorry."

I sniffle at the burn in my nose. "Thanks."

"Are you doing okay?"

My nod is too quick. "Yep, just fine."

The lingering grief is too much to unpack for a simple exchange. Blubbering in public is a real mood killer. My focus slides around the busy coffee shop to give me a moment to collect my thoughts. In this brief lapse, I realize nobody seems to notice or care that Drake Granger is in our presence. He fits right in, which isn't surprising in the least. But it does spark awareness and clarity.

Our reunion special distracted me from how this interaction started. Drake is still cradling my phone in his large palm as if it's precious. The sight provides a welcome reprieve from the heavy topic we'd just waded into.

His attention follows mine to where the device rests. A furrow creases his forehead before his brows take a hike to his hairline. It takes me several seconds to realize he's reading what's on my screen.

I gasp. "Hey! That's private."

"Fuck yeah it is." Glee is thick in his voice. "This is a dirty book, babe."

The nickname—regardless of how generic—spreads tingles through my lower belly. That desire is only spurred on by the context of our conversation and what he just read.

"There's nothing wrong with spicy romance," I defend.

"Couldn't agree more." His tone is raspy as he returns his focus to the open page on my screen.

"Give me that." I snatch my phone from his grip. "Nice catch, by the way."

"Kinda known for it. Couldn't let my record slip, even if I'm retired." He cocks his head while I tuck away the evidence. "That's pretty steamy stuff. Cassidy Brooks has a naughty streak. Who knew?"

I roll my eyes. "Quit overthinking it. I love to read when I have a moment to spare. Simple as that. It's a guilty pleasure and helps me unwind."

"Mhmm, I can see why." His timbre is still saturated in suggestive undertones.

"Must you make it sound so crude?"

"Not my fault this subject matter is so… titillating. Is there any other choice?"

"Nope, guess not." A huff escapes me, and I begin packing my things.

Drake clasps my elbow. "Hey, don't run off. I wasn't trying to make you uncomfortable."

I pause my retreat. "You didn't. I'm just tired of defending my books."

"Did you think I was being a judgmental dick?"

"It's fine. I'm used to it."

He blanches. "I sure hope not, or I'll be collecting their names."

I wave off his concern. "The only romance I can manage is fictional. It's why I'm perpetually single and prefer the company of horses."

"Well, that answers that." His comment doesn't make sense until I notice where his attention has swerved.

I inwardly groan at the shirt I'm wearing, not having the courage to glance down. But my avoidance doesn't erase the picture stamped across my chest. A cartoon kitten is meowing the words *One Whisker Short of Crazy Cat Lady*. It's comical, but slightly embarrassing in this instance.

"Give me a break. It's laundry day. Had I known a man who puts book boyfriends to shame would be here, I would've dressed the part."

A sly grin slants his lips. "And what part is that?"

"Uh…" Shit, I'm horribly out of practice. "Just something… more appropriate."

"Such as?"

I pull in a deep breath. Might as well step into character and make it worth his while. "Thigh-high boots, fishnet stockings, and a lace garter belt for starters, big daddy."

An obnoxious groan spills from him, paired with a full body shudder. His display snags the attention of several women sitting nearby. "Fuck, yeah. I'd love to see that."

My lashes flutter at an exaggerated speed. "In your dreams."

A dimple pops in his scruffy cheek. "Or you could let me lend a hand with your laundry."

"What does that have to do with anything?"

"I'll strip off your clothes and toss them in the washer before scrubbing you clean. Vigorously."

My mind whirls in a flustered spin cycle. "Oh, boy. Are you… coming onto me for real?"

"Coming onto me," he echoes like a breeze. "Um, yeah. I'd very much like to come all over you."

A low tune whistles from me. "You're really quick with the smutty banter, huh?"

His brows bounce. "Only with proper motivation."

"Good grief. Does this usually work for you?" I motion at him and his attempt at getting in my pants.

"You tell me."

"Yeah, no. We're not on equal playing fields. I'm going to leave before I make a fool of myself." My shoes squeak on the tiles as I begin a hasty backpedal.

Drake's large hand returns to my arm, his skin toasty against mine. "Whoa, whoa, Cass. What's the hurry?"

Other than him acting like we're fuck buddies after being reacquainted for five minutes? I knew him as a flirtatious boy, but this man is something else entirely. It's not entirely unexpected considering his career in the spotlight. That doesn't mean he should assume I'll become his latest conquest. Our previous connection is the only reason I'm still standing here.

A quick peek at my watch reveals that my precious free time has already dwindled to ten minutes. "I'm giving a lesson at one o'clock. My day is booked solid from there."

"How do I make an appointment?"

I quirk a disbelieving brow. "You want to ride a horse?"

"Or a very sassy redhead. Allow me to slide into this tight schedule of yours."

Hysterical laughter nearly bends me in half. This must be a joke. "Pass."

"What can I do to change your mind?"

"Nothing," I quip. "I'm not interested."

"That's a shame. We could recreate that scene you were reading, my beauty."

I huff at the familiar term of endearment. "Not funny."

"C'mon," he urges. "Let me be your Dixon."

My amusement fades. "You're serious?"

His smile is a slow upward stretch, like a gambler about to win the jackpot. "I'll help you unwind. Personally. Intimately. Carnally."

Neglected arousal attempts to cloud my better judgment and I almost agree. Resolve straightens my spine in the next instant. "I'm not going to sleep with you."

His eyes dance with humor. "You're totally thinking about it."

"I'm not." But I most definitely am. Most in my position would do the same.

Drake's expression turns almost sheepish. "Will you at least give me your number? I'll behave moving forward. For the most part. Promise." He releases a weighty exhale. "In all honesty, I'm not sure what came over me. There's just something about you that struck me deep, but I've clearly overstepped. Can I get another chance?"

For a blissful moment, I imagine doing just that. He'd call. We'd flirt. A passionate fling would kick off from there. It would be unforgettable and satisfying—but ultimately temporary.

That reminder bursts my bubble. Reality replaces wishful thinking. I'm not the type to do casual. Hell, I can't even fathom a quick bang to scratch an itch. My responsibilities are complicated and demanding.

A drawn-out sigh escapes me. "Unfortunately, my availability is very limited."

"Lucky for you, I'm wide open and very flexible."

I roll my lips between my teeth to trap a giggle. "It's probably best to appreciate this moment we were given and go our separate ways. We're obviously in the market for different things. I enjoyed bumping into you, though."

Drake chuckles. "Is that your attempt at letting me down gently?"

"Sure?"

"I do like to go down, but there's nothing gentle about my methods. More like thorough and complex." The determined charmer winks. "You'll learn that about me as we get to know each other better."

"But—"

He shakes his head to cut me off. "Just let it happen. What's meant to be will find a way, right?"

"If you say so."

"I do," he rasps.

"Um, okay. Until then, I guess." There's not much else to say. I have a sneaking suspicion that he's not the sort to surrender willingly.

As if to prove my point, Drake steps into my space until he's towering over me—but then smirks, those delicious dimples on full display. I feel my resolve crumbling in real time. "Same time tomorrow, beauty?"

CHAPTER TWO

Drake

THE PEN IN MY GRIP TAPS OUT AN AGITATED beat to match the restless energy inside of me. I can't stop picturing wild red hair, freckled cheeks, green eyes, and a blinding smile. The girl from my past has become the endgame I've been hoping to find. Sappy as fuck and I couldn't care less. Seeing Cassidy again after all these years feels like destiny. And it's about damn time.

Garrett and Ridge give me shit for picking the worst women to date. Those two can kick rocks, even if they're right. The guys I consider my best friends—not to mention business partners—are blissfully attached while I remain the last singleton standing. But I'm about to hit a home run and be out of this slump for good. I'll be relentless now that I know Cassidy is in Knox Creek. How I didn't notice her around town sooner remains a mystery.

Maybe the delay was for our benefit somehow. That's what I'm telling myself to avoid traveling down the road of missed opportunities. What matters is that we've been reunited and she's still Cassidy Brooks. It's a miracle she's never been married. Not sure how that's possible, but I have every intention of claiming her as mine. Once and for all.

Cassidy isn't planning to make that task easy for me if the past three days are any indication. If only I could casually bump into her again. That would save me the trouble of looking like a stalker. Or she might be flattered by unconventional methods of seeking her out.

I snort at my irrational logic. It's unlikely, considering she didn't return to Bean Me Up as requested. Two more failed attempts followed. Not that I expected her to drop into my lap. That visual earns a groan. My cock twitches as desire thrums through my veins. I recline in my seat to relieve the mounting pressure behind my fly.

"Hey, boss? Are you able to—?" Harper's voice cuts off abruptly as she appears in the doorway of the office. "Why are you smiling like that? You're supposed to be doing inventory, which you *hate*. I don't like that look of elation spread across your face." A thought seems to occur to her and she dry heaves. "Oh, gross. Please tell me I didn't interrupt you doing something unmentionable to yourself. At work, Drake? Really?"

I chuckle at the snarky blonde. She gives us endless piles of shit, but hiring her is one of the best decisions we've made for Roosters. Without her influence, our sports bar would be a total dive rather than a popular staple on Main Street.

"Can't I just be in a good mood?"

She scoffs, flipping her ponytail in the process. "Not with your track record."

My laughter booms across the small space. "That's harsh."

"But accurate," she chirps.

"What's up, Harps?"

"You tell me." She leans against the doorframe, abandoning the original reason for intruding on my so-called private moment.

"I wasn't doing anything."

"But you were thinking it. I'm a bit perved out."

"Shouldn't you be mixing a cocktail or stroking Jake's ego?"

Harper's eyes sparkle at the mention of her husband, but she's glaring at me in the next breath. "Shouldn't you be elbows deep in paperwork?"

"Already done, mama bear."

"Mhmm." She studies me under intense scrutiny until I'm ready to squirm in my chair. "Who snagged your attention this time?"

"Not sure what you mean," I deflect. Like hell am I going to reveal Cassidy's identity. The rumor mill will catch wind of my infatuation and news will spread faster than a fart in the breeze.

Harper frowns, something teetering on pity tightens her features. "Seriously, Drake. I hope she's decent. You've gotta stop picking bad apples."

I resume tapping my pen to drown out the reminder. "Does Sydney like ponies?"

She blinks. "Where did that come from?"

Purposeful deflection. Not that I'm admitting that either. "It's a simple question."

Air pushes through her pursed lips. "Does my daughter like ponies? Um, duh. What seven-year-old girl doesn't?"

The confirmation—no matter how

unnecessary—kicks my pulse into a jog. "How would she feel about a riding lesson?"

"She already does those."

"Really? Where?"

Harper stares at me for another lengthy delay. "Why are you asking?"

"I had a recommendation for you."

She nods but suspicion still puckers her forehead. "Well, we're pretty happy with Cassidy's methods. I'll let you know if that ever changes."

My grin returns with renewed excitement. "Cassidy Brooks? At Greener Pastures?"

"Uh, yeah?" The bartender straightens and crosses her arms. "This is getting creepy."

I pump my fist and forget about concealing my obsession. "When is Sydney's next lesson?"

Harper takes a noticeable step backward. "I'm beginning to think I shouldn't tell you."

"Why?"

"Would you like a mirror to see how you're chomping at the bit?"

"I'm hot to trot about horses." I neigh for dramatic effect.

She guffaws. "Or the redhead who owns the herd. Did she put those hearts in your eyes?"

I avert my gaze to hide the evidence, but it's too late to stop the loop from replaying her captivating features. *My beauty*. The nickname reminds me of the filthy excerpt Cassidy was reading, which reignites the lust in my veins. I snuff out the flames with a grunt before Harper reports me to her other bosses.

"Maybe," I grumble.

A hum scolds my evasive maneuver. "Maybe my ass. Either way, I approve."

My focus flings forward. "You do?"

"Sure, but how did you meet her? She rarely leaves her property from what I've heard."

"Well," I start but pause while deciding how much to actually reveal. "Cassidy and I went to middle school together. Hadn't seen her since, but we just bumped into each other at Bean Me Up. Got to talking and… yeah."

Her jaw hangs open. "Oh. My. Gosh. That's too freaking perfect. Why don't you just text her?"

I scrub over my face. "She told me she's not interested, but mutual attraction and chemistry like ours can't be faked. I've thought about her a lot over the years, which might sound crazy, but I can't stop. Maybe that's why my other relationships failed. Every other woman falls short of her and what's meant to be for us."

Harper blinks quickly as she digests my romantic mush. "She's the one, huh?"

"I think so. Actually, I know without a doubt. Right here." I clutch the fabric over my heart. "We're unfinished, but I'm going to change that."

"Oh, this is so perfect. I can tell you're super smitten and already halfway in love. It's one of my many talents. Look at Ridge and Callie. Totally called it."

I grunt. "Anybody with decent vision could see their happily ever after from a mile away."

"Mhmm, you're right. Ridge wouldn't have it any other way. But how about Garrett and Grace? I could take credit for them."

"That was a group effort," I correct.

"Whatever. Just don't fuck it up."

"Not planning on it," I grumble.

She pauses, that shrewd focus pinned on me. "Horses are your point of entry, huh? Have you ever been around them?"

"Just with Cassidy when we were kids. It'll be a cinch."

Harper laughs. "Your confidence is adorable."

"I've thought this through. Mostly. There's nothing she loves more. They go together as a package deal." I twine my fingers together in a unified formation. "Figured there's no better place to start than getting acquainted with the furry beasts."

"Calling them that will go over really well." She clucks her tongue before waving a hand in a dismissive gesture. "It doesn't matter. I'm not going to involve my kid in your latest… romantic exploits."

Can't really say I blame her but this isn't a random date I shouldn't have gone on. "I just want to tag along. No funny business."

"That's doubtful. Go on your own, weirdo. It will look super suspect if you randomly show up with us. Besides, Sydney doesn't have a lesson until Monday. Can you wait that long?"

That's almost a week away, which feels like an eternity. Desperation has already crawled under my skin and it's only a matter of time until drastic measures seep out. "Won't it be more strange if I just stop by?"

She shrugs. "Boarders come and go as they please. Just act like you belong."

"But I don't."

"Says who? You've taken on a very sudden interest in horses. Cassidy has at least a dozen to choose from, not including her fine hindquarters. Might as well toss yourself in the arena."

I rub my chin at the double meaning. "Yeah. Okay."

"Great. Glad we settled that." Harper brushes invisible crumbs from her palms. "The toilet in the men's room is clogged. Garrett said it's your turn."

A groan tumbles from me. "Of course he did."

"He's slinging drinks while you're in here fantasizing about a cowgirl riding you. Get plunging, boss." She mimics the action.

But I barely hear her after the explicit scene she paints. Down the drain and into the gutter my thoughts swirl.

"Hey, Harps. You've been gone forever. Is Drake getting off his—?"

"Yeah, yeah," I bellow to my so-called friend who put me on poop duty. "I've got this shit."

CHAPTER THREE

Cassidy

I SHIELD MY EYES AGAINST THE SUMMER SUN AND watch the young rider ease her horse to a standstill in the center of the outdoor ring. "Great job today, kiddo. You're a fast learner."

Polly beams from astride her trusty steed. "Thanks, Miss Cassidy. It's 'cause you're the best instructor ever."

My smile mirrors hers as I approach to assist in her dismount. The horse stands patiently, more than accustomed to this process. "That's a rave review. Be sure to tell your friends."

Her boots hit the dirt in a puff. "Uh-huh, I talk about Fire Engine nonstop. They're super jealous I get to ride such a big horse."

"And he's such a good boy." I pat the Appaloosa gelding on his spotted shoulder.

This guy is practically bombproof and the most reliable babysitter I own. Every beginner starts with him. Fire is responsible for carrying the weight of many who became professional equestrians.

"So sweaty." Polly rubs the gelding's neck under his mane where he's wet. She flips the thick hair over to the other side and blows on the slick area.

"He's not the only one." I fan my face, which does little to cool me off. "It's a scorcher."

Her nose wrinkles. "Huh?"

"It's a very hot day," I rephrase.

Even though most of the arena is shaded by trees, the July heat is beating down on us in relentless rays. My skin is slick and I haven't moved much in the last thirty minutes. Fire hardly got a workout himself but that's on purpose. I schedule the low impact lessons on afternoons like this, if I even do them at all.

"Should I walk him around?" Polly slides the reins from over Fire's head and holds them in a tight grip as if he's an unpredictable weanling.

"Great idea, kiddo. Take off your helmet and give yourself a breather too."

"I almost forgot." The little girl giggles while unclasping the strap under her chin. "Much better."

She plops the sparkly dome on a nearby post before guiding her mount around the edge of the ring. I watch their lazy gait until a dust cloud coming from the driveway steals my attention. An unfamiliar truck winds along the gravel path. My eyes strain to identify who's behind the wheel but they're too far away yet. A sinking feeling drops in my stomach that it might be another lackey from Sutherland Homes. The construction company has been hounding me for months.

Polly and Fire finish their lap, pausing beside me. "Is that good?"

I check the gelding's slick chest to make sure he's not too warm. There's foam forming under his breast collar but he's good to go. "Would you like to hose him down? He loves getting pampered after a ride."

"Oh, yes! Please, please," she whines.

"You've got it." I grab the walkie from where it's clipped to my pocket. "Hey, Anna?"

Static crackles through the speaker before the boarder who assists with chores answers. "What's up, Cass?"

"Can you please come get Fire and rinse him off? Polly is going to lend a hand."

"Absolutely. Be right there," Anna replies.

After the trio disappears into the barn, I refocus on the approaching vehicle. The Ford Raptor handles the turns like a new toy. Wealth gleams in the black paint and chrome accents to confirm my earlier assumptions. I square my shoulders and prepare for another confrontation with the rich pricks.

But then the man's face comes into view. He's wearing a hat and his eyes are hidden behind a pair of aviators but I imagine the baby blues crinkling in the corners. Relief streams from me in a long exhale.

I exit the arena to greet my unexpected guest, and I'm not alone in that feat. Our two Australian Shepherds wake from their snooze on the porch to hop on the welcome wagon. Their chorus of barks pierce the humid air as Drake parks his truck in front of the garage. He steps out and strides to where I'm leaning against the fence. Or at least he attempts to.

The dogs weave between his legs, nearly tripping him with every pass. He leans down to pet them, which only doubles their efforts. I whistle and the pair quickly backs off to give him space.

"Appreciate that. Wasn't sure I'd ever reach you," Drake laughs.

"Yet here you are." I take a moment to admire how his faded jeans are sculpted to his ass.

He returns the favor, his shielded gaze roaming over me in a languid perusal. "You look… hot."

"Thanks for noticing." I pluck at my tank top that clings to me like an extra layer of skin.

"Nice boots."

I glance at the worn leather caked in shavings and hay. The grime matches the stains on my denim cutoffs. A pat to my head bobbles the oversized bun keeping my hair tied up. Once again, my appearance leaves much to be desired.

"Dressed to impress," I joke. "You caught me in the middle of lessons and mucking out stalls."

"What's that?"

"Shoveling shit into a wheelbarrow."

"That sounds… thrilling." Drake adjusts his baseball hat to sit lower. "I had to plunge the toilet yesterday."

I twist my lips to one side. "That's almost the same thing."

"It's really not," he chuckles and scrubs the back of his neck. "Don't know why I brought it up."

A nervous energy surrounds him, which is endearing. I find myself smiling at the idea that this sports icon could be a bumbling goof around me. It must be the weather.

"So," I prod.

"Buttons."

"Good one," I quip. "But what brings the great Drake Granger to Greener Pastures?"

"You." His mirrored lenses reflect my shock.

I avert my gaze and kick at a stray pebble. "What about me?"

"Everything."

Which is too farfetched to believe. "It's the smell, huh? You've missed the scent of manure and farm animals. Feel free to stop by whenever you need a whiff."

Drake steps closer and breathes deep. "Careful, beauty. With an open invitation like that, I might never leave."

An ache rooted in loneliness makes it difficult to swallow. My gaze catches on his truck. "What're you hauling with that horsepower?"

He quirks his mouth at my deflection. "A boat."

"Why am I not surprised?"

"I'll take you for a spin on the lake. Just say the word."

A moan almost slips free at the thought of dipping under the cool surface for a reprieve. But that's a slippery slope, especially when referring to Drake's abs while wet. "Want to learn how to ride a horse? I can saddle up one of the green broke colts for you. Doesn't matter which one. They all need to get their bucks out. Western okay?"

"Maybe someday. We don't need to rush into anything."

My grin spreads at the uncertainty in his voice. "Slow and steady it is then."

Drake whips off his sunglasses to compel me with an unwavering stare. "Still can't believe you were under my nose this entire time."

"Just a few years," I argue. "And not that close. I'm at least ten miles from Main Street. To be honest, I drive into Moose River more than Knox Creek."

He stumbles backward, clutching his chest. "You're cheating on me already?"

I roll my eyes, but a giggle squeaks out to betray me. "That's where the feed store is. If Knox Creek gets a Spikes or Tractor Supply, be sure to tell me right away."

"Yeah, I'll keep you faithful." His assessing gaze shifts to study the place I call home. "Speaking of dependable, the house looks the same."

I follow his stare to the log cabin design that's stood the test of time. The rustic style has always made me feel like I belong. And now that my mind is wandering, I absently wonder what Drake thinks of Greener Pastures.

One hundred acres sprawl in slopes and valleys around us. There's a stream that cuts across the back forty where we swim with the horses. The grassy pastures are a sight to cherish. It's been almost two decades since his last visit. To my knowledge at least. He was only here once or twice along with our other friends during summer break. I'm curious if he notices the differences, much like those between us.

"The barn is bigger," he notes randomly as if answering my unspoken musings.

I swing my attention to the large building that stretches into an L-shape. "A storm wrecked the original. Mimi was able to build the stable of her dreams with the insurance money."

"Do you love it?" His voice is soft.

"Of course. Horses are my passion. That's why she left Greener Pastures to me. My parents and brother couldn't care less. To have my own barn is a dream." I gulp around the grief forming in my throat. "But I'd love it more if she was still here with us."

"She's always with you," he says gently.

I nod but the motion is jerky. "Yeah, I know. It's just... hard."

There's a sheen misting his blue eyes. "Let me know if there's anything I can do to make it easier for you. I'll share the load, beauty. You don't have to struggle alone."

"Thanks, but I have help." My sniffle ends on a snort. "And trust me, you don't want my baggage."

"I think that's for me to decide." This man. He doesn't have a clue what he's offering.

"Well, you know where to find me."

A rumble rolls from his broad chest. "Are you going to give me a tour?"

As if volunteering, the dogs return to his side. Yips and whines reveal their excitement. Their tails whip against the ground as they scoot forward, eager to be useful.

"You shouldn't disappoint them," I say.

"Hello again," he coos and crouches to their level. "What're their names?"

"Chester and Cheeto."

Laughter shakes his entire upper body. "How clever."

"Just wait until you meet Billy and Gruff."

Drake rises to his feet. "Who are they?"

"Our goats."

His straight teeth sparkle, framed by a wide smile. "Are you responsible for naming them?"

"Nope. That credit goes to my daughter."

He freezes and holds the unnaturally still position for several seconds. "You have a kid?"

"Two actually. They're twins." I flutter my lashes at his dubious expression. "Deal breaker?"

Shock melts into happiness. The joy illuminating his features is nearly blinding. "Quite the opposite. Why didn't you tell me you have children?"

"You didn't ask," I reply slowly.

"Well, this is fantastic. I love kids." His voice is starting to remind me of Blippi, which I recognize from being forced to watch entirely too many episodes.

I pop my lips. "You're straddling a fine line into unlikely territory."

"What? Why?"

"If you have to ask..."

He waves off my unsaid meaning. "It's not farfetched unless you make it that way."

"Are you sure about that?" I roll my lips between my teeth to stifle a laugh.

"I've always wanted kids. I'll be the coolest stepdad ever." His claim threatens to choke me.

"Drake, just no. Stop talking," I wheeze.

He does, but only because his attention diverts to the little boy exiting the barn. My son skips toward us as if summoned. Drake stares at him in awe, like this is the moment he's been preparing for his entire life. The gift he's never received is suddenly within reach.

"Don't be creepy," I mumble.

"Shit, sorry. It's just that I see myself as a family man. I'm ready to be a father, but it hasn't happened." He clears his throat and stands straight.

"Do you usually tell women this straight from the gate?"

A blush stains his cheeks and I almost swoon. "No, this is a new development."

"Ah." I bob my head, the mystery of his single status still evading me. "Maybe switch up the strategy from now on. Play it cool on the 'desperate to be a daddy' speech until things are more serious, huh?" As if I'm qualified to give dating advice.

"The past is irrelevant." He swats behind him to chase off the memories. "I'm concentrated on the future standing in front of me."

My entire body flushes. "Uh-huh, yeah. You're ready to settle down and have a family, but—"

"Exactly. Glad we're on the same page. I already knew you were the one for me, but this is just... better than my imagination running wild." He wags his eyebrows.

I hold up a palm. "Oh, no. Nope. We barely know each other and you're moving at a speed I can't follow."

He smirks. "I'm not afraid to fight for what I want."

"No fighting necessary," I argue. "You're looking to be a baby daddy—"

"Only if those babies are yours too," he cuts in.

My emotions run in separate directions, ready to split me apart. "Let's just pump the brakes."

The time for smacking him with a dose of clarity ends when my kiddo cuddles against me. "Hi, Mommy."

"Hey, monkey moo. Where's your sister?"

"She's teaching the kittens tricks," he explains.

"And how's that going for her?"

"Not well. They won't sit or roll over." His expression turns solemn on his twin's behalf.

"Bummer." I snap my fingers.

A sideways glance finds Drake practically vibrating in place. Freaking goofball. I've never met a guy this excited to meet a child that didn't belong behind bars. Maybe I should be more concerned, but my heart clenches at his eager expression. This man is too genuine to have a predatory bone in his body.

He's been patiently waiting for his intro, but my tongue ties over what to call him. Hesitation must pinch on my face because he takes the opportunity to let his personality shine.

Drake squats. "Hey, dude. It's nice to meet you."

My son squints at the proffered high-five, making no move to accept the gesture. "Who are you?"

I glance at Drake, allowing him to fill in the gap. It'll be entertaining to hear how he labels us when he's ready to race down the aisle.

The guy doesn't skip a beat. "I'm Drake. Your mom and I go way back. We're old friends."

The suspicious kiddo narrows his eyes further. "You don't look very old."

Drake chuckles. "What I meant is that we've known each other a long time."

He doesn't appear convinced. "My mom doesn't have many friends."

"Ouch," I complain.

My son gasps. "Did you hurt yourself?"

"You hurt my feelings. I have plenty of friends," I tell him.

Drake cups a hand around one side of his mouth to aim a stage-whisper at the little boy. "She's sensitive about her social life."

His freckled nose crinkles. "What's sensateve mean?"

The charmer rubs his stubbled chin. "It's like being soft or delicate. Touchy. We need to be really nice to your mom or she gets sad."

A shrill giggle rips from my sweet boy. "Uh-huh. Mommy has lotsa emotionals."

"And that's not a bad thing. It's good to express ourselves," Drake boasts.

My son's expression screws into a twist. "Um, okay."

"What's your name, big guy?"

The little kid puffs out his chest. "Charlie like my Grandpa Charles."

"Awesome!" My old friend holds up his palm again.

Charlie lunges to complete the high-five. "You're kinda cool, Rake."

I snort a laugh. "Totally tracks."

Drake ignores me, too focused on his new bestie. "How old are you, buddy?"

"This many!" He sticks out his hand.

"Wow, that's a lot of fingers."

"You've gotta count," my son insists.

Drake pauses, mulling over the answer. "Five? Is that right?"

Charlie is nodding. "Yes! Good job."

"Thanks. That was a tough one." He wipes fake sweat off the brim of his hat.

"Kenzie is five too. We're twins. That means we

were born at the same time. But guess what? I'm older. Mommy told me."

"Just by a few minutes," I interject.

"Whatever that means." He shrugs his skinny shoulders.

"All that matters is you're the big brother. They're the best."

Charlie hops on the balls of his feet. "Are you a big brother too?"

"Sure am." Pride shines in his response.

"Ohhhh, you got tattoos," my son blurts.

Drake straightens his arms for inspection. "Quite a few."

"Sooo many colors. Mommy, look!" Charlie tugs on my shirt. "He's got a baseball right there. You looooove baseball."

"Is that so?" Humor struts in Drake's gaze.

"I've watched a game or two," I deflect.

My kiddo scoffs. "She cheers super duper loud for the Mustangs. That's her most favorite team. I think it's 'cause she loves horses."

"Interesting," Drake murmurs.

I cringe at the sky, searching for a cloud or an escape from this conversation. "Beautiful day."

As if suddenly recalling an urgent issue, Charlie goes still and widens his eyes. "I've gotta go pet my bunny."

He spins on his heel and dashes off without further explanation. I smile at his retreating form. Meanwhile, a gritty chuckle tumbles from the man beside me.

Drake returns to his full height, pinning me with that addictive stare. "The Mustangs, huh?"

I shrug but can't escape his notice. "They're our home team."

"Is that the only reason?"

"Hush," I mutter.

"Well, well. You watched me play." His giddy tone is more appropriate for winning the lottery.

"You just happened to be on the Mustangs."

"Do you have my jersey?"

"No!" I wince at my sharp voice and how it sounds. "I mean, not a chance. I'm more of a Peterson fan."

Drake hoots. "Damn, woman. That's a straight shot to the junk."

"You asked."

"For the truth," he purrs.

I'm saved from the interrogation by a buzz in my back pocket. A glance at the caller ID sours my mood faster than a bad case of hemorrhoids. I dodged them earlier thanks to mistaken identity. Twice is asking too much apparently. A huff spews from me while I chomp on a foul curse. My finger stabs at the ignore button in rapid succession.

"Hey, killer. Easy." Drake circles my wrist to stop the attack on my screen. "What's going on?"

"Nothing," I spit.

"Let's not start off this relationship with more lies." His admonishing tone is too much.

Laughter bubbles from me, but the humor quickly fades into a sob. "It's this awful construction company. They're trying to buy a bunch of land around here for their stupid development plans. Freaking bullies."

"Okay, just relax. Deep breath in." He inhales and I mirror the action. "And now out."

I release the hot air along with some of the upset. "Mother truckers are such a trigger."

"They can't force you, right?"

I nod. "It's just nonstop pressure to sell. Their tactics are dirty."

"They have no power over you. Fuck 'em."

"Yep, they're not getting an inch from me. Ever." I tuck my phone away, and then swipe at my cheek that feels wet.

"Better?"

"Getting there." I take another slow breath in and out.

"Good girl." Drake is still staring at me even after I've collected myself.

"I'm fine now," I say to reassure him.

"You have a little something..." He points at his jaw.

I scrub at the area. "Gone?"

"It's worse," he laughs. "Allow me."

His touch is gentle as he sweeps at what I assume is a smudge of dirt. After several brushes, his fingers linger on my skin. He tips my chin upward to check his work. Electricity seems to spark from the contact, but that must be my imagination. Until our eyes connect and hold. Heat consumes me, the kind that burns from deep inside and spreads.

"Oh," I breathe.

Drake leans in. "Go on a date with me."

"Okay."

"So agreeable," he murmurs. His exhale skates across my lips. "I'll touch you more often if this is the reaction."

"Holy shit." I pull away from his hold. "You sucked me into your dicksand. That was… whew, mister. You're dangerous."

"Only to your panties. Never your heart." He winks and both naughty dimples pop in his cheeks.

Another wave of warmth travels through me. "I find that hard to believe."

Drake's smirk tips higher. "How's Saturday?"

"For what?"

"Our date."

I'm already shaking my head. "No, no. We're not going on a date."

"Sure we are. You already agreed."

"That doesn't count. I was under the influence of Drake Granger. I've recovered and reinforced my priorities. There's too much for me to do around here."

"You can spare an hour or two."

"I really can't." Especially if I'm this susceptible to him.

"All right," he drawls. "If you're that busy, I'll just swing by and help you. Free labor."

"That's not necessary."

Drakes crosses his inked arms over his chest. "I insist."

I torture my bottom lip between my teeth. "Why me?"

"Why not you?"

"I'm nobody special," I retort.

"Beauty," he chides. "You're the total package."

Several choice words lodge in my throat. "You're very persistent."

"I've been called worse than that too."

My laughter teeters on hysterical. "Okay, you win. The kids will be with their dad this weekend. I'll meet you in town for a drink."

Drake is quiet for a moment, too many thoughts swirling in his gaze. Eventually he settles for, "Does this mean I finally get your number?"

"I suppose." My palm lifts to accept his phone.

Time is suspended while he watches me typing on the screen. "You're gonna love the cock den."

I swallow another giggle. "Is that code for sex? I barely agreed to a drink."

His chuckle caresses mine, blending into a synchronized tune. "Roosters is the bar I own with two friends. Regulars started calling it the cock den and the nickname stuck."

"How cute," I coo.

"But we can put sex on the menu for the night. Just our table."

"Don't push your luck, trouble."

Drake's eyes gleam like sapphires in uncharted waters. "I'm going to have fun properly earning that title from you."

CHAPTER FOUR

Drake

THE FRONT DOOR SWOOSHES OPEN TO announce a new arrival. Like a dog expecting immediate gratification, my gaze whips in that direction. It only takes a second for another punch of disappointment to sink in. This is the nineteenth or twentieth flop since seven o'clock struck. I've lost count, but hope remains.

Cassidy confirmed our plans when I texted her a few hours ago. My phone sits silent and heavy in my pocket, but I'm not surrendering to the urge. I can control myself. Mostly. It's too soon to unleash my crazy. That obsessive side needs to stay benched a bit longer or she's going to regret giving me her number.

"She'll be here soon," I say.

The words are as much for me as they are for the peanut gallery in attendance. My friends and their significant others deemed this occasion worthy of their presence.

"Uh-huh, right." Garrett pops the caps off several beer bottles in rapid succession. "No one would dare to back out on a date with you."

"Didn't say that. Plenty have and still would if given the opportunity. Cassidy is different."

"She must be. You're herding her into the cock den

for your first date." Garrett motions around our bar and the debauchery to come.

"This is my home away from home. My favorite dicks are here to pump me up. Couldn't ask for more." I blow kisses to my hype squad.

He makes no attempt to catch one. "We're not going easy on you."

Ridge snorts. "Fuck no we're not. You deserve to be roasted while she has a front row seat."

"It's about damn time I get my turn in the spotlight." I tuck my hands behind my head, reclining against the cooler behind me. "Feel free to get started now."

The two guys I've known since freshman year of college exchange a look. Ridge shakes his head. "He's not very fun to heckle."

"Just hold your horses. We're about to get new material when he's stood up." Garrett doesn't bother lowering his voice, volleying the prediction down the rail to where I'm getting the best view of Main Street.

Ridge's glare scans the room, just waiting for another man to attempt polite conversation with his future wife. That last dude didn't realize what hit him until his ass spanked the floor. Now the space surrounding Callie's stool is protected by an invisible force field that nobody dares to cross.

"I give her another five minutes," the possessive grump adds to the conversation.

Garrett rubs his palms together. "Wanna bet?"

The former defenseman shrugs. "You're on. Ten bucks?"

"That's all my love life is worth?" I glance at my so-called best friends. "I'm hurt. Deeply."

That gets a grunt from Ridge. "Fine, make it fifty."

"Decent, but you're still selling me short. Spending too much on that fiancée of yours, Crusher?"

The sharp edges in his expression melt into sappy goo while he shamelessly ogles Callie. "If only she'd let me."

"I don't need your money." Her voice is barely audible over the growing crowd.

"Doesn't mean you can't have it, sweetness." Ridge leans forward to cradle her blushing cheek.

Love floods Callie's gaze in a downpour that requires a splash guard for us soggy bystanders. "You already give me too much."

"Gonna give you more of me later," he growls.

Her breath hitches. "Promise?"

"All right, you two." Garrett claps until the couple's intimate bubble bursts. "Drake already has to go home alone and lick his fresh wounds in private. We don't need to rub his face in our happiness on top of it."

Callie blinks quickly, glancing at me from the corner of her eye. "But Harper said Cassidy is the one for him."

Ridge's smirk is fifty dollars richer. "She's gonna show."

Garrett slices through the air. "Nope. The deal is off. You had an advantage."

"What can I say? We don't keep secrets from each other." He gestures between Callie and himself.

"Soulmate." Garrett groans and turns toward his

fiancée. "You need to get the daily dirt from Harper. I'm starting to look bad."

Grace flutters her lashes from where she sits at the rail. "You keep me too preoccupied, bartender."

He scratches his chin. "Well, shit. Guess I only have myself to blame."

I exhale roughly as more unrecognizable customers stroll in. "Or I shouldn't share personal information with someone who passes the beer around for everyone to take a sip."

Ridge pinches the bridge of his nose. "You and your nonsense idioms."

"It makes sense," I argue. My focus slides to our suspiciously silent employee. "Right, Harps?"

The blonde blabbermouth beams with pride. "The news was too juicy and thick and creamy. It burst out of me."

"See? That's how you properly support me during my time of need."

"Quit while you're ahead, Granger." The threat spews from the corner stool steeped in shadows.

I roll my eyes at Jake, also known as Knox Creek's favorite asshole. "Your wife started it."

"Doesn't matter. Finish it or I will."

My laughter meets his malice. "Calm down and carry on nursing your drink while picturing Harper naked."

"Ugh, don't encourage him. I can't handle more." Yet she winks at her husband.

A low rumble that can only be described as satisfaction is Jake's response. The guy has less tact than a butt pimple, but he treats Harper like a queen. His little girl has him wrapped around her pinky too. The grouch is a total softie where it counts.

Much like the loyal pack that gathered at Roosters once I told them I had a date. Regardless of the shit they talk, these hecklers care. They're like my family. It's obvious in the way Garrett winces after another minute ticks by. Ridge's fingers drum an impatient beat on the bar top that I feel in my soul. Even Jake arrived on the scene much earlier than usual tonight. They're in my corner, rooting me on. Warmth spreads through my chest as I take a moment to soak in the encouragement. The only person missing is my plus-one.

That's when the door opens again. I do a double-take and nearly lose my footing. Cassidy struts into my bar like an exclamation point. Her entrance punctuates the rambling sentence these nameless faces created.

As she crosses the threshold, I swear a gust of wildflowers and unbridled passion billow toward me. My legs carry me forward until I crash into the counter. I grip onto the barrier as my gaze feasts on the beauty staring back at me.

Cassidy's playful gaze skips over the framed jerseys and sports memorabilia on the walls. The oversized booths and exposed beams might as well be a muted backdrop. Not even the reclaimed barn wood that's repurposed throughout the room earns a glance. She doesn't seem to notice anything except my smirk aimed at her.

I allow myself to indulge, as if there's another choice. Admiring Cassidy Brooks demands my complete concentration. Fiery auburn waves are gathered in a loose braid to hang over one shoulder. Curly wisps frame her face, wild and free. Her green eyes are smoky from makeup. Glossy red is a hypnotic stain on her lips. A peek of her cleavage is on display in a white tank top. The stretchy material molds to her breasts in a tight fit meant to captivate. And that's only her upper half.

There's a steady throb in my dick, getting more insistent as my perusal travels lower. On the bottom, she wears a long skirt cut into strips that reach above mid-thigh. I gladly give the garment a closer look. The black fabric is purposefully designed to resemble Western chaps. Her toned legs are on full display through the sheer material and multiple slits. A thick belt is cinched low around her waist. Conchos and rhinestones decorate the leather, catching the light with every subtle movement. Fancy cowboy boots polish off the outfit. She looks ready for a reckless night that I plan to provide.

"Dibs," stumbles from the depths of my awe. I wasn't blowing smoke up her fine ass the other day when I told her that she's the whole package.

"Holy. Shit." The expletive comes from Grace. "Pour that woman a Wife Material."

Garrett scoffs and makes no move to fill the order. "That's your drink, soulmate."

"I'll let her borrow it."

"That's not how specialty cocktails work. Those mixes are custom crafted for one," he argues.

A frustrated noise escapes her. "Are you watching this? Forget eye fucking. They're ditching the condom and making babies."

"She's his unfinished love story. They're going to

write the end together and literally ride off into the sunset." Leave it to Harper to be the eloquent one in the bunch.

"I'll be expecting a wedding invite in the mail," Ridge mumbles. "Probably before you receive one for mine."

My grin spreads until I resemble a much more attractive Joker. I point at Cassidy and announce loudly, "I'm coming for you, beauty."

Her painted lips tip higher on one side before she crooks a finger to beckon me. "Do your worst, trouble."

I vault over the counter and clear the stools tucked into the rail. Garrett boasts about me stealing that move from him, but I barely hear him over the pulsing desire. My shoes begin eating concrete the second I land on the floor. People scurry from my path, granting me unrestricted access to Cassidy straight ahead.

"Hi," she breathes.

I inhale a hit of her addictive scent. Crisp and fragrant like lilacs after a rainstorm. "Hey, you."

"Sorry I'm late. Billy and Gruff chewed through a fence. A few horses bolted free from the paddock, but they didn't get far. Botched escape attempt. Typical Saturday." Her hurried explanation adds to her undeniable appeal.

"You're here now. That's what matters."

"Couldn't skip out on you if I tried," she laughs.

That sultry rasp wraps my cock in a fist and tugs. "Can I kiss you?"

"Wouldn't be the first time, and after that entrance?" Cassidy motions down the length of her body. "You better."

In a fluid motion, she's braced against me with my palm flat on her upper back. The other hand clutches her waist as I lower her into a dipped position. She gasps, her fingers clinging to the front of my shirt. My primal instincts roar at catching her off guard. The crowd agrees, encouraging me with whoops and hollers that pound my eardrums.

Cassidy's eyes skewer mine as I swoop down and drop my mouth onto hers. Tingles spark from where we're connected, confirming what I already know. I snag her bottom lip between my teeth, sucking gently. The pressure melts her shock and she relaxes against me. Her breathy exhale grants me entry to glide my tongue along hers. I groan into her mouth. She tastes better than pitching a strikeout to win the series.

I slide my hand into her hair and several strands tumble loose from the braid. My grip cradles her head to steer the kiss. In response, Cassidy slings her arms around my neck and holds on for the ride.

This is meant to be chaste and quick, much like our first peck as kids. But my need for her rushes to the surface and consumes me. I'm not alone in this desperation to get closer. Cassidy hitches her leg higher and hooks herself to my hip. Our mouths form a tight seal that feels unbreakable.

We feed off this undeniable chemistry. I devour our combined heat until the threat of combustion thrashes through my veins.

It's just us in this room. The crowd is drowned out when she mewls for more. That decadent tune repeats, spilling into my mouth like a shot of pleasure. My lips slide along hers to get another dose. Every slick lash from her tongue gets me higher. More intoxicated. Totally fucking gone. I lose myself in her and our second kiss that's much more potent than the first.

My blood pumps faster and hotter, surging south at a record-breaking pace. The strain in my jeans doubles, along with the realization that we're in public. I'm about to give the folks in Roosters a side of sausage they didn't order. Nobody gets my bulge except the woman in my arms.

I don't want to stop, but our spectators are getting rowdy. The chorus of cheers and shouts is almost deafening. Cassidy smiles into the last brush of our kiss and I sip on the curve of her mouth. After a final sweep of my tongue along her lower lip, I pull away and set her upright.

Our foreheads touch as she wobbles on her feet. I tighten my grip to anchor her to me. Letting go isn't part of the plan. Cassidy's grin spreads wider as if she can hear those possessive thoughts swirling through my head.

"How was that?" I exhale across her lips, which are somehow still painted.

"Way hotter than in my books."

I whistle. "That's high praise."

"You deserve it." This woman is a surprise from every angle. Her soft sigh could knock me sideways.

I can't wait to see what else she's capable of doing to me. "What's gotten into you? Not that I'm complaining. This reaction is just... unexpected."

"It's been a very, very long time since I've had a night out. I'm taking advantage."

"Well, this is the first of many."

She hums in response. "Where are we sitting?"

"Your choice." I thrust an arm toward my domain that's hers for the taking.

Her striking gaze scans the space. About half the tables are occupied. "There."

My attention swings to the high-top in the far corner hidden by shadows. "Very private."

"Precisely."

I motion her forward into the cock den. "Give me a second. Gotta grab something."

Cassidy nods and begins weeding through the throng while I snag her gift from behind the bar. I keep my chin tucked to avoid distractions—mostly my friends and their nosiness—but a bottle of bubbly demands recognition. Two glasses join the bundle and then I'm crossing the room to our chosen spot. Her gaze tracks me, green flames burning brighter with each step I take. It's a miracle I'm not incinerated by the time I reach her.

She quirks a brow at my choice of beverage. "Champagne?"

I get myself situated on the tall chair. "We're celebrating."

"Oh?"

"It's our anniversary."

Confusion morphs her expression into an unreadable mask. "Come again?"

"Again? Did you have to take the edge off before our date? I'm flattered that I get you so hot and bothered."

Her freckled cheeks turn crimson. "Such trouble."

"Later, beauty. You'll come until your clit is numb. But be patient," I chide. "This is for you."

Cassidy studies the wrapped mason jar I'd been holding and now nudge toward her. "I was beginning to wonder."

"Just don't tip it upside down," I warn.

"That's a big hint." She begins to open the paper folded neatly at the top.

Once the contents are revealed, I watch the memory splash across her expression. Seventh grade was seventeen years ago but the past floods back to me in a vibrant wave. She opened her locker on the Monday after our first kiss to find a single sunflower and a note. *To brighten your day like you've brightened mine.*

Her eyes lift to mine. "You remembered."

"How could I forget?" I'd said something similar when we reconnected last week.

She pets one of the yellow petals. "We were just kids."

"Doesn't make your impact on me less significant. I knew you were special. Even back when I was a clueless teenager fueled by hormones and Mountain Dew."

Cassidy is quiet for a moment, capturing me in her unwavering stare. "Who are you?"

I chuckle. "Is that a trick question?"

Her smile rivals mine. "You're not what I expected, Drake."

That could become our tagline. "How so?"

"I'm not sure how to describe it other than pleasantly unexpected."

"Great description." My laugh booms louder.

"Can you blame me for being flustered? You've caught

me off guard. Again. This"—she points at the champagne and flowers before gesturing to me as a whole—"is very extraordinary. Above and beyond romantic. I kind of assumed we'd have a drink and call it a night. But now..."

"You want to see what happens," I guess.

"I do."

My stomach flips to catch the gallop in my pulse. "A toast then."

A glance at the label proves this brut is worthy of the occasion. I unwrap the foil and pop the cork with expert efficiency. My friends erupt in applause for our benefit. Cassidy's attention whips in their direction. Recognition flits across her expression when she notices Harper standing behind the bar. The others earn a wave in greeting.

"Your co-owners?" she asks once her focus is on me again.

"Garrett and Ridge. You'll get a proper introduction soon," I promise.

Once the flutes are filled to the brim, she raises one along with a questioning eyebrow. I lift mine to clink against hers.

"To us and our anniversary."

"Ah, yes. The cause for celebration." Yet she sounds unsure.

I sip the champagne but don't take my eyes off her. "It's been a week since we bumped into each other at Bean Me Up. We've accomplished so much in such a short amount of time."

"You're ridiculous," she laughs.

"Nah, I'm just dick-ulous. For you." I smirk, flashing her my dimples.

Cassidy watches me from over the edge of her glass. "You've been in Knox Creek since leaving the league?"

A phantom ache screams from my elbow at the reminder. "Yep, pitching is a young man's game. Garrett proposed the bar concept and I couldn't refuse. Here we are, four years later."

She nods slowly. "Uh-huh, makes sense. You're a star athlete, extremely attractive, and own the most popular place in town. How are you still single?"

"I've been waiting for you to find me."

Her eyes roll twice for good measure. "What a line."

"A straight shot to your heart."

"Very smooth," she praises.

I prop an elbow on the table and raise my flattened palm. Cassidy doesn't hesitate to press her hand against mine. We intertwine our fingers together, as if the link is expected and comes naturally. I like that. A lot.

The years apart have enriched us. I've honed my appetite and diet to fit a specific flavor palate. She's refined, more supple. Complex and layered. Eager for my touch. Exactly what I've been craving.

This is more than a public display of affection.

Cassidy rolls her lips between her teeth. "I have so many questions, but most can wait."

I stay quiet for her to elaborate, but she just drinks her champagne. "Which one can't?"

Emerald desire smolders from her gaze when she asks, "Did you put sex on the menu?"

CHAPTER FiVE

Cassidy

GLEE TICKLES MY BOLD SUGGESTION AS I WATCH several emotions play across Drake's features. Initial disbelief puckers his forehead before the wrinkles smooth and his jaw unhinges to hang slack. Heat paints his cheeks an endearing shade of pink. His hand tenses in mine. That combination plus too much excitement opens and closes his mouth on a soundless loop. The sweetest reward is confirmation that I've knocked this confident man off-kilter.

Drake clears his throat, but it does little to remove the frog stuck there. "Come again?"

My heart kicks to a giddy rhythm. "If all goes well."

His dumbfounded expression hasn't lifted. If anything, another round of shock stuns him. I wait patiently. This is more entertaining than Billy and Gruff getting the herd riled up.

"You want to have sex? With me? Now?" He stabs the table to punctuate each point that requires clarity.

"That's the idea." I giggle like the carefree version of myself that I'd forgotten existed. I turned him down last week but my willpower is no match for his charm. "If you're still interested..."

Drake launches from his seat. The loud screech of metal on concrete rouses notice from those nearby. Any attempt at being discreet flies out the window, especially when the chair topples over from the abrupt movement. He doesn't pause at the noise, just rushes to get me standing and at his level. I wobble on weak knees like a newborn foal. Laughter spews from me hard enough to blur my vision.

It's a challenge to remain upright while he spins us in a slow circle. "Where are we going?"

"Not sure yet." His gaze is unblinking and crazed as he searches the bar. A thought must occur to him, and he tugs me toward a closed door on the opposite wall.

"Wait," I laugh. "What about the champagne?"

His determined stride plans to leave the bubbles behind but he decides to double back for the booze. I grab the sunflowers while we're at it. Once we're in motion again, a revived round of applause and wolf whistles come from his friends. My face bursts into flames from the attention. I duck my chin and watch our hurried steps. There's no doubt they know where we're headed and why.

Drake guides me into a small office and shuts the chaos out behind us. The room is plain and has minimal furnishings, but the leather couch will do the trick in a pinch. That's where he leads us.

Before making myself comfortable, I set the flowers on the solo end table. My plan to take a seat is derailed by the imposing force of a man in this space with me. He guzzles a swig of champagne straight from the bottle and swoops down to kiss me. My lips part for him automatically. I moan into our shared exhale. The tart flavor lingers on his tongue as he swipes inside my mouth.

A dizzy spell that has nothing to do with the alcohol content makes the room spin. This guy is too much, but I can't get enough. I lower myself onto the sofa to avoid an ungraceful tumble. Drake follows me down, only breaking our kiss to tip the bottle back for another drink. I notice he doesn't swallow before our lips are reunited.

Liquor dribbles into my mouth from his and I sip from him eagerly. None escapes, caught between our desperation for each other. The smooth taste compliments his feverish desire for me. Our tongues glide together, exchanging what remains of the bubbly refreshment.

Drake pulls away until only his ragged breathing teases me. "More?"

I'm already nodding. "Please."

His smolder burns hotter on mine. He repeats the act to quench my thirst as a different need builds. Hunger gnaws at me, an urgency to have him. I want to gorge myself on this heated moment so I can feast on the memory in the morning. That's what I'll have to keep me company when this is over.

"You're so sexy," he rasps before kissing me again.

I allow my hands to roam, appreciating his body towering over mine. Rigid muscles bulge under my exploration. A solid wall I want to climb. He's enthusiastic and passionate and mine for now. A hollow clench beckons from between my legs, requesting to be filled. I arch to bump our hips together and spur him in the downward direction.

Drake groans into my mouth and sets the bottle aside. His palm cups my breast through my shirt but doesn't linger there. Our lips disconnect as he trails nibbles along my jaw and throat. I tilt to give him better access, which he greedily accepts. Rough stubble nuzzles into the slope where my neck meets my shoulder. He inhales deeply, pulling my scent into his lungs. I tremble beneath him when he expels a guttural sound.

My hooded eyes watch while Drake kneels on the floor. He unclasps my belt in a deliberate display. I lift my ass off the couch when his fingers hook into the elastic band of my skirt. He strips off the black frills in a whisper of fabric against skin. Next is my thong. Cool air kisses my slick arousal and I shiver. I'm bared to him from the waist down.

"Perfection," Drake rasps while admiring my most intimate bits.

The urge to cover myself is deeply ingrained but I refuse to cower. Instead, I inhale a slow breath. His sandalwood cologne might as well be labeled as an aphrodisiac. After I get a good whiff, I'm a puddle for him to splash in. My lashes flutter while I drag in another lustful dose. The thrill that I'm about to sleep with Drake Granger is intoxicating. He could have anyone, but he's here with me. As I told him earlier, I'm taking advantage. Reality can scold me tomorrow.

"What's that look for?" He squints at the unfocused glaze clouding my vision.

"I can't believe I'm doing this," I confess the truth.

"Don't make a habit of initiating sex on the first date?"

My giggle is shrill. "Especially not with someone like you."

Drake's pout could convince a square peg to fit in a round hole. "Hey, we're on an even playing field."

"Yeah, right." A snarky brow quirks at his claim. "I'm not delusional, trouble."

"That's reassuring. Hallucinations can be a real bitch. I'd still put a ring on it, though."

"You and your cheesy lines." I bite my bottom lip, calling upon an inner seductress who doesn't exist. "Are you sure this isn't a dream?"

His palms roam my inner thighs, spreading me wide. "Does this feel real?"

Warmth collects in my lower belly and I slouch deeper into the sofa. "I'm not sure. Keep going."

He drapes my knees over his elbows, using the hold to scoot me down until my ass is hovering off the couch. His grip is what keeps me from falling. I gawk at his inked arms clutching my naked flesh. The sight punches me with another strike of arousal. There's a decent chance I'm going to drench the leather seat.

My breathing is labored from just ogling him positioned to feast on me. "You're actually going to..."

Drake's gaze flicks to mine. "Eat your pussy?"

I'm sure my face flames redder than my hair. "Mhmm, yeah. That."

"Couldn't stop me if you tried." He squeezes my legs in his grip.

"Uh-huh," I mumble absently.

"Gonna gush down my throat." His exhale ghosts along my exposed center.

A twitch attacks my limbs. "Ohhhh, gosh."

Drake chuckles. "This should be fun."

I don't get to question his statement. A hoarse cry rips from me as his tongue swirls around my clit. The guy doesn't need a detailed map to find the hidden gem. He lands on the spot with expert aim. It's some sort of miracle I'll have to process later.

Any further deliberation melts into wonder when his lips form a tight seal. The gentle suction makes me thrash against him. But I'm locked in his hold, at his mercy. Gladly.

Sparks crackle from where his mouth is latched onto me. I'd forgotten how good this feels. Drake smiles along my slick center when I tell him that very thing. When I glance down, his gaze is waiting for me. The intense eye contact makes me squirm.

"I wanna see you fall apart for me, beauty."

He slides a finger into my empty core to accomplish the small feat. My slippery walls clench to greet him. He's quick to spear a second into me along with the first. There's a dull ache as I stretch to accept his shallow thrusts. Drake's pace is steady as he stimulates me from the inside out. Neglected pleasure blooms and flares outward.

I'm overly responsive to his touch, already on edge. It's embarrassing to recall how long it's been since I've been treated to such sensual concentration. The friction of his scruff against my bare center is provocative. It's as if he's branding me with the abrasion. I jolt from the slight sting but roll my hips for more.

"My girl is needy. Show me how bad you want to come." Primal lust drips from his voice to pair with the fire thrumming in my veins.

I buck against his hold but don't get far. My legs strain in the pinned cage of his broad frame. We're wedged together as he pulls passion from me.

An explosion simmers just beneath the surface. I allow myself to voice the delight spreading through me. Garbled pleas and choked whimpers become more deliberate.

"Yes!" I wail. "There. Oh, right there."

He groans into my slit, burying his face deeper to reach my trigger. "Ride my face, cowgirl. Use me how you wish."

The cue washes over me and I'm eager to obey. I stab my fingers into his hair, using the grip to bring him impossibly closer. My hips grind to a frantic tempo. His tongue lashes at my clit in relentless swirls while he presses against that secret spot inside me.

Sensation swarms me in an overwhelming flood. I gasp while struggling to accept the onslaught of carnal bliss. The low buzz in my veins builds into a heavy throb. Pressure expands in my lower belly. The need for relief grows restless until I'm consumed.

I'm suspended over the peak, almost there. My hips rock forward to gain that last push. Drake gives me a final swipe to send me soaring over the edge.

A scream wrenches free from my mouth. I clench my eyes shut as trembles rack my entire body. The climax is more powerful than the bite from an electric fence. My teeth clack together from the ripples of intense euphoria. It's like a live wire zaps me with a white-hot surge. All the while, Drake continues suckling my sensitive flesh until I'm a boneless heap.

The orgasmic lull carries me in a peaceful daze for several minutes. Once clarity begins to resurface, my thighs attempt to clamp shut but Drake still pries me wide open. I scramble to prop myself on a wiggly elbow. It's a valiant effort that makes me resemble a floppy fish. My energy is depleted, spent wisely on that toe-curling release.

Hair sticks to my forehead thanks to the layer of sweat and lowered inhibitions. I'm a mess, but Drake's gaze burns a scorching path along my exposed curves. "C'mere, trouble."

His knees remain firmly planted on the floor. "My view from down here is tough to beat."

I try to claw at his jeans but he evades my reach. "Don't be shy."

"Trust me," he chuckles. "I'm not lacking in the confidence department, especially when it comes to what's below the belt."

My blink is coated in cement. "Why aren't you freeing the cock from the den?"

"Still eating," Drake rasps very close to my quivering folds.

A squeak tears from my exhausted vocal cords. "You're not doing that to me again."

"Do you have something against multiple orgasms?"

"I probably won't recover, which would make having sex challenging."

He shrugs. "We'll save that for next time."

There's a low hum in my ears that sounds a lot like my brain misfiring. "You don't want to have sex with me?"

"I didn't say that." Drake's tone is too earnest, which only heightens my confusion.

"The post-coital glow is messing with me," I grumble under my breath. "Level playing field my ass. I'm way out of practice."

He squeezes my legs that remain locked in his unyielding grasp. "This is serious for me, beauty. You're not going to get this prize penis for one night only. I'm yours and you're mine. Until you believe that, we're not having sex."

My mouth drops on a wheeze. "What?"

"Don't worry about going without. I'll eat this pussy whenever you need a release." His focus caresses my thoroughly sucked bits that are on full display.

"But what about you?" I fasten my gaze on his hard length ready to burst through denim.

"I'm satisfied with you feeding me sweet honey on a platter. This"—he takes a long lick through my center—"pleases me."

A shudder rolls through me and my eyes roll to the ceiling. "You're really denying me the dick?"

"For now." Drake flattens his tongue to swipe along my slit again. "I have this feeling that if we have sex, that'll be the end of it."

"And what's the problem?" But the protest is weak as I settle into the cushions.

He scolds me with a harsh tap to my clit. "We're just getting started. I'll never be done with you."

"Will you at least let me return the favor?" I poke my tongue into my cheek for the universal blowjob symbol.

He adjusts on the floor but doesn't rise from his

squat. "The first time you make me come, it won't be with your mouth."

My exhale sputters. "You won't let me suck your cock?"

"Not tonight."

I squint at him. "Anal isn't an option."

His nod is resolute. "Not without proper preparation and lube. We'll build up to that."

"What?" I shake my head. "No."

"Sounds like we're in agreement that I should keep feasting on this pussy," he chuckles.

I snatch the bottle of champagne, suddenly in desperate need of a drink. "Thirsty?"

"Parched." But he doesn't accept the pucker I form on my lips.

The bubbles fizz along my throat with a long swallow. "I thought we were sharing."

"Drink the rest. You give me enough to drown in."

"Definitely not what I expected," I breathe.

Drake's smirk flashes me a dimple before he returns to his favorite meal. "I plan to keep it that way."

CHAPTER SiX

Drake

THE DARK ROAD APPEARS ENDLESS THROUGH my windshield. I allow my thoughts to wander, accompanied by the measured thump from the truck's tires. Cassidy's face replaces the black landscape stretching in front of me.

Her tangled hair and flushed cheeks are the picture of passion. She falls apart in my clutches, eager and effortlessly like we're established lovers. Pleasure saturates the air until she's all I breathe. The hours pass too quickly, as if we only shared a few minutes together.

And that's already a memory. It was difficult to watch Cassidy leave, but she insisted four orgasms were adequate. I snuck her out the rear exit to avoid a walk of shame. Her words, not mine. Personally, I didn't see what the fuss was about.

I strutted to the front of the bar like a champion stallion who just won the Triple Crown. Cassidy's essence smeared all over my face makes a far sexier trophy than a blanket of roses. My friends goaded me for being drunk on pussy, and I wore the evidence with pride. Still am, in fact.

The taste of her still lingers on my tongue. Echoes of her breathy demands fill my ears. I'm painfully hard.

My cock aches for the release I've denied myself. Not for much longer.

Pavement switches to gravel when I turn onto the long driveway. The truck coasts along the bends framed by trees and rolling hills. I'm on autopilot with a singular goal as I park in front of the garage. Motion sensors spot me and illuminate a direct path to the house.

My boots hammer on the porch stairs to announce my arrival. Loud barking erupts from inside to confirm I've been heard. The door opens before I can knock, but the screen divider remains between us. At least until Chester and Cheeto claw at the flimsy barrier. Rusty hinges screech as the pair is set free to maul me.

The dogs rush forward to neutralize the threat. A few quick sniffs is all it takes before they're trotting off to do their business in the yard. Cassidy leans in the doorway, screen snapped shut to protect her from the swarm of mosquitoes. A soft glow from the porch light reveals her grin. She makes no move to let me in, happy to watch me get eaten alive.

We stare at each other in silence. Only the chirps from crickets and intermittent squeaks from the windmill break apart the calm of midnight. I take the opportunity to drink in her appearance. She's washed off her makeup. The outfit I drooled over earlier this evening is gone, replaced with an old, baggy t-shirt. Her hair hangs free in red waves. My fingers itch to feel the silky strands again.

"Drake." The purr of my name rolling off Cassidy's tongue has my dick punching forward in greeting. "Did I forget something?"

"Yeah, me."

She blinks. "Huh?"

"I changed my mind. Sex is back on the menu."

There's a brief pause while my words register. Her eyes widen before narrowing into molten pools of lust. That heat engulfs me until sweat prickles my nape. It's suddenly difficult to take a full breath.

"Gonna let me in, beauty?"

Cassidy licks her bottom lip, trapping the pouty flesh between her teeth. I groan and slap a palm against the siding for moral support. This woman is trying to drain every drop of blood from my brain to make my dick even bigger. Before I can beg, she pushes the screen open to grant me entry.

The dogs barrel past me as I step into the foyer. Cassidy shuffles to the side to give me space that I don't want. Our gazes collide while anticipation crackles in the air.

We sever the distance in a simultaneous rush. I lunge at her while she leaps into my arms. Lips and teeth smash in a sloppy union while I cinch her legs around me. My palms roam under the hem of her shirt to discover naked skin. Only a tiny scrap of lace conceals her pussy. I snap the elastic at her waist and she bucks against me.

Something crashes to the floor but I don't pull away to assess the damage. Not while Cassidy is wrapped around me like a Christmas bow. I'm about to give her the package that keeps on giving. As if listening to my plans, she grinds into me again. The motion strokes along my cock. I stumble in desperation, blindly searching for the nearest surface to get balls-deep.

She rips her mouth off mine. "This doesn't mean I'm agreeing to your terms."

"Uh-huh."

"I'm serious."

"Me too."

Additional protests fizzle on her tongue as I kiss her again. I tug on her bottom lip, smoothing the sting with a gentle lick. Heat streaks up my spine in a demand I can't ignore. This frantic urgency locks me in place even when my feet shuffle restlessly.

Cassidy loops one arm around my shoulders and uses the other to stab in an unseen direction. Her body shifts in my hold, tilting backward to gain momentum. I try to follow her guidance but trip on the rug. After a thorough sweep of her mouth, I force myself to regain composure. Just an ounce. To get where we're going.

A downward glance snags on a familiar logo I didn't notice before. "Are you wearing a Mustangs shirt?"

Cassidy huffs, sending red curls flying. "Don't let it go to your head."

"Too late," I chuckle. "Bedroom?"

She tries to nudge me along again. "Upstairs."

Which requires a steep climb. "Here works."

She gasps as I push her up against the wall. My spread thighs support hers while I rip off her panties. Message received, she fumbles with my jeans. Her haste to free my cock from the restrictive confines aligns with the thunder in my pulse. A collective sigh of victory exhales from us and I steady our position for maximum impact.

Her hand seeks to stroke me but my patience for

foreplay has left the building. I slide my length through her slippery arousal. She moans as I lube myself and bump her clit in the process.

My tip is notched at her entrance when a vital detail occurs to me. "Please tell me you're on the pill."

"I have an implant. Why?" Cassidy's heavy-lidded gaze searches mine, and then she stills. "Oh, shit. We need a condom. I can't believe I forgot."

A powerful surge of devotion rises in my chest. "I don't want anything between us."

"Is that safe?"

My nose drifts along hers. "I've never gone without. You'll be the only one to ever ride me bareback."

"Unprotected sex is risky. Not that condoms are indestructible," she mumbles absently. "The number of past partners—"

A kiss quiets that unpleasant statement. "I don't want to talk about anybody but us right now. In this moment. Do you trust me?"

"Yes." She seems startled by the blurted response.

I smile against her lips. "That's just what I wanted to hear, beauty. Are you ready for me?"

Her expression is dazed. "I think so?"

"You're not sure?"

Cassidy wiggles, feeding herself a taste of me. "I haven't gotten a look at this prize penis you promised me."

"By all means," I rasp and brace myself. "Take every inch."

Her mouth drops on a soundless scream when I thrust. Hard. One shove gets me halfway. A second slides me home to the hilt. The sensation of being bare inside of her strikes me as a lit fuse. Warmth like I've never felt envelops me. I slump against the force, nailing Cassidy on my shaft and the wall at her back.

She goes lax, her head lolling, as I pause to let her accept my size. The adjustment period is for me too. Her tight walls clench around me like a fist trying to suffocate.

She sputters and squirms. "That's... um, a lot."

I blink at the spots in my vision. "Are you okay?"

Her nod is bobbled. "Just out of practice, remember?"

"We'll go slow." Which is also for my benefit.

Pressure already squeezes my balls. At this rate, I'll blow my load after a third plunge. Cassidy tests the limits by sinking her weight on me. The slight change pushes my cock deeper. She trembles, which seats her even lower. We're joined as one. Finally.

Slick heat welcomes me in this paradise. "Fuck, you're so wet."

"Good thing or you'd never fit." There's a smile in her voice.

"Would've given me an excuse to go down on you again."

"You might be addicted."

"Guilty," I murmur into her neck. "You'll never get rid of me."

Cassidy doesn't answer, but the curve on her lips is bliss. I rest my forehead on hers. Our labored breaths mingle and dance. With her in my grip, I gingerly withdraw and glide back in. My palms rest on her ass to set the pace.

"This is..." Cassidy's comment trails off on a whimper when I slap our hips together.

"Unexpected?" I grind against her, trying to hit a certain spot.

Her eyes bulge. "What...? Is that...?"

I chuckle at her garbled speech. "Ah, you've become intimately acquainted with my pubic piercing."

"Your...?" She quivers when I press harder to stimulate her clit. "Ohhhh, Drake. You really are trouble."

"Just for your panties." I nod to the discarded heap I have every intention to pocket later. "Also your pussy. There's no replacing me."

Cassidy quakes as I stroke deep. "Ahhhhh... don't stop. Not sure what magic you've got below the belt but give me more."

"Gauged for your pleasure." The barbell imbedded at the base of my cock is thick and wide precisely for this purpose.

"I've never felt anything like this," she mumbles.

"And you'll never have to go without ever again."

"Trouble," she sighs.

I double my efforts to send her reeling. My dick punches in and out at a fluid tempo meant to reach that pivotal peak. The moan spilling from her lips encourages me to push faster. I bury my face in the notch between her neck and shoulder. A long inhale fuels me with lilacs and renewed purpose. This is just the beginning for us.

Her nails scratch along my scalp before securing a grip. My vision swims while desperation sinks its claws in. There's a noticeable tension in my balls that squeezes harder with each thrust. Her pussy is just too damn irresistible. I'm not going to last much longer.

Cassidy is shamelessly swiveling her hips to the

erratic beat I'm composing. The fact that she's getting off on me strokes my ego in a vise grip. I straighten to watch her, finding her gaze already locked on me. Each forward drive pounds us to release.

"Come on my cock, beauty." The command is more of a plea.

"Oh, oh," she chants. "I'm gonna—"

But she doesn't finish her sentence as relief comes for her. A spasm clamps her muscles around me. I punch my hips into hers, creating an unbreakable seal where we're joined. Pressure spreads and spurts from my cock. Warmth explodes throughout my entire body, spilling into hers.

Somehow, the momentum remains fluid when I lose myself to the pleasure she wrings from me. I feel disjointed yet complete. My hands splay across her ass, shoving us tighter together until no end or beginning exists. She scrambles to hold on but the climax sweeps her away in a thrash of limbs. We ride the waves together until a calm settles.

Our heavy exhales fill the quiet house. No words are spoken as we bask in the recovery phase. Sweat slicks our skin. We smell like sex and endless orgasms.

When sensation returns to my legs, I push off from the wall. Cassidy sags in my arms where she belongs. I keep myself lodged deep inside of her. There's zero chance I'm letting go.

My jeans slide down, reminding me to ditch them. I blindly toe off my boots and manage to leave the discarded denim behind without falling on my ass. The elastic from my boxers restricts my movements as I begin to climb the stairs, reminding me that I missed a step. My hitched stride rouses Cassidy from her stupor.

"Where—?" Her groggy voice tickles my throat.

I nuzzle against her. "We're not done."

"No?"

"No," I state firmly.

Muscle memory steers me in the correct direction. We hadn't spent much time at the farm, but she invited me and our other friends over once or twice. I wouldn't have assumed that she would still be in the same bedroom as her childhood. A gut instinct told me otherwise.

I perch on the edge of the mattress with Cassidy straddling my lap. Even in the dark, I admire the flush staining her cheeks. My thumb brushes over a patch of freckles and she leans into me. She wiggles closer, her eyes rounding when my cock twitches. Our combined pleasure is sticky between us but I only feel her coating me.

Her bottom lip pokes out. "You're still dressed."

"So are you." I tap at the Mustangs logo stamped on her chest that revives my arousal.

Cassidy gathers the hem of my shirt and begins to lift. My gaze feasts on hers while she strips me. Her touch drifts along muscles and ink. The gentle caress pumps my shaft to stiff mast.

"You're like..." Cassidy's gulp is audible. "Really hot. Super fit. Sculpted from clay. You must belong to several gyms. How often do you go? Daily? Who has time for that? But you're not too bulky. Just the right amount of strength to toss me around." She exhales while squeezing my biceps. "Yeahhhh, that's... nice. Wow. Excuse my blabbering. My mouth is watering. The drool is loosening my tongue. Maybe it's laced with something."

My chuckle jostles our position and we share a moan. I shuck my boxers with a downward swoop before scooting to the center of the bed. Cassidy adjusts her position astride me while I prop myself up against a mound of pillows. The action draws her focus to my upper body. She doesn't bother hiding the blatant desire in her eyes. That need sweeps over me in a fiery blaze, skidding to a halt on the enhancement rooted into my pelvic region.

"Damn, there's a book boyfriend spreading my pages."

My palms travel along her thighs. "Glad to hear we're officially dating."

She swats my abs. "You know what I mean."

"That I'm the man of your fictional fantasies brought to life? You're madly in love with me? We're about to have sex again? Yes, that came across loud and clear."

"Uh-huh, right. Stop distracting me." Cassidy's hand hovers above the protruding barbell pierced under my skin. "Can I touch it?"

"Please do. That's all yours."

She prods at the bump, rolling her fingers back and forth. "Did it hurt?"

I glance at the impulse embellishment. Only the platinum spheres holding the post in place are visible. "Not too bad. Switching to a bigger gage was worse than the initial pain."

"Well, I appreciate you taking one for the team. And you're not the only one with surprises." Cassidy whips off her shirt in a practiced motion. "I'm pierced too."

My eyes feast on the sight while saliva collects in my mouth. Silver hoops decorate her nipples. Thin and delicate but brazen. "Holy shit, that's sexy."

"It's no pubic piercing." She rolls her hips to hit the spot.

My fingers pause inches away from her tits before I've even realized I moved. "May I?"

"Yes," she murmurs and thrusts her chest at me.

I cup her breasts, gently sliding the metal through her pebbled peaks. "Fuck, beauty. You're blowing my mind. I knew you were incredible, but this is..."

She trembles from my fondling. "Shock and awe?"

"To put it mildly," I breathe.

"These are a gift from me to myself. After nursing twins for almost two years, I developed a strange relationship with my boobs. They didn't feel like mine anymore, if that makes sense. I'd become a mother and a food source and lost my personal identity in the process. This"—her palms lift to cover mine playing with her pierced nipples—"helped me feel like a woman again. My most important and sacred role is being a mom, but I can also look at myself as sensual. Seductive. Desirable."

At some point, I begin moving inside her again. Just a lazy rhythm to stoke the smoldering embers. "You're the most beautiful woman I've ever seen. I couldn't be more attracted to you if we were magnets."

Cassidy's smile flirts with mine. "Such a line."

"But true," I vow.

"Show me," she urges on a whimper.

And I do just that. There's no hesitation as I buck upward to fulfill her request. Her back bows when I strike hard. One of my hands drifts along her spine, fingers tangling in her hair. She clutches my head to her breast and matches my strokes. I tongue her nipple, tugging lightly on the jewelry.

"I hope you weren't planning on getting much sleep," I murmur into her flesh.

She gasps when her clit rubs along my piercing. "Who could deny this?"

"Not you."

"Not me. I'm choosing to indulge," Cassidy confirms. Her grip on me tightens and she adds, "Just this once."

CHAPTER SEVEN

Cassidy

SUNLIGHT STREAKS IN THROUGH THE WINDOW to alert me that morning has arrived. With my eyes still shut, I smile into my pillow and stretch until the stiffness in my joints recedes. There are more tender spots than usual, especially in my lady business. My lips tip higher.

I'm sore and barely awake but I haven't felt this refreshed in years. There's a lingering scent of sandalwood and orgasmic bliss surrounding me. I'll have to wash the sheets or my dreams will be a constant replay of the best sex I've ever had.

My fingers reach for the opposite side of the bed. The spot Drake had occupied while cuddling me to sleep is now cold. A pinch of disappointment clenches my heart. Stupid. This is what I wanted. I had every intention of kicking him to the curb but he saved me the trouble.

Just then, a clang rings out from downstairs. I shoot upright, pulse leaping to the sky. My breath catches as I wait for Chester and Cheeto to sound the alarm. Not a single woof confronts whoever just dropped something. My ears strain to hear a voice to identify. The racket continues with more clinks and clatters. There's definite rummaging. Nobody speaks.

I shiver, suddenly very aware that I'm nude. There's a lump of fabric within grabbing distance and I yank the cotton over my head. Drake's scent washes over me but I'm too distracted to appreciate the comfort.

I grab clean underwear while noting the clock strongly suggests my kids shouldn't be home yet. It's possible that Shawn dropped them off early but he would've called.

As I creep down the stairs, the most likely intruders come to mind. I slump against the wall for a moment and gather my scattered wits. Several members of my extended family live just up the road. Auntie June is notorious for dropping by unannounced. She caught the horse bug at an early age, unlike my mother. The unmistakable aroma of freshly brewed coffee points a guilty finger at my cousin.

I stroll into the kitchen and stumble to a stop. The scene in front of me takes a solid minute for my brain to compute. It isn't Paisley raiding my fridge. Auntie June is nowhere in sight. Charlie and Kenzie wreaking unsupervised havoc would be more believable.

Drake is standing at the stove with his back to me. Smoke and steam curl around him like a caress. There's a distinct sizzle from whatever he just flipped in the frying pan. But it's not the possibility of food that captures my appetite.

An apron string is tied at his lower back, leaving his ass on naked display. That firm bottom is something to admire. Especially in the soft light fondling him. My mouth waters and I have the sudden urge to nibble on a juicy peach.

Those sculpted cheeks flex as if aware of my intense admiration. "Hungry?"

"I could eat," I croak.

Drake peeks at me over his shoulder, a smirk waiting on his lips. "You look freshly fucked."

"You're one to talk." But the retort is weaker than my vagina's willpower against him.

Between the dimple buried in thick stubble and twinkling baby blues, this man can get whatever he wants. He couldn't be unattractive if he tried. Meanwhile, my hair resembles a nest that most birds would abandon. It's entirely his fault I'm in this disheveled condition.

I tug at a snarl while slinking toward the large island that occupies the center of this open concept layout. The butcher block surface provides support for my unsteady limbs. His bare butt is within chomping distance. It wouldn't spoil my appetite to take a nibble.

As if listening, Drake's attention returns to the stove. "Breakfast is ready."

"Just making yourself at home, huh?"

"It felt right," he croons. "The goal was to serve you in bed. Here will have to do. Plans are meant to be rearranged, right?"

"Um... I guess?" That's not how the phrase typically goes, but it does remind me that he didn't leave.

The swoop in my belly is uncalled for. Drake should be long gone by now. That's what I expected. But I can't ignore the giddy flutters that take flight seeing him in my space like he belongs.

He turns off the burner and plates an oversized

omelet. The smell of melted cheese and fried onions has my stomach growling. But then I get a peek at his apron.

Written across the front in bold letters is the word *Vagitarian*. There's a definition scribbled underneath but he turns away before I can read the whole thing. Something about frequently dining between her thighs. I'm still trying to digest what he's wearing while he pours a cup of coffee. The words are a blur as he strides back to me.

Without spilling a drop, Drake hoists me onto the island and kisses me from the stupor. "Good morning, beauty."

"Morning," I mumble absently. I accept the steaming mug while my thoughts swirl. "Where did you get that?"

"This old thing?" He tugs at the strap around his neck. "I found it in your pantry."

"What?" I sputter. "No way."

"Must've been a forgotten gift," he muses.

"There's not a chance you found that in my house." Unless it belonged to my grandma, which would add another twist entirely.

The sparkle in Drake's gaze brightens. "Ah, you caught me. The apron is mine."

I'm laughing hard enough to shed tears. "And you conveniently had it in your truck?"

"Optimism is its own reward." He steps into the space between my parted legs.

Somehow, I missed the tented fabric until he bumps against me. "Oh, wow. Is there a pony hiding under there or does my kitchen excite you?"

His lips brush over mine. "Ignore that. He's always preening for you."

Once again, sandalwood teases my nostrils. "I can't have sausage for breakfast?"

"Don't tempt me," Drake warns.

I hook my knees to his sides, hauling him closer. "As if you didn't see this coming."

"The food will get cold." But his voice already wavers.

"We can do two things at once." I sip at my coffee before setting it aside. "For the sake of time management."

Drake's palms roam up my thighs, lifting the hem of my shirt. The coarse scrape of his calluses chafe my skin in a zing. "I'll cook for you more often if this is the response I get."

"It's been a very long time since someone made me a meal in my own home. I'll admit that it's very... disarming."

"Oh?"

"Mhmm, and we shouldn't waste your efforts." The omelet is waiting for recognition and I spear a piece with the fork. "Can I feed you?"

"Ladies first." He snags the food to reverse our roles while simultaneously whipping the apron barrier out from between us. "And I'll pleasure more than your taste buds."

My lips part automatically to accept the extended bite. Savory flavors burst on my tongue. "Ohhhh, that's delicious."

His gaze heats when I moan. "Surprised?"

"Not really. You seem capable of just about anything."

His thumbs tease the lace concealing my slick arousal. "Like filling two of your holes at once?"

There's a noticeable gush in my basement to reveal what his words do to me. "That's filthy."

"You love my dirty mouth." He nips at my bottom lip.

"It's just okay," I blatantly lie.

His chuckle curls my toes against his ass. "I bet your pussy is drenched for me."

"Only one way to find out."

"Brace yourself, beauty." Drake rips the crotch of my panties and slams into me.

"Shit," I hiss. My sore muscles weep at his harsh intrusion.

He stills. "Too much?"

"Never. Just out of practice, remember?"

"I thought we fixed your squeaky wheels."

"You'll have to grease me better than that," I taunt.

His arm loops around me, splaying a palm on my back. "You want it fast and hard?"

"Yes," I breathe.

"Rough?"

"Please."

That's the permission he needs. I grab onto him as he withdraws and slams into me again. From there, his hips piston in and out at a feverish pace. My inner walls ache at his quick tempo, but the twinge is somehow pleasant. I hike my legs higher around his waist to adjust our angle. His piercing rubs at my clit and I sigh at hitting the spot.

I'm overly sensitive. Tingles are already spreading

after a few thrusts. Drake takes the cue to grind against me, pumping faster.

This man already knows how to play my body like a professional sport. His technique is finely tuned to pluck at my desire as if we're performing a choreographed script. It's like he's reinventing me, which is too screwed up for me to consider right now.

But our compatibility thrums through my veins, surging hotter each time he sinks into me. This type of chemistry can't be denied. Drake is determined to prove that. It would be careless—not to mention naive—to fall headfirst into the fairy tale he's selling. I'm realistic. There's no time for romance. These heated moments will have to be enough.

"Fuuuuuuck," he groans. "Have I told you how incredible you feel?"

"Not today."

Devotion floods from his unyielding gaze. "I had no idea sex could be like this."

"Too sweet," I murmur. The flimsy scold is more for myself than him.

"Ah, damn. I almost forgot myself."

Drake gathers my hair in a fist and pulls just tight enough to sting. My head tips back to alleviate the burn, a gasp spilling from me. He's in control but I'm confident he would yield if I asked. Another furious shove jostles our position and I wheeze. To be honest, I don't mind how he dominates the scene. I trust that my pleasure is his priority.

More than that, he's handling my needs without any guidance. Each sure stroke allows me to surrender and pass him the reins. For years, I've had to take care of everything myself. Drake is granting me relief from the weight of endless responsibilities.

That freedom is dizzying, especially when paired with his cock stretching my tolerance to the brink. His lips travel along the extended column of my throat, the gentle caress at war with his brutal fucking. The contrast propels me toward the edge. Pressure builds until I'm trembling for release.

The plate clatters beside us, reminding him of my other hole he can fill. "Still hungry?"

"Uh-huh."

Drake manages to fork another section of omelet to feed me. "Open wide."

I do and my eyes nearly cross at the onslaught of sensations. "Might be the best thing I've put in my mouth."

"Until you choke on my cock."

I slurp on the excessive amounts of saliva that visual manifests. "Should've taken me up on that blowjob when you had the chance."

"I'm enjoying your pussy too much."

"Sounds like a personal problem."

"But how does this feel?" He pulls out just to hammer me with his thick girth.

My teeth clack from the force. "So close."

His grin stamps mine. "We can do better than that."

"By all means," I urge.

Drake is gracious to include me, but this isn't a collaboration. Not when his piercing presses against my clit and I see stars. I cling onto him as he pounds us to the peak. His dick strikes at that sacred area to finish me off.

My nails dig into his shoulders while a spasm clamps my core. He curses and his steady motions stumble. A final thrust tips us into oblivion together.

I'm a quaking puddle of bliss when Drake cuddles me against his chest. We drift on a peaceful tide that prove simultaneous climaxes aren't a myth. My ear absorbs the heavy thump of his heart, coaxing me into a trance.

His hand travels the length of my spine, dragging me deeper under his influence. "How are those squeaky wheels?"

"Thoroughly greased," I exhale.

Drake kisses my temple. "Are you full?"

"Didn't we just confirm that?" I mumble.

His chuckle bounces me on his pec. "There's more omelet if you didn't get enough."

"You stuffed me to the brim." My mind wanders through the afterglow. I could get used to this treatment if I'm not careful. That warning can be ignored for another five minutes. "Do you like to cook?"

"Yes, but it's not very satisfying to eat alone."

"Just like sex," I whimper as his cock twitches inside of me. My vibrator collection is stellar but there's no replicating his level of stimulation.

"Just as I predicted." He tucks my head under his chin. "We were meant to find each other."

Before I can argue his commitment status, the front door opens. I freeze in Drake's hold. My pulse thunders as I wait for our unexpected guest to identify themselves.

"Cass?"

I exhale for a full minute when my cousin's voice

calls to me. She's the best option in this scenario. Had it been my children, I'd probably expire on this island like rotten milk.

"In the kitchen," I tell her.

Drake falters. "The fuck?"

"What?"

"I'm still inside you." His eyes lower to where our bodies are joined at the hips.

"Time to go, trouble." I straighten and push at his shoulder.

He slips from me and I hiss at the loss. There's no time to mourn the fleeting connection, which is entirely my fault. I slide off the counter and straighten my shirt, the hem falling beyond mid-thigh.

"Looks good on you," Drake comments.

"Hmm?" I mumble absently.

He nods to the oversized garment. "Something to snuggle when I'm not around."

My focus narrows on what I'm wearing. How I didn't notice this was his before is another mystery. "Damn."

"You can say that again." His laugh is slightly unhinged. "I can't believe you invited someone in here after what we just did."

"It's only my cousin." My hand swats at his misplaced concern. "And to be fair, I didn't know she was coming over."

"You could've told her to wait a minute."

"That would've raised suspicions."

"And this won't?" He motions to his mostly naked form.

"I don't see a problem." But the fib is transparent.

My ruined underwear does little to soak up the evidence of our morning sexcapades. I cross my legs and flex every Kegel muscle possible. A hollow ache spreads to remind me of the wreckage Drake left behind. My vagina will never be the same.

He shrugs, reading my bluff like a context clue. "No? Fine. Let her get an eyeful. Didn't take you as one to share but—"

My lips flatten and I back him against the cabinets. "Don't move."

"Why not? Afraid she'll see my hot ass?"

"Yes," I say before logic can muzzle me.

"Is my cum leaking down your inner thighs? My shirt is the only thing concealing you from view. You're covered in me, beauty. If I thought you looked freshly fucked before..." He trails off on a chuckle, scrubbing at his stubbled jaw.

I glare at the possessive gleam in his gaze while trying to tame my hair. "Just hush over there."

"Howdy, cowgirl. How's it—?" Paisley jerks to a standstill at the kitchen entrance. "Oh! You have company."

My elbow misses the counter when I try to aim for calm and collected, which only adds to my frazzled state. "Don't mind him. He's just... someone I used to know."

My cousin's eyes bulge as she gawks at Drake. "Are you—?"

"Cassidy's sexual servant? Yes, guilty as charged. I'd shake your hand but I'm under strict orders to stay in the corner." The incorrigible flirt winks at me.

"You're her...?" Paisley's gaze swings my way. "Wow."

"He's joking," I blurt. "Obviously." But the needy clench in my pussy calls me a liar.

"I see," she drawls. "You have Drake Granger in your kitchen, wearing a *Vagitarian* apron, claiming to be your sexual servant."

"That about sums it up." His smirk exposes those naughty dimples.

"Well done," Paisley praises me before waving at the man who has officially overstayed his welcome. "We haven't met but you don't need a proper introduction. I'm Paisley, if you were curious. Cassidy would be horribly lonely and even more anti-social without me."

"I'm glad she has your moral support," Drake laughs.

"Right? I don't think I get enough recognition for that."

My arms slide across my chest in a feigned pose for nonchalance. "Uh-huh, thanks a lot. Both of you. Was there a reason you stopped by, Ley?"

"We're supposed to do pattern work with the futurity prospects today. You asked me to help you." Her attention returns to Drake. "But it looks like you're busy."

"No, no. I'm ready to ride." Even if I totally forgot about our plans to do so. I send a pointed look to the man responsible for distracting me. "He was just leaving."

"I wasn't," Drake interjects. "You on a horse is always a sight to see. It's been too long."

"Am I interrupting?" Paisley glances between us but makes no move to offer us privacy.

"Nope, we—"

"Just finished," Drake cuts in.

"Good grief," I mutter.

Paisley laughs. "Heck of a reunion."

"You have no idea." Drake blows me a kiss.

My face goes up in flames. "Well, this has been fun..."

The blonde bombshell parks her hip against the dining table. "I'm not going anywhere."

"Wasn't talking to you."

Drake drops his jaw. "Are you trying to get rid of me?"

I huff. "Maybe you can get dressed."

"Kinda hard when you're wearing my shirt."

"Just try your best. Please," I add through clenched teeth.

"Always do." Drake saunters toward the stairs but pauses to give my butt a soft spank. "Don't miss me too much, beauty."

CHAPTER EiGHT

Drake

THE WOMEN AREN'T IN THE KITCHEN WHEN I return downstairs. Their whispers lead me to a cozy room at the opposite end of the house. The space is designed for cuddling on the couch to watch a movie or hiding from a certain someone who isn't familiar with the floor plan.

I smirk while studying Cassidy huddled in a secretive formation with her cousin. They aren't aware that I've found them, which allows me to admire the sassy redhead at my leisure. She changed clothes in the five minutes I was gone. Snug jeans conceal the toned legs that were very recently draped around my waist. The denim molds to her round ass like a wet dream, especially in her bent position. A stretchy crop top does the same ample service to her breasts, as if offering them to me on a shelf.

A pleased rumble announces my presence. The hushed tones cut off instantly and the women whirl to face me. Cassidy's cheeks are flushed, displaying the freckles on a map to her getting caught. Paisley smiles as her gaze noticeably dips to my groin. Satisfaction spreads through me. The fact that my cowgirl couldn't wait to share intimate details about me might as well be a marriage proposal.

"Um, hi. You found us." The uncertainty in Cassidy's voice stretches my grin wider.

I close the gap separating us, drifting a thumb along her blush. "Were you talking about me, beauty?"

"Yes," she breathes. Her lashes flutter, but then she straightens. "I mean, no. Freaking dicksand. Why would we be?"

"It's been an eventful morning." I rock on my feet.

Paisley giggles. "That's putting it mildly."

Cassidy nudges her cousin. "Zip it."

"I'll warn you now," the blonde drawls. "It's unlikely I'll ever shut up about this."

"Just great." Cassidy rolls her eyes, catching sight of my outfit in the process. Her blink is slow as she gives me a once-over. "Is that...?"

"Yours?" I pluck the cotton tank practically glued to my chest. "Figured it was only fair seeing as I gave you mine to have and hold from this day forward."

"Oh, my," she exhales.

"Fits perfect," Paisley muses.

Cassidy snaps out of her dreamy stupor. "Are you ogling him?"

"Can you blame me? Especially after what you just told me." She adds the second part under her breath.

"This is going straight to his big head," Cassidy gripes.

"Already there." The cheeky smile curving my lips has reached clown status.

My better half admires me again. "Consider that shirt yours now that it's sculpted to your... bulging bulges."

"Bulging bulges?" I whistle. "Damn, beauty. You know how to wrap me around your little finger."

The red splotches on her cheeks burn brighter. "I'm a tad out of my element. Give me a break."

"What's bothering you?"

She flails an arm in my direction and huffs. "Um, hello."

"Would you rather I take it off?" I begin peeling the hem off my abdomen.

"No!" Cassidy blurts while her cousin says the opposite. That earns the blonde a fierce glare. "Seriously, Ley?"

Paisley shrugs. "He offered."

I hold up a palm. "No need to argue. I'll stay decent."

"Not sure that's possible," Cassidy mumbles.

"This is the thanks I get after everything I've done to make our one-week anniversary special? Ouch." But my smirk isn't fooling anyone.

Paisley's jaw drops. "I didn't know it was your anniversary."

"It's really not," Cassidy argues.

"Definitely is," I counter and give her a thorough perusal. "The celebration isn't over based on what I'm seeing. You look better than a Sunday brunch buffet after eating salad all week."

Paisley chokes, which morphs into a cough as she levels her cousin with a stare. "Wow, that's worth spreading yourself out on the counter as a holiday feast. Why are you still standing here?"

Cassidy hangs her head. "Don't encourage him."

"Too late," I chuckle.

"Okay, trouble. This has been super fun, but we have chores to do." She makes a shooing motion.

"Awesome." I clap and then rub my palms together. "Where do I start?"

Cassidy blinks. "Huh?"

"How can I help?"

"By going home," she deadpans.

I frown. "That's not a preferred opinion."

"For you."

"Are you trying to get rid of me again?"

"My kids will be home this afternoon. I have piles of shit to clean up before then. Literally." If she actually wants me to go, I will. But the humor in her eyes tells the truth.

"Just let me lighten your load for an hour or two. It's my fault you're behind."

Cassidy inspects my muscles, which flex for her approval. "Have you ever worked on a farm?"

"No, but I'm a fast learner."

"I'm sure he can be useful," Paisley comments.

Cassidy's lips pinch together. "Whose side are you on?"

"The one where I get to continue watching this play out." Paisley gestures between her cousin and me.

"Fine." Cassidy tosses her hands in the air. "You can feed the chickens and goats."

"What else?" I ask while we walk to the foyer and put on our boots.

"Just start with that," she says.

"Really? It's gonna be a breeze. Animals love me."

Chester and Cheeto dash outside when I open the door. "See?"

"Missed your calling as a dog whisperer." Her grin is tipped high enough to cause concern but I'm too happy to see the expression to question it.

The morning sun beams down on us while we stride into the stable elements. Apple blossoms and horse manure are fresh in the air. Cassidy prattles off instructions that seem easy enough. I swerve toward the coop as the women walk to the barn, going our separate ways.

"Good luck," she calls over her shoulder.

My smirk is smeared in confidence. "Won't need it."

Cassidy's response is carried off on a breeze but I catch the laughter in her tone. That sound strokes me to distraction while I scoop feed from the labeled bin. My head is in the clouds, replaying her orgasmic bliss from earlier, when the metal latch lifts in my grip.

"Holy flock!" I stumble backward and nearly fall flat on my ass.

Countless chickens rush at me in a whirlwind of feathers and gratitude. Their clucks flutter the silence as they escape the confines without a care for breakfast. A whiff from inside the coop reveals why they're in such a hurry to leave. It smells like dust and poop had a dozen babies in this hot box. The sweltering heat predicted for today must make the environment inhospitable. I hold my breath before dumping the grains and seeds into the dishes.

There's a swarm of birds surrounding me once I evacuate, as if applauding my efforts. They totally get it. Clean oxygen has never smelled so good. My lungs greedily soak in several breaths while I mentally check off the first chore.

An impatient clatter shakes me from the reprieve. The bang rattles the chain link fence again. I squint at the pen a few paces away where two goats demand an audience.

"Hey there," I croon. "You must be Billy and Gruff."

Synchronized bleats confirm my assumption.

"I thought you'd be bigger. Are you a miniature breed?"

The gray and white pair bump their heads into the cage, proving to be mighty regardless of size.

"Got it, dudes. Hungry?"

Their strikes against the enclosure gain momentum to prioritize a plan of action. Forget fetching the pellets. Freedom to roam can't wait.

I swing open the gate and wisely step aside. Unfortunately, my sole clips a divot in the yard and I tumble to the ground. Next thing I know, I'm splayed out in a starfish position. The blue sky mocks me while I collect my wounded pride. Muffled clops approach and a nose snuffs me. I ruffle the goat's coarse hair, which he views as permission to climb on top of me like a very masculine mountain.

A wheeze is stripped from me when his front hooves stomp my chest. "Damn, you're stronger than you look. Give me space, yeah?"

Billy or Gruff—not sure which—doesn't do boundaries. The little guy nibbles at the cotton stretched tight over my nipple. I squirm while trying to dislodge him without causing injury.

A shove at his neck does nothing. "Whoa there. I'm spoken for."

The goat chomps on the fabric, chewing until an unmistakable rip sounds.

"Dude, did you hear me? I'm a taken man."

Our conflict of interest gains the attention of his buddy. He trots over to us, a gleam in his beady eyes.

"Oh, hell no. I'm not getting double teamed by you two."

A threatening thrash stops the incoming one in his tracks. By the time I wrangle the other horny goat off me, there's a large hole torn in my shirt. I shrug and accept the damage as free air conditioning. A whistle purses my lips while I dust myself off and get the goats fed. They barely sniff the pellets, too preoccupied following me into the barn.

Cassidy is saddling a horse in the center aisle when I strut inside. I don't get to admire her methodical technique for more than three seconds. Paisley whizzes past me, pushing a full wheelbarrow. Her dedicated concentration on the pile of shit narrowly misses slicing off my toe. I leap from her path, which allows me to inspect the spotless interior.

"Damn, how long was I gone?" Not that I saw it before, but this must be an improvement.

"At least thirty minutes," Cassidy answers as she finishes tacking her steed.

"What? No way."

"Rookie." She glances at the condition of my shirt. "Doing okay over there?"

"Your goats took advantage of me."

Her grin slides to the naughty duo loitering behind me. "They'd never do such a thing."

"I feel violated, but I've put myself back together again. Just call me Humpty Dumpty."

Paisley laughs, returning from her poop duty. "I like this guy."

"You can keep him company while I ride Levi." Cassidy gives the horse's neck an affectionate pat.

"Gonna make me jealous, beauty."

"Good." Cassidy winks and takes hold of Levi's reins, his hooves clomping on the concrete to announce their exit.

"C'mon, lost cause." Paisley claps my back. "We'll get you turned on."

I lock my knees. "Excuse me?"

She rolls her eyes. "Cassidy is sexy in the saddle. You won't be able to control yourself."

"Oh." The strain in my posture deflates. "That's nothing new."

"You've seen her ride before?"

I nod. "Years ago. When we were in middle school. She was at the county fair for a barrel race or something. Her horse was scary fast, but Cassidy handled him like a pro. I imagine her skills are even more impressive now."

"Ah." The blonde's features pinch. "She's such a natural talent. Meant to be on the back of a horse. Too bad she doesn't compete anymore."

"No?"

"Nah, but that's not my story to tell." And her hasty retreat tells me she's done talking about it.

When we get to the outdoor arena, Cassidy is already

sitting on Levi. Her untamed hair blows in the slight breeze while she steers him to the outer edge and urges him to trot. The gait seems bouncy, but she's one with the horse. Their pace increases in speed until it seems like Levi's legs don't even touch the ground. Cassidy hovers in the saddle to avoid jolted impact, at least I assume. It's like they're both floating.

She guides him at a diagonal across the ring. There's a mutual respect while they appear to get cues from each other. I notice she barely touches the reins, controlling him some other way. The training that requires goes way over my head. All I can do is watch in stunned silence.

"Damn," I breathe.

"Told you." There's a smug edge in Paisley's voice.

It's only then I remember she's beside me. I was too caught up in Cassidy. "Aren't you supposed to be helping her exercise the prospects or whatever?"

"Yeah, yeah. We have all day. Want me to get one saddled for you?"

I burst out laughing until I realize she isn't joining in the amusement. "That's a negative."

"Have you ever been on a horse?"

"Nope."

"Do you plan to?"

"When Cassidy's ready to teach me."

"Excellent answer." She spots something over my shoulder. "Pussy incoming."

"The fu—?" My question cuts off as sharp claws pierce into my legs. A peek behind my shoulder reveals two kittens climbing me like a scratching post.

"Meet Ethel and Ester. Such rascals but very loved. They're Kenzie's pride and joy."

The mention of Cassidy's daughter forgives the felines' antics. "I'm beginning to believe the animals are testing me."

Paisley assists in plucking the kitties off my jeans, and then proceeds to cradle them like babies. "Welcome to your Greener Pastures initiation."

I scratch Ester and Ethel behind their ears. "Does this mean I'm accepted?"

"Meh. If her kids approve of you, then you're golden."

Warmth spreads through my chest. "Hopefully I'll get the chance to know them and plead my case. I met Charlie, but haven't seen Mackenzie yet."

Paisley studies me for a moment, long enough that my skin starts to itch. "Can I give you some advice?"

"By all means." I gesture for her to let me have it.

"Cassidy is a rare gem. She's the type you meet once in a lifetime and want to smother in so much love that she can't deny how much you appreciate her. I get it, but you need to understand she's fiercely independent."

My attention returns to the spirited redhead who's loping Levi in figure eight patterns. Her body sways into the horse's stride. I find myself mesmerized once again. "There's nothing wrong with that."

Her head bobs to agree with me. "Her barn doors have been sealed shut until you barged in somehow. She might've agreed to let you tickle the twat, but there's no way she's ready to go all in. I bet she's planning on walking away after whatever happened last night."

"No," I snap.

Paisley just rolls her eyes. "You doubt me?"

"Why would she do that?"

Paisley shrugs. "Cassidy has been on her own, raising her kids, building a name for herself in the horse training industry. She has a load of crap on her plate. It's everywhere. If you push her too hard or fast, she might buck you off. Permanently. Not because she doesn't like you, but she's accustomed to doing things her way. It's no secret that you're coming on really strong. I admire your devotion and determination, but there are limits for a reason. Too much change to her routine will spook her."

I frown at the possibility of not having Cassidy at my side. It doesn't take more than a quick glance at our surroundings to expose her responsibilities, and that's only on the surface. I've always worked best on a team—but she's running this entire operation by herself. Unless I can convince her to let me on the stable squad. This type of labor isn't my wheelhouse, but I wasn't lying about being a fast learner.

"What do you recommend?"

"Be patient. Give her time and space."

"But—"

She presses a finger to her lips, telling me to shut mine. "You asked. Don't argue."

I slump in defeat. "If I back off, she might go about her business and forget about me."

Paisley snorts. "She won't."

"How do you know?"

"We're family, but she's also my best friend. Honestly, just this morning is a huge sign. I've never seen her act the way she does around you. She's flirty and funny and just… herself. It's refreshing."

That's a term I'm well versed with when it comes to Cassidy Brooks. She isn't a blip on an overgrown path I once traveled. She's the permanent mark where I'm meant to plant roots.

Whatever expression I'm wearing has the blonde smiling. "There we go. You're listening. Now, don't fuck it up. Let her come to you."

"And if she doesn't?"

Paisley's focus returns to Cassidy, her grin spreading. "That won't be a problem."

CHAPTER NiNE

Cassidy

"MOMMY, MOMMY!" CHARLIE TUGS ON THE HEM of my shirt and points at a nearby food truck. "They got cotton candy. I want some. You said I could."

"Yep, that's great." My eyes sweep the festival crowd again.

Kenzie tries to yank me in the opposite direction. "The face painting lady is over there. We're doing that first."

"Nuh-uh, my tummy is hungry. I need the cotton candy."

"But I want my face painted," Kenzie demands.

"We can do both," I mumble absently.

"M'kay," Charlie chirps. "Me first."

"No, me! I go first." Kenzie stomps her foot.

My son shakes his head of shaggy hair. "I'm the oldest. I get to choose."

"That's not fair," my little girl whines.

"Please don't argue." But the request lacks authority as my attention wanders across the sea of people clogging Main Street.

Kids and their parents have flooded Knox Creek to attend the annual Daze & Knights carnival. Most of the attractions are meant for children, but adults are encouraged to join in the fun. My knees and bladder are already preparing for the bouncy houses. The inflatables portion is in the park, which requires us to wade past rows of vendor booths along the way.

Tents and stands from dozens of small businesses line the road. A familiar brick building is ahead on the left. The logo makes my belly flip, and I avert my gaze.

I'm most definitely not searching for Drake. There's not a chance his cock den is included at a family-friendly event. It doesn't bother me in the least that I haven't heard from him since last weekend. The fact that it's Saturday and I've seen him the past two didn't register. Nope. We had a quick—but very passionate—fling and it's over. That's exactly what I predicted.

The pang in my chest calls me a liar. Dammit. This is the part I planned to avoid.

A harsh jostle to my arm whips me from the melancholy. "Mommy? Are you listening?"

"Mhmm," I answer.

Kenzie parks a fist on her cocked hip, not buying my noncommittal response. "Then why'd we stop walking?"

"We did?" I realize my sandals are firmly planted on the pavement.

Charlie gasps. "Oh, oh! We know that guy."

I glance at my son and try to follow where he's pointing. "Who, monkey moo?"

"That's your boyfriend!" Charlie stabs at a very specific spot and begins hopping higher than a bunny.

My cheeks blaze like I have a fever. I already know who he's referring to without seeing the proof. "Um, weren't we getting a snack somewhere?"

Kenzie relaxes her sassy stance. "Mommy doesn't have a boyfriend."

"Does too. He came to our house," Charlie insists. "His tattoos are awesome!"

My daughter blinks at me. "But boys are yucky."

"Girls are grosser." Charlie sticks out his tongue.

"Ewwwww," Kenzie complains. "You're rude."

The twins stare at each other, exchanging glares and silent insults like they often do. Meanwhile, I gather the courage to peek at Drake. A baseball hat shades his eyes but I'm certain that steely blue gaze is pinned on me. He turns more fully toward us and I'm captivated by his presence. I shiver despite the warmth rushing under my skin. Half a block separates us but we might as well be a foot away. It feels like his focus is touching me, reminding my body of how easily he can provide pleasure.

Charlie catches wind of our staring contest. "See! Mommy looooooves Rake. She's got those googly eyeballs just like when Pam looks at Daddy."

Kenzie starts nodding along. "They're gonna get married. Maybe we can throw flower petals in that wedding too. And then they'll take a big trip and be gone for a suuuuuuper long time. Mommy will get a baby in her belly and need to take lotsa naps. Her boyfriend husband will rub her feet. It's like when they all live happily ever after in the movies."

My son wrinkles his nose. "But are we gonna be in the happiness too?"

She shrugs. "I dunno. Is Mommy's boyfriend nice?"

"I think so?"

Kenzie smiles. "He'll let us stay and we'll have another daddy."

"That sounds cool," Charlie breathes.

"Okay," I sigh. "That's enough of that. Mommy doesn't have a boyfriend. You're not getting a second dad. No babies in my belly either."

As if waiting for a cue, Drake waves both of his arms straight in the air like he's flagging down an airplane. "Hey, family!"

I hang my head, the heat in my face reaching a level that burns. My fingers offer a limp wiggle before I duck into the crowd as a shield. Unfortunately, many of them are gawking at me.

"Such trouble," I mutter.

A shrill whistle slices into the distance between us, demanding notice. "Stay there! I'm coming."

"We gotta go." I usher the kids to the cotton candy stand, which conveniently hides us from view.

"But your boyfriend told us to wait," Kenzie says.

"He's not my boyfriend," I repeat for hopefully the final time.

Charlie huffs. "Rake is a boy and he's your old friend. That makes him your boyfriend."

"The terms don't quite..." I start but my tongue ties. "That's not how it works."

My daughter squints at the teenager spinning sugar onto two paper cones. "But—"

I pay for the sticky treat and steer my kids to the next stop. "What design do you want on your face, bunny boo?"

Kenzie's eyes sparkle, blue fluff already glued to her lips. "Elsa!"

"What a surprise." I laugh and glance at my son. "And for you, monkey moo?"

"Venom," he growls.

I startle. "Oh, that's… interesting."

"He's super scary and has sharp teeth." Charlie gnashes his own into another bite of cotton candy.

"Um, okay."

We slide into the line and I breathe easy for what feels like the first time since we arrived. The kiddos chatter about whose face paint will be better while munching on their sweet snack. I take a moment to soak in the sunshine. We shuffle forward, making progress. Rinse and repeat.

A buzz vibrates my back pocket. I slip my phone free and peek at the text.

Trouble: Hey, beauty. Where'd you go?

I consider not responding, but the silent treatment isn't nice. Especially when he's done nothing to deserve that.

Me: There's stuff the kiddos want to do.

Trouble: Can I join you? Unless you're not ready for that. I don't want to overstep.

I stare at his words, imagining the honesty thrumming in his tone. Indecision churns my thoughts into whipped butter. There hasn't been a man in my life since Shawn, but he barely counts as anything except a fantastic father for our kids. He and I didn't work out, but that doesn't mean we can't be co-parents. The twins accepted Pam as another parental figure once their dad made it official.

Kenzie mapped out a similar fate for me with Drake before even seeing him up close. Charlie met him and isn't traumatized. Unless I consider the boyfriend assumption. That's more problematic for me, though.

A heavy exhale slumps my shoulders. "Hey, moo-boo?"

They swivel toward me as a cohesive unit. "Yes, Mommy?"

I grin when they don't fuss about the conjoined nickname. It's hit or miss these days. "Would it be okay if Drake stopped over to say hello?"

Charlie's forehead crinkles. "You mean Rake?"

"His name is actually Drake," I laugh.

"Is that your boyfriend?" Kenzie's voice lifts to a dreamy tune.

"He's just a friend," I reiterate.

"And a boy," Charlie adds.

My daughter giggles. "He wantsa hang out with us. I think he's your real boyfriend."

"Maybe he should stay where he is," I mumble to myself.

"Noooooo!" Charlie shakes me until I almost drop my phone. "I wanna see Rake."

"Don't make me regret this." I motion from my eyes to theirs.

Drake gets the same message when I reply to tell him where we are. Kenzie skips to the open seat when the artist is ready for her. Charlie gobbles the rest of his cotton candy, his skinny limbs twitching with the incoming sugar rush. I brace myself for the unknown.

"There's the lovely bunch I've been missing." Drake's approach parts those blocking his path to us.

I don't fight my smile. "Didn't expect to see you here."

His stance widens beside me. "Why not?"

My lips curve higher. "This doesn't seem like your usual scene."

A quick shake of his head scolds me. "I'll have you know that Roosters is donating all proceeds from today to a charity that feeds starving children."

"That's... really incredible." And crumbles the puny restraint I'd attempted to build against him.

"Much more than a sordid cock den." Drake winks.

"I'm done! Your turn, moo." Kenzie hops off the chair and inspects her transformation in the provided mirror.

"Yay!" Charlie eagerly replaces her, explaining his choice to the artist.

"You make a beautiful Elsa," I tell my daughter as she does a twirl.

"Thanks, Mommy." Her eyes slide to the man next to me before returning to her reflection.

A bubble expands in my throat and I suddenly lose traction in this situation. He's just a guy. They don't have to like him. My heart is far from invested. But a clench in my chest argues that the beating organ isn't falling for lies.

Drake appears content to allow the scene to unfold

naturally. His expression is relaxed and open for engagement. My kiddos exchange a silent glance that holds an entire conversation without a word.

"What're they doing?" Drake asks from the corner of his mouth.

"It's a twin telepathy thing. They've probably been doing it since they were wombmates. I think they're feeling you out."

"Ah, okay. I've got this." He rubs his palms together. "Should I be concerned?"

"Only for what you're wearing under those shorts." His left dimple blows me a kiss and I sway.

"Oh, my." I haven't regained my bearings when Drake spreads his arms wide in greeting.

"Mac and Cheese! Thanks for letting me tag along. I'll make it worth your while."

Kenzie squeaks and a sparkle enters her gaze. "Is that our nickname?"

"Absolutely, Mac." The man responsible looks too pleased with himself, especially when my little girl begins bouncing in a circle.

"I love it!" Kenzie shouts.

"Me too!" Charlie cheers as the artist finishes his design.

"Is that a monster on your face, Cheese?" Drake motions to his own cheek.

"I'm Venom. Feed me tater tots and ice cream," my son demands in a demonic tone while curling his fingers into claws.

"Whoa!" Drake stumbles backward. "Please don't hurt me."

"I'll save you, Rake." Kenzie flutters fake wings and zooms in front of her brother, tapping him with a pretend wand. "There. Now he's frozen."

"Save me," Charlie wails. "I'm sooooo cold."

"What should I do? I'm conflicted." Drake hesitates, unsure whose side to be on.

"Don't worry," I murmur. "They'll work it out."

As predicted, Kenzie spins around her brother and boops him with her invisible magic. "You're melted, Venom. But you better behave or I'll lock you in the dungeon."

"M'kay, promise." Charlie smiles wide. "Let's fight bad guys!"

Drake laughs as the twins whack and slice a fleet of villains into thin air. "Wow, you didn't tell me your kids belong in movies."

I roll my lips between my teeth but a giggle escapes. "They're very theatrical."

He applauds them. "I'm here for it."

"Which reminds me..." My attention swings to the line behind us. "We should get out of the way."

Before I can grab my wallet, Drake dumps entirely too much cash in the woman's money jar. "That should cover it."

"You don't have to do that," I rush to say.

His thumb traces the shape of my jaw. "I want to, beauty. Is that allowed?"

I lean into his touch, accepting whatever he's offering at this point. "Uh-huh."

"Should we play a new game? Mommy picked the

last one." Charlie resembles a tornado as we leave the small tent.

That shakes me from the stupor. "I did?"

"Yep! You hid and seeked with your boyfriend," Charlie giggles.

"He found her. Good job, Rake." Kenzie gives him a thumbs-up.

"What's my prize?" Drake asks, playing along.

"You get your face painted! It'll match the tattoos on your arms." Kenzie squeals.

"Only if you choose the design," he tells her.

"Bold move," I warn.

But it's too late. My little girl is already at the display boards, hovering her finger over the colorful options. Charlie and I share a laugh, giddy over what's about to happen.

Drake catches our amusement. "Don't worry about me. We're bonding."

I bite my bottom lip to trap a smile. My heart is the consistency of romantic slop. "Endless amounts of trouble."

"You love it." He squeezes my hip.

Kenzie arrives at a decision, but zips her mouth shut. "It's gonna be a surprise. 'Kay, Rake?"

"Sounds like a plan, Mac. I'll get it done right after these fine folks." He motions to the mom and her son waiting their turn.

"Oh, you can go ahead. I'll pay to see this." The woman's eyes are entirely too trained on Drake. There's a familiar heat wafting from her loins that makes misplaced tension coil inside of me.

I flick the green goblin off my shoulder. "This one is my treat. Give him the deluxe. We can afford to splurge."

Drake grins while he takes a seat. "Business is booming?"

"I sold two horses this week."

He whistles. "Well, shoot. Congratulations."

Emotion steals my speech for a moment, but I swallow the lump down. "Thanks. It's a needed boost. The market is tough but heavily in the seller's favor."

"Good on you, beauty. You're doing the darn thing." His eyes track Kenzie whispering to the artist. He slouches deeper into the chair and flips his hat backward. "All right, I'm ready. Do your worst."

"Nah, only the best for you. My line will wrap around the block after this." She dips a brush in water and gets started.

Humor climbs my throat when pink paint is slathered on the majority of his face. Laughter spews from me in unladylike snorts as the design takes shape. By the time glitter is added, my eyes are leaking tears.

The artist sprinkles on a few finishing touches and grabs a compact mirror. "What do you think?"

Drake is speechless for a moment as he inspects the transformation. "That's me? Holy smokes, I've never looked better."

"You're like the coolest ever." Kenzie stares at him in awe.

"Uh-huh," Charlie sighs. "I'm so super glad you're Mommy's boyfriend."

Drake clutches the area over his heart. "Is this what it feels like when dreams come true? I can't believe your mom is my girlfriend and she has the best kids in the whole wide universe."

A protest tickles my tongue but I let the label stick. Just for today. My children flock to him as if he's been their favorite person forever. They're totally smitten, not that I blame them. The warmth in my belly spreads until I'm sweating.

Another generous wad of cash is added to the lady's money jar before we return to the crowded street. A glance at Drake standing tall and proud folds me in half. I'm unable to contain my glee as it quakes my entire body.

"What's so funny?"

"She turned you into My Little Pony," I laugh.

"Pinkie Pie," Kenzie corrects.

He neighs and stomps the ground. "Your mighty steed has arrived. Wanna ride?"

Lust replaces amusement in a fiery wave. "Yes, please."

"This is doing it for you?" He points to the paint job that's turned him into single mom clit bait.

"Big time." I fan myself.

But I can be patient unlike my kiddos. The twins swarm him, tugging from both sides. It's no surprise they begin arguing about who goes first.

"Hey, hey," Drake shushes. "Guess what? I have two legs. You can ride at the same time. Hop on!"

Kenzie dances on her toes. "We totally get to be part of the happily ever after."

"Yessssss! This is the best day everrrrr," Charlie hollers.

They squeal and attach themselves to him. Their little arms hold tight as they balance on his feet. Shrill giggles spill from them, rising above the festival noise. Drake whinnies again and begins walking forward in exaggerated strides. People turn and gawk. He waves at the admirers shamelessly. I follow behind, almost tripping head over heels from the view.

Drake glances at me from over his shoulder. "Hey, beauty?"

My leisurely stroll speeds to a trot so he doesn't have to shout. "What's up, trouble?"

"I know you're busy and we're taking things slow"—he chuckles when I falter at that second point—"but there's a surprise party for one of my best friends and his fiancée next weekend. Will you be my date? If that's not convincing enough, the Roosters crew demands a proper introduction."

My lashes flutter at the whole package beside me. It's impossible to deny him while decked out as Pinkie Pie. "I'd agree to just about anything right now."

"Probably shouldn't have told me that."

"Don't push it. There are limits," I tease.

Drake swoops slightly while maintaining his choppy gait. "I look forward to discovering them."

"And why's that?"

"I'm going to swing for your fences and head straight for home."

CHAPTER TEN

Drake

"WELL, WELL, WELL," I DRAWL AND STRAIGHTEN off the building that had been propping me up. "Sure is fancy bumping into you on Main Street again. How many Saturdays in a row does this make?"

Cassidy laughs, her eyes rolling skyward as she steps down from her truck. "As if you're not counting."

"Humor me."

Four fingers wiggle at me. "Are we celebrating? Other than this secretive party that starts at noon."

"We have time to honor our anniversary first."

I admire the view as she struts toward me. Another pair of heavily tooled cowboy boots cushion her feet, but those barely earn a passing glance. It's the one-piece denim contraption barely concealing her curves that has my dick twitching. The snug material is a combo of shorts and a sleeveless shirt. My mouth goes dry as I continue to gawk. Frayed bottoms end just below her ass and the buttons down the front don't start until well beyond her cleavage. That plunging neckline strikes a match to my insatiable hunger. I bite my fist and growl.

"Like what you see?" She spins in a slow circle.

"Fuck my friends. Tell me how to get that thing off you and we'll have some real fun."

"It's complicated," she purrs.

"I'm not afraid of a challenge, and I'll sweeten the pot. These are for you." I reveal the sunflowers from behind my back, which she immediately accepts. "And this is for me."

She smiles when I cradle her chin between my thumb and forefinger to lock our lips in a chaste peck. "All I had to do was show up? I'll thank you extra for that."

My groan slips into her mouth as she opens for me, taking the kiss to an elevated public display of affection. "Damn, beauty. You're the gift that keeps on giving."

"Makes sense since it feels like a special occasion whenever you're around." She tucks the sunflowers into her purse and then clutches the front of my shirt, tugging me into a tight embrace I never want to leave.

I tremble when her tongue slides along mine. "Did you miss me?"

"Yes," she freely admits.

"Love hearing that."

"Yes, yes, yes," she chants.

My chuckle interrupts our heated exchange. "Careful or you'll attract a crowd."

Cassidy drifts her nose along my stubbled jaw, inhaling me on an audible breath. "You do that on your own, trouble. I'm surprised you didn't announce my arrival to the entire town."

"Thought about it. I want everyone to assume you're mine."

"Afraid someone else will catch my eye?"

"Only every day."

Her laugh is vibrant as she pats my chest, smoothing

the wrinkles she created. "You have nothing to worry about."

I cinch an arm around her waist, hauling her against me. "Does that mean you're agreeing to be mine?"

Not that she has to admit it aloud. The truth is that Cassidy has been mine since she kissed me when we were kids. But I'll let her believe whatever she wants. For now.

She flutters her lashes. "It's a bit early for labels, hmm?"

"Not according to your children, and I respect their opinions."

Her grin spreads. "Until they disagree with you."

I scoff. "That's not gonna happen. They love me."

"Oh, yes. What was I thinking? Kids always behave and go along with whatever you say is best."

"Your sarcasm clashes with my optimism," I grumble.

"If it makes you feel better, you've totally won them over. Charlie and Kenzie haven't stopped talking about you or your pony rides."

A pressure I didn't realize was in my chest suddenly loosens. "The feeling is mutual."

She hums. "Your texts were cute too."

"Had to make sure I'm never far from your mind. I almost drove to your house a dozen times this week, but I didn't want to crowd you."

Her eyes sparkle. "Since when?"

My palms roam along her sides, as if offering comfort on their own. "I see how much you have going on. The moments you sacrifice for me are already a strain on you. Like right now, I'm sure there are a million other things you'd rather be doing."

Cassidy cuddles into me. "I'm exactly where I want to be."

"On the same page as me," I murmur into her hair.

Her gaze latches onto mine. That unwavering attention feels bottomless. "I had every intention of making this a one and done."

"Oh?" Paisley's words haunt me, the truth clanging against my skull. "But now?"

"I've realized you might be irresistible. Charlie and Kenzie more than likely influenced my decision." She pulls away slightly and goes quiet for a moment, studying me closely. "The twins are your biggest fans. Please don't take that for granted."

I flinch. "You think I could do that to them? Or you, for that matter?"

"No, but shit happens. Just consider their feelings before acting like a dick." She kisses any chance of an argument off my lips.

I grunt into her distraction method. "What's best for you and your kids is my top priority. I hope you trust me enough to believe that."

She's already nodding. "It was mostly a precaution."

"Completely unnecessary." The start of our conversation circles back to me while we're discussing the kiddos. "Where were Charlie and Kenzie that first Saturday we saw each other? If my math is mathing correctly, they should've been with you that weekend."

"Somebody is sensing a pattern," she laughs. "Shawn and I switch if there's something going on that the kids should be part of, or a conflict that's better for them to avoid. The flip flop is frequent, so good luck keeping track."

My pulse drums faster. "Am I allowed to ask about him?"

"I'm shocked you haven't already," she guffaws.

"It's been a hard-fought battle."

Cassidy quirks a brow and shrugs. "I commend your patience, but there's not much to tell. We were little more than fuck buddies when I got pregnant. Shawn was really involved and there for me, but it was obvious we weren't a love match. Thankfully we get along and respect each other. That's made co-parenting a breeze."

"Huh," I say. "That sounds very... civil."

"It is. We've got a good system. No jealously or animosity. Shawn is married to a lovely woman named Pam and they have a baby girl. The twins already told him about you." Her tone is nonchalant like this is a normal conversation, and it probably is for her.

But my blood pressure is trapped on a rollercoaster. "He's okay with that?"

She blinks. "Yeah, why wouldn't he be?"

"I dunno." And I really don't. This is a situation I'm completely unfamiliar with.

"You'll meet him eventually, if this goes anywhere serious." She motions between us.

"Isn't it already?"

Cassidy's grin softens. "Maybe? I like you a lot and we're having fun, but I'm not expecting a commitment. This isn't me sending mixed signals or playing games. I'm realistic. There's no spare time for romance. My responsibilities and priorities come first, always."

"I feel like you've rehearsed that speech. Didn't we already tuck this under the covers?" We share a laugh but hers sobers much faster than mine. "I'll settle for whatever you're willing to give me."

"But you shouldn't have to, Drake. You're sexy and rich and hung like a bedazzled horse. Why would you want to saddle yourself to a single mom with no spare time and spends her days shoveling shit?"

"Don't sell yourself short," I chide. "Don't act like you're not the woman I've been dreaming to find my entire life. Don't make your situation sound like a burden to me. It couldn't be further from the truth. You're the one for me and your kids are an added bonus. Like you said earlier, I'm exactly where I want to be."

"Damn," she chokes. "That's a great speech."

"It's my truth. I'm already yours. Can't you see that?" My thumb drifts along her upturned jaw.

She leans into my touch when I tuck loose hair behind her ear. "Logic and common sense suggest you're too good to be true."

"What do your heart and gut think?"

"That you'd rather cause yourself pain than hurt me intentionally. You're the most considerate, dependable man I've ever met. Not once, but twice."

"I'll accept that answer," I chuckle.

Cassidy bites her bottom lip as a blush blooms across her freckled cheeks. "I should be counting my lucky stars that you even glance in my direction."

My lips slant into a smirk. "I'm the lucky one."

"We don't have to lie to ourselves," she laughs.

"Believe in me, beauty. I'll never give you a reason to doubt me."

Her throat works with a thick swallow. "I trust you, trouble."

"There we go." My mouth brushes against hers. "I look forward to you falling in crazy extreme, unconditional love with me, Cassidy Brooks."

"My goodness." She fans her face. "You wear confidence like a favorite outfit."

"It's easy to feel invincible when I have the prettiest woman in my arms." My grasp on her wanders and latches onto her hips. I can't stop touching her, but she doesn't seem to mind.

"Such a line." Cassidy cuddles closer, returning my affection while basking in our chemistry.

"It's more than fluffy words and I'll prove it. My friends will too. Let's go meet them." I slide her fingers between mine and turn in the direction that leads to Ridge's house.

She glances at our clasped palms, clutching tighter to me. "This is nice. I can't remember the last time I held someone's hand just for the simple pleasure of it."

"It's the little things that allow intimacy and companionship to thrive in a relationship. Solid foundation."

"I think it's working already. Oh!" Without releasing me, Cassidy whips out a key fob and locks her truck. "Before I forget."

"Good call." I admire her Ford pickup that puts mine to shame. "That's quite the beast you're driving. What're you using all that horsepower for?"

"Nothing much," she quips. "I just really like the vibrations from such a big motor. It really hits the spot."

I gulp, now imaging the fiery redhead in the throes

of passion while swerving along a back country road. "That stick shift handles your needs."

"Mine is automatic. Push start. Slides into gear smoothly. Gets me there faster. No hassle with a third pedal."

"There's still a crank shaft," I croak.

Her laughter is a pleasant chime in the wind. "I don't even know what that does."

My brows wiggle. "Keep me around and find out."

"Trouble, trouble," she sighs. "Remind me why we had to park in town?"

"Ridge would know something's up if he saw a bunch of cars near his place, especially ones he recognizes. That would ruin the surprise."

Cassidy nods. "Smart. Do you live nearby?"

It could be considered odd that she doesn't already know, but her responsibilities at Greener Pastures demand that she stays onsite. "Not close enough to walk from there."

"I'm curious where home is for you," she muses.

Wherever she is, but it's too soon for that. "You've got a lot happening on your property. There's nothing to worry about at mine. We'll swing by someday when it's convenient."

"Mr. Granger?" A man I don't recognize waves, pausing on the sidewalk. "Ah, I thought that was you. I'm Alan, a sales consultant for Sutherland Homes."

Cassidy visibly stiffens beside me, but doesn't speak.

"Nice to meet you," I say and shake Alan's proffered hand.

"We're grateful for your investment toward our

construction plans. The contact information for Mr. Kenner is also much appreciated. Thanks to you, we're one step closer to breaking ground." He beams at me.

"Glad we found a solution."

The woman beside me gasps and untangles her fingers from mine. I reach to reclaim her palm but she crosses her arms. My smile dies in a tragic flatline.

Alan reads the mood and resumes his stroll. "Well, I'll leave you to it. Just wanted to say a quick hello and let you know we're indebted to you. Please give us a call if you'd like to collaborate again in the future."

I barely hear him or his retreating footsteps. My focus is trained on Cassidy and the hurt shimmering in her eyes. She begins backing away without a word.

"Hey, where are you going?" I clasp her arm.

She rips herself from my hold. "Don't touch me."

My frown is met with a wounded expression. "What's wrong, beauty?"

Her eyes narrow into daggers. "The fact you even have to ask is incredibly insulting."

"Why are you mad?"

A lone tear slips free from her glare, slicing into me with lethal precision. "How could you?"

"I'm lost."

"Seriously?" She scoffs and betrayal distorts her beautiful face into a pinched mask. "What did I just say about acting like a dick? And to think, my heart was opening to you."

I blanch. "How am I acting like a dick?"

Her lips press into a firm line. "I can't believe you'd willingly work with that company."

I hold up a hand. "To be fair, I didn't know who they were until you told me."

"I didn't tell you their name," she shoots back.

My hands swat at the sudden space separating us. "But it wasn't difficult to connect the dots. Process of elimination."

Another tear traces her freckled cheek. "You're unbelievable."

"Does it help to hear that I gave them money to protect you?"

"Are you kidding me? No, never. Not even a little bit."

I cringe. "Really?"

"Yes, really. Those people are ruthless predators. Truly awful. Preying on those they believe are weak. They're trying to destroy my home. The legacy my grandmother built and passed down to me. How could you support them?" The raw emotion cutting from her voice stabs me in the gut.

I nearly double over. "It's not what you think."

"How can it be anything else? You invested in their plans to turn farm country into mass-produced houses."

A tight knot forms in my throat. "Only to get them away from you."

"And harass some other unsuspecting landowner? How nice." She rolls her watery eyes.

"Not quite. Robert Kenner is very willing to sell."

"That's beside the point. They've made my life miserable. I detest everything about them and now you're their partner."

"But I did it for you," I try again.

"You shouldn't have." Her dry tone is almost comical.

"Do you want me to kill the deal?"

"Yes," she says without pause. But then she sighs. "If that Robert guy wants to sell his property, it's not my business. But I don't like that you're involved with Sutherland Homes."

"It's not ideal, but they agreed to stop bothering you and your family."

"Yeah right," she scoffs. "For how long?"

"Indefinitely."

She pauses, a breeze kicking up her wildflower scent. "How much did you give them?"

"Less than my limit."

"Is this bullshit bargain worth selling your soul to the devil?"

The urge to touch her lifts my arm, but I drop the limb seconds later. "Your happiness means everything to me, beauty. That's why I did this. You haven't heard from them in over two weeks, right?"

"I figured they were on vacation," she grumbles. "What's to stop them from coming after us again?"

"Me."

She tugs at her hair. "You'll fund them to build elsewhere until you're broke."

I shrug. "If that's what it takes for you to be left in peace."

Cassidy hangs her head. "You should've talked to me first."

"But then you would've convinced me not to invest."

"Exactly! It's a shitty position you've put me in." She bites the inside of her cheek, avoiding my gaze. "I wish you hadn't paid them."

"Will you forgive me?" I reach for her fingers, threading the tips with mine.

"It's hard not to. Your intentions were decent. Not another penny, okay?"

"But—"

"No, they don't deserve it. We can get rid of them the old-fashioned way."

"Like feed them to the pigs?"

She laughs, which is a great sign. "Ignore them until they lose interest."

My smirk makes a miraculous comeback. "Obviously, I was just testing you."

"Uh-huh, I'm still not pleased about this. You're earning your nickname." Cassidy clucks her tongue.

"Will you let me make it up to you?" I pull her flush against me, wrapping us in a hug that soothes the ache.

She rests her chin on my sternum, fluttering her lashes. "How might you do that?"

"I can be very creative and thorough." A peek at my watch spurs me into action. "But first, we need to hustle or we'll miss the surprise."

The amused curve lifting her mouth flips upside down. "You should go without me. I'm not the best company right now."

"What? No way. You can't ditch me after our first official fight as a couple. I need to grovel until you agree to makeup sex."

She snorts. "Good luck with that."

"It's going to be an afternoon to remember. I'll make it worth your while," I vow. "You agreed to believe in me."

"Mhmm, and then look what happened."

"That was a tiny detour, but we're back on track."

"It isn't that simple. I should probably be alone. My feelings are... complicated and conflicted."

Something sharp stabs my chest. "About me?"

"We've moved really fast, and I'll accept the blame for that. Space might be a good idea. It's a jumble up there." Cassidy taps at her temple.

"Is that what you really want?" If it is, I'll quit pushing. At least until tomorrow.

She sniffs and drops her gaze. "No."

"You'll let me fix this? Starting now?"

"That doesn't seem right." A deep furrow creases her forehead. "Am I overreacting?"

"Nope, I crossed a line. You're justified in getting upset. Your feelings are valid. I hear you and I'm sorry."

"But you didn't know how much this would hurt me."

"I do now. I'm listening. It's a learning curve. We're communicating and working through it." I tuck a bent knuckle under her chin. "Don't give up on me yet."

Cassidy melts into me. "Not sure I could if I tried."

"Does that mean you're still my date for this shindig?"

"Maybe..."

"Don't make me toss you over my shoulder."

"You wouldn't dare."

"Do you doubt me and my devotion to our relationship?" I squat and lift her off the ground.

Cassidy squeals, wiggling in my grip. "Okay, fine. I'll go with you."

"Damn straight." I lower her feet to the sidewalk and snag her hand. "Stay beside me, beauty. Right where you belong."

CHAPTER ELEVEN

Cassidy

A LARGE OAK SHIELDS US FROM THE WORST OF the late July heat. I stare across the decorated backyard while we wait for the guests of honor to arrive. Too many names clog my brain, the introductions a blur. My wits are still scattered after Drake's unfortunate revelation. The sour taste in my mouth further proves Sutherland Homes is toxic.

"Is this too much?" The question in his expression expands wider than the small crowd gathered to celebrate Ridge and Callie.

I shake my head. "It looks perfect. The party planner deserves a raise."

"Thank you," Harper chirps as she pauses next to us. "Minimal hiccups except the happy couple is nowhere to be found. There are murmurs about penis candy too."

I lift my brows at the blonde, one of the only faces I recognize in the bunch. "Penis candy?"

She holds up her palms. "I'm acting oblivious. Just cross your fingers that Sydney doesn't find them, if they do exist."

A snort rips from me just imagining her little girl's reaction. "That would be an awkward conversation."

"One more for the list," she muses.

I nod and take a long sip of my pineapple mimosa.

A silence creeps in. That lull oozes and festers like a scab that hasn't fully healed. The tension swirls until I can choke on the fumes.

Harper's keen awareness shifts from me to the man hovering at my side. "Are you two okay?"

"Yep," I say at the same time Drake provides his own answer.

"I fucked up," he admits.

She purses her lips. "Why am I not surprised?"

A sheepish grin matches his downcast gaze that looks far too innocent. "I got into bed with her enemy. It was supposed to be heroic, but I didn't consider the consequences. Botched banger."

Harper's eyebrows disappear into her hairline. "Ummm…"

All I can do is laugh. "That sounds much worse than it is."

"Uh-huh," she drones. "This one"—her thumb hitches at Drake—"has a tendency to exaggerate."

He shrugs. "I prefer the term overindulge. Enthusiastic. Dedicated. Vigilant. Committed."

"Don't know when to quit," she adds.

"Exactly." His blue eyes sparkle in that hypnotic sense. "What did you expect after I got reunited with the woman I'm going to marry?"

A wheeze lodges in my throat and I almost cough up a lung. This doesn't ease my rattled thoughts. Unintelligible nonsense sputters from me in response.

Meanwhile, Harper appears positively giddy as her grin stretches to hit a world record. She cups one side of her mouth and leans toward me. "He's a really great guy."

"I know," I whisper just as loudly in return.

She smiles. "Are you gonna keep him around?"

Woodsy spiced cologne and undeniable temptation blow on the breeze. My scattered wits collect themselves, allowing me to picture us years down the road. "I'd bet on the odds."

"Yes, cowgirl. Giddy up!" Harper stills. "Did you get him on a horse yet?"

"Nope, but his butt will be in the saddle soon." More stress seeps from me at that visual.

"Whatever she wants. I'll step up to the plate." Drake pretends to swing a bat.

"Wrong sport," I laugh.

"Similar mechanics."

"Not even close."

"My athletic abilities spread beyond the pitcher's mound." He winks.

"You'll see once certain muscles are stiff and you can barely walk." I mimic the sore, bow-legged motions.

"Damn, beauty. At least buy me a drink first."

"I'll make your refill a double." The alcohol table was properly stocked by a bartender after all.

"Welp, you don't need me to loiter on the romance. This has been a blast. Cheers, lovebirds." Harper begins backing away while glancing at her phone. "And on that note, there's a Ridge and Callie sighting. That's my cue. Stay sharp!"

We linger in the shade as she trots off to handle her host duties. Silence finds us again. The pause isn't awkward. More like a calm between chaos.

A sideways glance finds Drake's gaze tracing my

curves. I take the opportunity to return the favor. Sunshine kisses his hair, the dark strands streaked to glow. The white tee he's wearing stretches over his muscles. Tattoos and ropey veins on full display thanks to the short sleeves. Faded denim hugs his ass and legs in a relaxed hold. My thighs flex, seconds from launching at him.

"Penis candy," I mumble.

His brow puckers. "What?"

"I'm in the mood for something sweet."

"You're hungry?"

"Okay."

"Is this too much for you?" he asks again.

I blink from the haze. "Not at all. Quit stressing, trouble."

And let's be honest, I'm mostly recovered from the ordeal. Other than the reminder that Sutherland Homes doesn't give a damn about who or what or where. They'll devour whatever bait is in front of them like parasites. If I'm off their radar, maybe I can finally relax a little.

"Does that mean you're agreeing to marrying me someday?"

"Oh, that." I laugh as his comment to Harper replays. "A tad presumptuous, but barely fazed me. You should hear the wild stories my twins whip together without trying."

He chuckles. "Mine isn't pretend."

I gape at him. "We've been on two dates. Maybe three if you're being generous."

"And?"

My mouth opens and shuts, speech absent. "A

relationship is already a stretch for me to believe. There's no way marriage is actually on your radar."

"Swing and a miss," he rasps. "I'll improve my game. Add it to the groveling."

"That's not necessary," I croak. "You have nothing to prove, remember?"

The potential of him trying harder unravels me. Heat floods me in a fiery wave and my knees wobble. I probably wouldn't survive the possibilities.

Drake rubs a bent knuckle along my overheated cheek. "I disagree, if you still doubt me."

"A man who isn't afraid of commitment. My imagination is running at a full gallop."

"Didn't we already prove I'm real?" He dips to brush his lips over mine. "I want the happily ever after with you and the kids. That's my dream. You're the only one who can fulfill it."

My inhale is sharp. He included my children in the equation. How I'm still standing and not in a puddle at his feet is some sort of superpower. There's a clench in my lower belly as if my ovaries are about to release every egg in stock.

That's the moment I decide to ditch the fear and restraint holding me back from this man. No more hiding. Loneliness isn't my lifelong bestie. Screw Sutherland and their seedy shit.

Something long overdue loosens inside of me. A rusty gate creaks open to release my worries and fears and allow acceptance to flood in. He's worthy of breaking my heart, but I'm certain that he'd be the last one to ever do so. Fizz tickles my nose as I suckle at my beverage, suddenly parched.

"I think you're my dream too," I breathe.

Drake's broad shoulders sag and he stoops over me. "Thank Cupid and his arrows for that. Now I don't have to suppress my urges with you. This means you're finally mine."

"Oh, my." I flutter a palm to my chest. "Are you asking me out, Drake Granger?"

"Didn't I already?"

"Not officially."

"I've only been practicing the line since seventh grade." He thumps his forehead and clears his throat. "Would you do me the honor of being my girlfriend, Cassidy Brooks?"

My heart soars as if I'm that teenage girl again, flirting with the boy she's been crushing on. "Better late than never."

"Is that a yes?"

My nod is fast. "I'm willing to fall."

A pleased sound rumbles from him. "You won't regret it, beauty. I'll catch you and treat you better than a cowgirl queen."

There's a drum thumping a giddy beat in my veins. "And I believe it. You already make me very happy. Give me something to look forward to and smile about. Deliver a sense of comfort I've rarely had. The struggles and responsibilities don't drag me down as far when you're around."

He kisses me again. "You have no idea what that means to me."

Our eyes catch and lock. Static buzzes in my ears as his unwavering focus dives beneath the surface. Birds chirp overhead, providing a soundtrack for conversation. I can practically hear Drake's mind churn over the weight of something heavy.

His throat bobs as he gulps. "Can I ask you something?"

My lips twitch. "I dunno. Can you?"

Drake chuckles but the amusement quiets almost instantly. "Why did you stop competing?"

I freeze, eyes wide. It's suddenly hard to breathe. The pressure in my chest is too familiar. A numbness threatens to settle over me in a protective layer. But my typical reactive response doesn't fit in this moment.

"Wow, that's… not what I expected." I struggle to swallow around the knob in my throat.

"You don't have to tell me, especially at a party." His eyes slide to those in the backyard with us, preparing to celebrate love and happiness.

The reflex to duck and cover sputters from me. "Too late. You already pried this lid open. We're being very personal and intense today. Might as well follow the trend."

Drake's concern studies the hot sting blurring my vision. "I didn't mean to upset you."

"It's a tough subject," I confess. "But it's nothing compared to what other people have gone through."

He pulls me into him. "Don't minimize your pain. What you're feeling is just as significant, regardless of the circumstances."

"Gosh," I blubber. "You always know what to say."

"One of my many talents when it comes to you."

Which gives me a necessary push. "I always loved the thrill of rodeos and barrel races, but the competitions lost meaning for two reasons. First, about seven years ago, my horse Pago got sick and died unexpectedly."

He frowns. "Oh. I'm sorry."

"Yeah. His loss hit me hard. I'd never experienced such a devastating blow. We'd been a team since I was eleven. To a young girl, there couldn't be a more loyal companion."

The reminder is a punch to the gut. Emotions get the best of me and I'm crying openly again. Drake is quiet as I grieve, holding me flush against him to provide support. That contact is appreciated more than I can voice. It takes a minute for me to regain my composure enough to continue.

"He was my first true love. My partner. My everything. That never changed. Our bond was unbreakable. Still is, even though he's gone. At least I like to think so." I exhale slowly. "Pago is irreplaceable to me, and I wouldn't dare try. I haven't competed since our last run. We won the overall championship that weekend. Hit an arena record too. Guess we were meant to end on a high note."

Drake rubs circles along my back, the gentle touch soothing me. "He was black, right?"

Confusion spikes, yanking me out of my reverie. "Did I tell you about him?"

"I saw you two at a show. You were really good together."

"The best. He ran so hard for me." I pause and lick my lips. "I didn't know you watched me ride back then."

Red blooms on his cheeks. "That was on purpose. I had a big crush on you, especially after our kiss."

"You should've told me. Maybe I would've kissed you again."

"And then we might not be standing here today. I'm okay with how we've found each other again. We're making up for the past." Drake's thumbs brushes wet sorrow from my cheeks. "I know it's not the same, but he's still with you. Like you said, that type of bond doesn't break. You've got yourself a guardian steed."

"Yeah, I do." Tears spill down my face and I don't bother stemming the flow. "It's nice to imagine that Kenzie and Charlie were miracle gifts sent to ease the ache. I stopped riding while I was pregnant, which was like a forced vacation. The break gave me a chance to heal and reset my priorities."

My lips attempt to form a grin, but the expression barely lifts. "Once the twins were born, they were my whole world. There wasn't time for much else but I was perfectly content. I almost left horses behind in my pre-mom life, but then Mimi passed."

"You don't have to keep going," he murmurs into my hair.

"It's okay. I'm almost done. You've already heard most of this stuff anyway. Greener Pastures became mine practically overnight. It's not like I could refuse her last wishes. Nobody else would do the barn justice. If it were up to my parents or older brother, the property would've been signed over to Sutherland Homes." I shudder and an icky lurch twists my stomach. "The responsibility of running the stable and managing my grief was difficult to balance. Not to mention two toddlers. It was a lot to juggle."

"Too much," he murmurs.

"I didn't have time to even consider getting back into the circuit, even if I wanted to. And you pretty much know the rest." I blow out a heavy breath, pushing the raw edges back into the shadows.

"Well, shit." Drake drags a hand through his hair. "I'm a dick for asking and making you spill your guts on Ridge's lawn."

"It's okay. I wouldn't have told you if I didn't want to." My shrug is noticeably lacking enthusiasm. "And this is the awkward part where you try to console me with words, but I just need a hug."

"Done."

His devotion wraps me in a tight embrace, shutting out the noise and fun-tivities surrounding us. A slow, deep inhale grants me his scent and I relax against him. I'm not sure how long we stand that way. Until my emotions regulate and I can breathe without pins jabbing into my lungs.

His fingers massage my shoulders. I imagine he's erasing tension and baggage stamped into the muscles there. Relief spreads from the area, turning me into warm putty.

"You're not alone, Cassidy. This is a team effort. That's why I paid off Sutherland. I want to take care of you." His exhale pours through me. "And I'm sorry I didn't run it by you. I should have included you in the discussion so we could figure it out together. That's what being on a team is all about. I'm well aware you're capable of taking care of yourself but I figured you wouldn't mind reinforcements. Have someone else go to bat for you."

"Good grief." I fan my watery eyes. "You're trouble for my composure. Where do you come up with this stuff?"

"It's just for you, beauty." His lips caress my forehead. "You bring out the best in me."

If I hadn't already thrown caution to the tumble-weeds, this would've done it. Drake is the type of man I wouldn't believe actually exists in real life. But here he is, telling me everything I've wanted to hear. My very own Mr. Full Package Hero as if a romance author created him just for me.

"Uh-oh," Drake mumbles suddenly.

"What's wrong?"

"We've got company headed our way."

I peel my face off his chest to take a peek. A mountain of a man escorts a petite brunette across the yard toward us. His large build towers over her smaller frame, acting as a protective shield, like she's a priceless treasure. Based on the process of elimination, I'm betting this is Ridge and Callie.

"Yikes. We missed their entrance." The urge to cower behind Drake trembles my thighs.

He holds me in place. "I doubt they noticed."

"Uh-huh, sure. Ridge's stony expression suggests otherwise."

That observation is met with a scoff. "Don't put too much stock into that mean mug. He always looks angry."

"You talking about me?" The grump's scowl hardens into steel blades as they reach us.

"Hey, Crusher. You finally made it." Drake claps his

friend on the back before waving to the brunette. "Glad you could convince him to be social for five minutes, Callie. The rest of us thank you for using that power of persuasion for the greater good."

"Don't be a dick," Ridge grunts.

"That's exactly what I told him." I toss my hands in the air.

"Ah!" Drake's eyes sparkle a shade of blue that should probably be taken as a warning. "This is Cassidy. She's the one who carries my balls in her purse."

I almost spit out my final sip of mimosa even though the creative title should be expected. He told Garrett and Grace that I'm responsible for his permanent erection. My blush was probably visible from the moon.

"It's very nice to meet you," Callie says.

"Likewise," I croak once I find my voice. "Congratulations on your engagement."

She sighs and gazes longingly at her fiancé. "Thank you."

Ridge scrutinizes me under a microscope that zooms in and detects my intentions. "You must be the unfinished story."

I bounce in my boots. "Oooooh, are we writing a book?"

The big guy shrugs. "Might as well. He can't stop talking about you."

"Unless there's another Cassidy with a set of testicles in her bag."

"She gets me." Drake lifts my hand that's clasped in his to kiss along my knuckles. "I can't wait to get your name tattooed on my ass."

"Yours is gonna look spectacular across my left boob."

His eyes heat. "Don't tease me, woman."

"Wouldn't dare."

"No wonder you two weren't part of the welcome wagon. Lost in your own world," Ridge grumbles.

"That's calling the pitcher offsides," Drake jests.

Ridge blinks. "The fuck?"

"Love is grand, eh?" Drake winks at his friend.

I ignore the flutter in my belly. He's not using the term for us, obviously. We're celebrating Ridge and Callie and the upgrade to their relationship.

"Thanks for having us. This is a great party," I gush.

Ridge narrows his eyes. "Thanks for barging into my house uninvited."

"We never stepped foot in your home. Harper let us into the yard through the side gate." Drake blindly gestures at the general area. "Besides, you're not mad about your future wife's smile. Thank the hostess of the roastest for that."

Ridge snorts, but a glance at Callie defrosts his steely exterior. The dude might as well be gelatin as he melts toward her. "You're happy, sweetness?"

She beams at him like he put the stars in the sky. "This was a great surprise."

He grunts again. "Harper deserves a raise then."

Drake hoots, pumping a fist in the air. "That's the spirit, Crusher."

The guys begin bickering like brothers. Their friendship is clearly ride or die, built on trust and loyalty.

Warmth spreads through me watching them interact. Drake deserves to have solid rocks in his corner.

When I shift my gaze to Callie, I notice she's already staring at me. "Is there something on my face?"

It's meant to be a joke, but she nods. "Were you crying?"

That's when I realize my makeup probably resembles a splotchy painting left out in the rain. I swipe under my eyes, that minimal effort smudging my fingers with black. Trash panda status is fully activated.

"Um, is there a bathroom I can use?"

"Of course," Callie rushes to say.

"I'll show you where it is, beauty." Drake rests a palm at the small of my back, using the other to point at Ridge and Callie. "Don't do anything I would do while we're gone, kids."

I laugh while allowing him to steer me across the lawn. "What's that supposed to mean?"

"That's for them to figure out."

CHAPTER TWELVE

Drake

CASSIDY STARTLES AT SEEING ME LOITERING IN the hallway when she opens the door. "I could've found my way. You didn't have to wait for me."

"And miss this opportunity?" I straighten and stalk toward her.

"What're you planning, trouble?"

My gaze carves a path along her curves. "I haven't tasted your pussy in weeks and I'm famished."

Her eyes round into saucers. "Now?"

I step into her at the threshold of the bathroom. "Can't think of a better time."

"We're at your friend's engagement party."

"And?"

"There's a bunch of people outside." She gestures wildly.

"Better make it quick then."

"Or we could wait until later."

A sharp shake of my head rejects her suggestion. "I'm going to get on my knees, worship your pleasure, and beg you to forgive me."

"You've already been forgiven."

"Not to my liking."

"Going down on me is what it takes?"

"It's a start."

Her mouth works soundlessly. "I'm not even sure how to respond to that."

"Just accept it."

Cassidy furrows her brow. "But—"

I swoop down to silence her with a kiss. She melts into me, which I interpret as a positive sign. My tongue swipes out to test the limits of her wavering inhibitions. Her lips part on a sigh and a green flag raises along with my arousal. But this isn't about me.

"Imagine this as a scene in one of your romance novels." The temperature in the small room spikes at least ten degrees when I shut the door. "I bet you've read one that's similar. We can turn fiction into reality."

Desire smolders in her green eyes and she squirms. "Yes."

"That's my good girlfriend."

A moan slips from her. "I think you might've uncovered a praise kink."

My cock twitches from that sultry rasp. "If you listen, I'll reward you."

"With an orgasm?"

"If we quit stalling." My hands hover over the one-piece contraption Cassidy considers an outfit. "How do I get this off?"

"Easier than you think." Which she proves with a fluid motion from her deft fingers.

As the buttons open, denim loosens to reveal her naked flesh. Soon all that covers her is a matching bra and panty set, the dark green lace little more than scraps.

"Impressive," I rasp.

She kicks away the garment pooled at her ankles. "Where would you like me?"

I glance at the options. None of them are ideal for comfort, but this is meant to be fast and efficient. "Park that hot ass on the toilet lid and lean back against the wall."

Like an obedient cowgirl, she positions herself as instructed. A tremble ripples through her. "Chilly."

"You'll be burning for me soon." My knees meet the tile floor. "Spread eagle, beauty."

She stretches her legs wide, propping one foot on the counter. "Planning to eat around my thong?"

"Absolutely."

It won't be a problem. I can see how juicy and ripe her cunt is for me. The skimpy material between her thighs is drenched. My thumbs trace the frilly edge hiding her from view. A purposeful exhale against that wetness is met with a shiver.

"Tease," Cassidy whimpers.

I chuckle, but that's all the warning she gets. A tug on her hips delivers her into my grasp. She squeaks at the abrupt change but the sound barely registers. I'm too preoccupied bracing her legs apart with my broad frame, wedging us together.

Another startled noise spills from her when my nose and mouth burrow in her slippery heat. My addiction is fed with a hit of sweet zing. The lace barrier does little to conceal her unique flavor.

"Fuuuuuuck, I've missed your taste."

Her fingers grip onto my hair. "Don't stop."

I cluck my tongue. The action strikes her clit and

she jolts. Her response is strong, but it could be better. A yank removes the flimsy barrier from obstructing my dignified palate. Her arousal instantly coats my lips and I guzzle the spiced sugar like a man who just escaped the desert.

"Flood my mouth, beauty. I want to feel your cum slide down my throat."

Cassidy arches, tilting to tighten my seal on her pussy. "Such a dirty boy."

I suckle her clit, the bundle already swelling. "Only the filthiest will do for you."

"More," she mewls.

I sink two fingers into her, the push and pull tempo matching the rapid flicks of my tongue. She quakes against me. Whether intentional or not, she begins a steady grinding motion. That hungry movement spanks her sex against my chin. The friction must add another level of intensity. Loud cries escape her on a constant loop, proving she isn't concerned about getting caught. Her enthusiasm fuels mine, spurring me to increase my pace.

"Tell me you're mine," I mumble into her folds. "I need to hear it."

"Yes, yes," she chants.

"Give me the words."

She squirms, "I'm all yours, trouble."

"Fuck, you're perfect. Exquisite. Giving me more than I've asked for. My beautiful girl," I praise.

Her wheeze in response is passionate and pleased. I glance up while feasting on her essence. Cassidy is already watching me. The cups of her bra are folded down, giving her unrestricted access to her pierced nipples. She plucks at the pebbled points, pinching until the tips are pressed flat. My eyes nearly cross from the sight.

"I'm almost there," she breathes.

Lust thrashes through me in a blaze. Damn, that's a stroke to my ego. I figured she could get off quick, but this might be a record.

That's when the doorknob rattles.

Apparently not speedy enough.

The plan was to get Cassidy to burst before we were busted, but that's why locks were invented. I double my efforts to give her relief. My fingers pump into her, curling to find that sacred spot. She's riding my face to a rhythm that will win her a trophy. Our rude interruption knocks as if that's going to do the trick.

"Shit," she mutters.

I shush her, the admonishment vibrating against her core. My actions have the opposite effect as I tap her clit in the process. Her hips thrust forward and she goes still.

"Yes! I'm coming," Cassidy shouts.

A sugary gush bathes my tongue, sluicing down my throat like dew. I groan and open wide for more. Her knees clap against my head to trap me in place. There's a clench in her core that suctions at my fingers. She bucks against me, chasing the peak to the highest point. I'm swallowing every drop she gifts me.

"Holy shit. They're totally doing it in there." Grace's voice is muffled but recognizable through the door.

"I don't blame him. A permanent erection is demanding. Get yours, buddy." The encouragement booms from Garrett, but I'm concentrating on the woman splintering apart for me.

Cassidy spasms in my clutches. I ease her back from the ledge with lazy licks to her pussy. It's mutually beneficial, allowing me to consume her to absolute completion. She regains some semblance of composure and straightens from her slouched pose. The afterglow shimmers in her eyes as they latch onto mine.

"Do you think they heard us?"

"Us?" I laugh, assuming she missed the commentary from the hallway voyeurs. "Oh, beauty. You broadcasted loud enough to overcompensate for me and my appetite."

The flush from her release brightens to a ruby shade. Cassidy glances at the door that's gone silent. "No."

I pepper her inner thighs with kisses. "Don't worry. I'll take all the credit if you'll let me."

CHAPTER THiRTEEN

Cassidy

I ROLL OPEN THE HEAVY DOOR WHILE MENTALLY reviewing my morning chores. The list is longer than usual thanks to a certain someone and his prize penis. My empty core clenches at the reminder of just how full Drake packed me over the weekend. A soft moan accompanies the lingering ache. Totally worth it.

Chester and Cheeto spin circles around my legs before spying a cat to chase. That sets my sights on the tasks straight ahead. The first signs of dawn stream inside the barn. Dust dances in the open space, welcoming a fresh start. Energy thrums in my veins to rejuvenate my tired body. Several whinnies greet me. A warm comfort soon follows, chasing off the early hour chill.

"Good morning," I croon to the sheltered herd.

"Morning, beauty."

I halt in my tracks. Once my eyes fully adjust, I notice the lights are on. Drake is leaning against a wheelbarrow in the aisle. I might've whimpered, not that anyone can blame me. A backward hat has never looked sexier. My gaze narrows onto his very naked torso. Colorful tattoos and gleaming muscles command admiration. His dimpled smirk isn't hard to drool over either.

Our stares collide, mutual attraction blazing hot. Static buzzes in my ears and a wave of heat crashes over me. Desire that should be thoroughly satisfied snaps hungry jaws at the sweaty man in front of me.

"What...?" My voice cracks and I gulp to try again. "What're you doing?"

Drake spreads his arms wide. "Mucking the shit out of these stalls. Literally."

"You're...?" I blink at him and his shirtless glory, taking up residence in my barn. "Why would you willingly do that?"

"To make a grand gesture."

"But we're not fighting, and you definitely don't owe me. Not after the orgasms you served on tap," I mumble.

"We don't have to be at odds in order for me to do something nice. Besides, I'm getting acquainted with my roots. Granger isn't my last name for nothing."

"Ummm...?"

His chuckle is rich and deep. "Grange translates to barn in French."

"Does it?"

"Not sure." He laughs again. "My mom told me that once. It would explain my irresistible charm. Right, *mon amour?*"

I suck in a sharp breath as the foreign term of endearment curls off his tongue. Crisp pine hangs heavy in the air, overpowering the scent of dirt and manure and horsey goodness. How I didn't notice the clean smell before can be blamed on the guy holding the pitchfork. Such a pungent level suggests that a major amount was used.

A peek into the nearest stall reveals that Drake didn't just scoop out the poop and pee. He replaced the old shavings with new stuff. I had explained the once-a-week, deep clean process while joking about my boss firing me for slacking off. Clearly, Drake was listening, and extremely well considering the task appears complete.

My focus returns to him. Everything else fades into a blur, which is becoming a habit whenever he's around. "This is more than nice, trouble."

He stretches, putting his captivating physique on display. "You flatter me."

I scoff, but the sound lacks ire. "This is a huge job. How long did it take you?"

Drake glances at the rising sun behind me. "Not sure. I started at three."

"It's after six now."

"Well, there you go. That explains why I had to pause and water your bushes."

"I bet you did."

His smirk isn't apologetic in the least. "Why have all this land just to pee inside?"

"No judgment. I can pop a squat as steady as the next cowgirl." My mind whirls in reverse. "Didn't you work at Roosters last night?"

He nods. "The bar closes at eleven on Sundays. That gave me a few hours of sleep before I drove over here."

That sends my curiosity in the opposite direction momentarily. "How's your elusive house? Still standing?"

A chuckle bounces from him to chisel at the tension. "You're always welcome over there. My bed is very comfortable."

"Yet you left it after a short snooze. Just so you could clean the stalls."

"Grand gesture," he repeats. "I'd rather be here with you. No matter the conditions."

I blindly reach for the closest surface before my knees give out. "It's very much appreciated, but you don't need to try this hard to get laid."

"That's not what this is about." Drake straightens, seeming to measure the distance separating us. "I'm after your heart. Your trust. Your love. Your future. I don't just want to date you, beauty. I want to keep you. Forever. I'm willing to do whatever it takes. Hard work doesn't scare me. Besides, you deserve a day off."

Good grief, this guy. The kindness in his tone strikes a very sensitive note. Conviction pulses from his broad frame and I'm captivated again.

Heat stings my eyes. I sniffle, wiping away the emotional evidence. Drake is too observant, already stalking toward me. His gentle touch swipes at a stray tear I missed.

Natural instinct has me leaning into him. "I can't believe you did this."

"Like in a good way?"

"The best. You saved me a lot of hard labor. My back thanks you."

He deflates as if my answer is responsible for removing a pallet of bricks from his shoulders. "It's good for me. I've been getting soft after leaving the league. Too complacent."

"Oh, puh-lease." I gesture to his chiseled abdomen. "Look at that stack."

"Feel free to stroke me while you're at it."

"Shameless." But I allow my fingers to trace the sculpted ridges.

His groan is paired with an obscene thrust from his hips. "Little lower, beauty."

I eye the bulge below his belt. "My kids are asleep, but not for long. I'd hate to leave you hanging."

He nods in understanding. "Blue balls is my least favorite color."

My palms drift along his arms, pausing to squeeze his biceps. "How about a massage for now?"

"Happy ending later?"

"Of course." I encourage him to turn, granting me better access.

His skin is still slick and I use that to my advantage. My fingers glide along his shoulders, curling into the impressive bulk. *Soft, my ass.* The man is a solid brick. There's no squish to be found, only tough spots. A tremble ripples through him when I knead at a knot.

Drake's head hangs forward. "Damn, baby. Go deep in there."

"Just the way you like it," I purr.

"Careful or you'll turn me on."

"Too late."

He chuckles but the noise drops into a sigh as my thumbs press harder. My knuckles don't stand a chance against his build. The pleasure oozing from him is distracting too. He's warm and clammy and irresistible. His big body slackens, pliant for me. My mouth waters to lick him.

Soon I'm basically appreciating his brawn through languid caresses. My technique is far from professional, more gropey than relaxing or soothing. He doesn't seem to mind based on the grunts and heavy exhales.

A quiet nicker on my left distracts me. "The horses are still locked in."

"Yeah?" The confusion in his voice is warranted seeing as my statement is obvious.

I failed to recognize the implication earlier.

"You cleaned the stalls without taking them out?"

"Is that a problem?"

"No, it's just much more difficult."

"Really? Huh. Maybe they took pity on me. Except that one." He points to a particular mare. "She kept nibbling on my pants."

I pause Drake's massage to stroke her velvet nose. "Doesn't surprise me. She's a bit of a troublemaker. You two have a lot in common."

He joins me in pampering her with a scratch under her chin. "She must've sensed one of her own. What's her coloring called?"

I pet her speckled coat. "Leita is a bay roan."

"Beautiful animal," he coos.

"Definitely a looker. Great on the barrels too. I haven't listed her for sale yet but there's already several very interested buyers. She has tons of potential."

A swift maneuver has him facing me again. "You're not keeping her?"

"For what?"

"To have as yours." His brows lift.

"She would just waste." But I'd selfishly considered the possibility of saving her for Kenzie and Charlie.

"Or you could take her to a show," Drake suggests casually.

A sharp pang hammers my chest. "Not gonna happen."

His lips press into a firm line, undoubtably trapping a retort. "Are you riding her today?"

"That's the plan, but a bit later."

"Fantastic." He claps, rubbing his palms together. "Is there a horse I can hop on?"

My jaw drops. "You want to ride? Voluntarily?"

"Been waiting for an invite. I didn't buy these boots for nothing." He taps a sole on the concrete floor.

A peek at the expensive Ariats suggests those soles wouldn't have met manure without my influence. The supple leather is still unblemished even after the hours he spent on chores. "Had those seen a speck of shit before this morning?"

"Nope."

"Better get some miles on 'em. Go open that gate." I point at the one on the opposite end of the barn. "We'll free the beasts."

Drake's feet remain firmly planted. "I'm not qualified."

"It's easy."

The cowboy in training doesn't look convinced and moves at a tortoise's pace to fulfill my request. It's actually very funny and cute to see his typical confident swagger replaced by apprehension. Once the route is clear, I begin unlatching the stalls. The horses exit their private quarters and form a single file line toward freedom. It's a smooth transition that they perform twice daily.

Drake watches the practiced routine as if it's a

Broadway show worthy of an award. His eyes bulge as his fellow troublemaker stops to sniff him for treats. My heart flutters faster at the sight but I ignore the sensation. The roan mare settles for a ruffle to her forelock before she trots off to catch up with her herd. She bucks at the air, showing herself out with a proper farewell.

"Better keep an extra eye on her." He shuts the gate while chuckling.

"Told you."

"That was impressive." His arm arches over the aisle where he just received our demonstration.

"They're highly motivated by food and playing follow the leader." I stand beside him, gazing at the paradise spread in front of us. "You're a very capable stable boy."

"Does the position come with benefits?"

"I could probably whip up a bonus structure."

Drake bites his fist and groans. "Don't tempt me or I'll give you a private tour of the tack room."

I snort at the mention of the random space. "Did you stumble in there by mistake?"

"Sure did, and it was hard to leave. The smell of leather and victory is very sexy. Those trophies are such a turn on," he rasps.

"Maybe I'll let you spread me over a saddle."

"Now?"

I shake my head and begin backing away. "Still no. Rewards come after chores."

"Delayed gratification? Kinky, beauty."

"Especially once Billy and Gruff get their hooves on you again." I wink and blow him a kiss. "Can you handle the goats and chickens? I'll turn the horses out to pasture, portion their grain for dinner, check on the cats, and sweep."

"Is it a race?" Drake stretches his legs, doing several lunges and flexes.

I study his effortless movements. Chester and Cheeto arrive on the scene, sensing the competitive shift between us. The dogs will herd the horses from dirt to grass for me. Too bad they can't unlock the chain and save me a trip. But that won't alter the outcome.

"Sure," I quip. "We can make it interesting."

"What do I win?"

"Presumptuous much?"

His eyebrows wiggle. "Just confident."

"You have to beat me first, grand gesture." My route to success is ready and set. "Go."

CHAPTER FOURTEEN

Drake

"I STILL THINK YOU LET ME WIN." MY BOOTS CRUNCH on gravel as we cross the path and return to the barn.

Cassidy's focus slides to me, a smile curling her pouty lips. "Is your pride wounded?"

A scoff spews from me while I flex my arms and chest. "Nope."

She eyes me as I the test the stitches on my shirt seams. "Are you complaining about your prize?"

My stomach sighs in full-belly bliss. "Nope, I don't regret my victory. You're a damn fine cook."

"Egg bake is easy."

"Not for me. Take the compliment." I trace the apple of her cheek with a bent knuckle before opening the door. "If only you'd let me act as sous chef."

"I couldn't risk a repeat of last time you were in my kitchen." She flicks the lights on and twirls into the aisle.

"Can't resist me, huh?"

Her gaze gobbles me from top to cock. "Which is a problem when my children are home."

I adjust my hat, flipping the brim backward. "You keep saying that but I have yet to see them."

"They're sleeping late. Don't complain."

The wise advice prompts me to shamelessly ogle her instead. Snug jeans with bling on the rear hug her ass like a lover's embrace. An athletic tank top stretches over her breasts, giving me a juicy shot of cleavage.

She cocks a hip. "What's up, trouble?"

"Other than me?" My dick twitches behind my zipper for her approval. "This cowgirl uniform of yours is extremely attractive. Sexy and practical, beauty."

"Lucky for you," she drawls. "I wear this getup on the daily."

My appetite rebounds as I give her another languid once-over. "How much longer will Mac and Cheese be snoozing?"

"I expect them to join us any minute. Add two or three onto that for breakfast."

"Gobble and go types," I praise.

"Especially if the twins recognize your truck."

The fact that they might after spotting the pickup once or twice realigns my desires in this moment. "Will they ride with us?"

"If you ask them to."

"I'd love that." The image of us on a family outing along the trail pops into my mind as if it's chiseled in stone.

Cassidy's grin brightens. "Wait here while I get our horses."

My devoted attention stays glued on her and her seductive self until she disappears into the tack room. I haven't moved when she reappears with two halters hanging off her shoulder. Once she's gone from view again, I decide to make myself useful. But a quick scan of the spotless barn mocks my intentions.

Chester and Cheeto zoom past me at a speed that

suggests Cassidy left them behind. There goes my idea of playing fetch with the pair. Although, I'm not certain Australian Shepherds enjoy that sort of chase. That question gets stored away for later.

It's too quiet. The squeak from the rusty windmill serenades the calm. Idle hands get me in trouble, even if I twiddle my thumbs. I'm about to wander outside when thundering footsteps approach. My heart rate spikes momentarily in fear that Billy and Gruff are about to have their way with me again. I'd barely dodged their earlier advances while feeding them.

Shrill giggles ease my concern and I turn toward the open door. Kenzie and Charlie dash directly at me, making no attempt to slow down until they crash into my legs. An exaggerated *oomph* wheezes from me strictly for their benefit.

"Pinkie Pie!" Kenzie's squeal shatters the silence and my eardrums.

Charlie winces but recovers quickly. "Hi, Rake."

"Hey, Mac and Cheese!" I rub their backs. "You're the entertainment I've been waiting for."

A twinkle shines in the little girl's hazel gaze. "Can we turn you into a scarecrow?"

"Absolutely."

"Yay!"

The synchronized cheer blasts to the rafters. They race to a nearby bale and begin plucking. It doesn't take long before they've gathered fistfuls, waving the straw in victory while speeding back to me. I kneel on the ground and bend my arms in the standard position. Kenzie shoves hay under my sleeves while Charlie decorates my collar. Alfalfa and laughter buzz in the air. Once their stock is depleted, they rush to collect more. This cycle continues until I'm ready to be propped in the field.

I chuckle as stray bits of straw and dirt skitter down my back. "Have you done this before?"

"Nope," Kenzie chirps while sprinkling my hat. Her auburn pigtails sway from the movement. "Mommy doesn't like hay on her skin."

I can understand why seeing as mine already itches. But it's too late. I've already committed to the role.

The clop of hooves echoes from the opposite end of the barn. Cassidy falters at the sight of me. "How long was I gone?"

"Rake is a scarecrow," Charlie announces.

"I can see that." She ties the horses to the front of two stalls, looping the ropes in a strange knot. "He's supposed to have his first riding lesson but I guess we'll reschedule."

"What can I say?" Dried grass and debris rain off me as I rise to my feet. "I got stuffed for a change."

"How does it feel?"

I wipe at my prickly nape. "Uncomfortable."

"You don't have to agree to everything they ask," she reminds me.

"Eh, this was an easy decision. I need to shower anyway."

Her gaze roves over me. "They're taking advantage of your inexperience."

"Meh, what's the worst that can happen?"

Cassidy's eyes widen. "You should never ask that."

Kenzie sticks out her bottom lip. "Why can't Pinkie Pie get his lesson?"

"You already taught him one. He's turned into a scarecrow. They're packed with straw and not so many brains. He might fall off."

The little girl blinks at her mom before glancing at me. "Just hold onto the horn. Really super tight, m'kay?"

"I won't let go." My fingers curl as if already getting a grip.

Kenzie's focus returns to Cassidy. "See? He's listening."

"Shocking." The snarky redhead winks at me.

"We wanna ride too," her daughter adds.

"Uh-huh," Charlie chimes in.

"Should I get Snowball or can you take turns riding Fire?"

There's no hesitation in the kids' reply. "We can share."

"That's probably best. Not sure what state I'd find Drake in if I leave again."

"Maybe short a few more brain cells," I tease.

"Can't risk that." Cassidy rolls her lips together to trap a cackle. "Hey, moo-boo?"

"Mommmmmmy," Charlie wails. "That's for babies."

"Ah, right." She winces and begins to count on her fingers. "I forget how old you are."

"So big!" He spreads his arms wide.

"Is monkey moo still okay?"

Charlie nods. "Yep."

Cassidy slides her focus to Kenzie. "And bunny boo?"

The little girl hops dutifully like the nickname. "I'll always be your bunny."

"Thank goodness." She wipes fake sweat from her forehead. "How about you brush Fire while Drake helps me with Leita."

The twins trot off to follow directions. They retrieve a wooden box from the tack room that appears to be overflowing. I'm still picking hay out of my shirt when Charlie hands me two different brushes. One is round and the other has long bristles. The little boy disappears before providing instructions. Logic dictates and I begin sweeping the clingy bits from my body.

Cassidy doesn't stifle her giggle. "You're adorable."

"Thanks, beauty. You're not too bad yourself."

"Those are actually for the horses." She points at the brushes.

"Obviously," I snort.

"Mhmm, right." Amusement embellishes her tone. "We use the curry comb first to loosen the dirt."

I study her circular motions with the rubber disc on Leita's hide. "Do they like this?"

She nods. "Especially under their belly and withers."

Confusion puckers my brow until she points to the slight bump between the mare's neck and back. "Gotcha."

"Go ahead."

I accept the curry comb from her and copy the technique. Leita begins rubbing her nose against the stall. "What's she doing?"

"Giving back." Cassidy grins at my dumbfounded expression. "That's her way of saying it feels good and she's trying to return the favor."

"How sweet," I croon. My focus centers on that area and the horse's nose moves faster against the wood.

Cassidy uses the bristled brush, following behind my strokes to remove the dirt. "She's such a good girl."

"Don't think I missed the fact that you chose to ride her first."

"She's somewhat of a favorite. Not that I'm getting attached," she rushes to add.

"But you could get attached."

"I already have trouble chasing me around." She nudges me.

"That's fair." I laugh, but don't believe the excuse. "When are you planning to sell her?"

"September at the latest. Otherwise people go on a buying freeze for winter when it's expensive to feed them."

"But that's next month." August just wandered into town, chasing off July.

Cassidy shrugs. "She might go even sooner. That's how the business thrives. I can't keep them all."

"You're not keeping any."

"Hush." Cassidy swats away my argument. "We have Fire and Snowball. The others come and go."

Yet the way she interacts with Leita seems special, even to a clueless novice like me. Even a simple task such as brushing her coat is done with careful consideration and precision. The horse obviously respects her in return. She stands politely while we finish grooming her until not a speck of dust lingers.

Cassidy's touch is gentle while she combs through the roan's mane and tail. "Done."

"Teamwork makes the cheese churn." I hold up a palm for her to slap.

"Ummm..."

"Just go with it." The unmistakable noise of goofing off snags my attention. I peek over and spy the twins lifting Fire's leg. "Are they okay over there?"

"They're picking his feet." Cassidy demonstrates on Leita, scooping muck out with a handheld tool.

"That doesn't hurt them?" I don't bother asking about the metal shoes nailed into the hoof.

"Not if you do it right. Just avoid the frog." She points to a triangular section that sticks out.

"I have so much to learn."

"Only if you're interested. Most of it isn't necessary if you're just riding once or twice for fun."

"Your passion ignites mine," I rasp.

Her throat works with a thick swallow. "Are we still talking about horses?"

"And everything else you're passionate about."

More giggles from the kids knocks Cassidy from her stupor. She blinks and the heat clears from those green depths I love drowning in. "You don't have to worry about them with Fire. He couldn't hurt a fly. That trusty Appaloosa is the reason I didn't quit riding as a kid after a few bad apples almost ruined the experience for me."

I release a low whistle. "Wow, he must be old."

Cassidy smacks my abs, the back of her hand bouncing off the muscle. "Rude."

"We're the same age," I drawl.

"Doesn't mean you won't trade me in for a younger model down the road."

"I'd never. You're it for me, beauty. Even when we're wrinkled and gray."

"We'll see." She twirls away, disappearing into the tack room.

A wool pad is in her grip, which goes on Leita's back. I rush to carry the saddle for her and heft it where she instructs. She explains the process to me, but most of the equipment terms and purposes resemble gibberish. That doesn't stop me from nodding along. Before I realize how efficient she is, both horses are ready to go.

"Question," I pipe up as we walk our steeds to the arena. Fire allows me to lead him easily, which I appreciate.

Cassidy's gaze slices across the yard to where Kenzie and Charlie are wrestling with the goats. "Just one?"

"For now. Doesn't a bridle usually have a bit?" I'm purposefully putting my fresh knowledge to the test.

"Not always. We use hackamores while training." She points to the curved rope on Leita's nose. "This keeps her mouth soft. It's a personal preference."

"You're my personal preference." I dip toward her for a kiss. Instead of a romantic gesture, the helmet she insisted I wear smacks her forehead. "This thing is a menace. Why don't you have one on?

She rubs at the bump. "I'm a professional."

"With my penis."

"You act like we didn't have sex twice yesterday," she mumbles.

"Can't get enough." I guide Fire into the large ring.

Cassidy shuts the gate behind us. "Keep it in your pants, trouble. You'll be stiff after this."

"Already am."

She hangs her head but can't hide the humor shaking her shoulders. "Do you want to use a stool to mount?"

"Can't I mount you? The kids are nearby, but discretion is one of my many talents."

"Good grief, just get on the horse."

"Why didn't you say so sooner?"

"I did," she laughs. "But chose the wrong phrase."

"Sex is on your mind again. Such a fiend." I *tsk*.

Cassidy rolls her eyes and swings onto Leita in a fluid motion. "You're on your own."

"Don't leave me hanging," I whine.

"We gonna teach Pinkie Pie the lesson," Kenzie calls while sliding through the fence boards.

"Good luck," their mother responds. "He's a tough student."

"Hard," I correct and blow her a kiss.

"Just for that, I'll let the twins swoop in and steal my thunder."

My eyebrows reach for the sky. "Is that wise?"

"Are you questioning my methods?"

"Of course not," I scoff. "But I'm still on the ground."

"Whose fault is that?" She pecks the air before trotting off.

I wait for Fire to get antsy about being left behind but he stays calm and still. "Guess it's just us, dude."

Charlie slams to a halt beside me. "You gotta get on, Rake."

"How do you suggest I do that?"

"Put your foot in the stirrup." Kenzie flanks my other side, pointing at the targeted spot.

"Seems easy enough." I lift my boot.

The little girl squeaks. "Wrong one."

I switch, managing to balance thanks to Fire's patience. "Now what?"

Charlie frowns. "Do you need a boost?"

"Hoist yourself up, trouble. Use the horn for leverage," Cassidy explains from across the arena.

The action breaks into simple steps. I stretch for the braided rawhide post, getting a sure grip. My pulse quickens as I launch upright and climb on. There's no reason to fear. Fire stands like a distinguished gentleman while I bumble through getting myself astride his back.

"You did it!" Kenzie claps.

Charlie gets my right boot tucked into the stirrup. "M'kay, you can go now."

"Just like that?"

Cassidy pulls Leita to a stop. Her stare is locked on me, roving over my flimsy attempt at playing a cowboy. There's no disguising the desire smoldering in her eyes. A blast of warmth envelops me and sweat prickles my scalp. The blistering sunshine isn't to blame.

"Are you good?"

"Couldn't be better." I relax my pose, the leather creaking beneath me.

"I wouldn't have wandered off if I didn't trust Fire to go nice and easy on you."

"Don't forget Mac and Cheese." I hitch a thumb at the pint-size horse whisperers.

Kenzie huffs, crossing her arms. "Mommy, we're the boss. You said we can tell Pinkie Pie what to do."

Cassidy presses her lips into a firm line to trap a laugh. "If that's okay with Drake."

"As if I'd say no." I chuckle, but the humor is strained. "Will you stay close, beauty?"

"Are you scared?"

"No," I scoff.

"Good. You're in very capable hands."

"Am I?"

A snarky brow quirks at me. "Who do you think they learned from? Besides, what's the worst that can happen?"

My brows spring upright. "I thought we weren't supposed to say that."

"This is different."

"How so?"

"Buttons." Her tone teases me.

"I see your point." My palm cups around my mouth to muffle what I say next. "But they're only five."

She gets the message, shrugging the concern off. "They started riding at eighteen months."

"Really? Wow. That's early."

"Advanced equestrians," she praises.

"We're the bestest," Charlie boasts. "You gotta listen to us, Rake."

"Just walk today," Cassidy interjects. "Focus on your seat and getting acclimated in the saddle. Learn how to steer. Control the direction. Fire will go where you choose or wait for the next move. Take your time."

I shift my ass that's already half asleep. "Got it."

"Don't kick him too hard." Kenzie wags her index finger at me.

"Why would I do that?"

"To make him go faster." Charlie rolls his eyes as if I'm not catching on quick enough.

"Maybe we should shake a bag of treats for Fire," the little girl suggests.

"And then he'll chase after us like suuuuuper fast." Which the little boy demonstrates by running in place.

"Yes!" The twins giggle, which sounds too much like a diabolic cackle for my liking.

"I'm fine standing," I admit as Cassidy's warning returns to haunt me.

Charlie smooshes his lips to one side. "You gotta walk. Mommy said. I'll hold the reins and lead you."

"Me too!" Kenzie grabs the excessive slack I haven't picked up. "Ready?"

"Yup." My response is far more confident than the drum pounding in my veins.

My chauffeurs set us in motion. The slow rock of Fire's gait tips me forward at first. I overcorrect and lurch myself backward. This might be considered a strike but I'm still swinging for a home run. The horn anchors me, stabilizing my position. There's a shift where the riot in my bloodstream calms to a dull roar. Our steady pace begins to feel natural. It's a consistent sway that lulls me into a sense of safety.

"I'm doing it." My fist pumps the air.

"Don't let go," Kenzie scolds.

"Whoops." But I'm starting to realize a death grip on the horn isn't necessary. My posture deflates, allowing the seesaw stride to swing me. "I could get used to this."

"Let's play Mac and Cheese Says," Charlie chirps.

"What are the rules?"

"Just like when you do whatever Simon says, but we're Mac and Cheese. Duhhhh," Kenzie giggles.

"I'm game."

Charlie exchanges a blank look with his sister. "No, the game is Mac and Cheese Says."

"Right. Go ahead," I laugh.

Kenzie taps her chin. "Mac and Cheese says to tap your head."

I knock on my helmet. "Now what?"

"Mac and Cheese says to stretch out your arms," Charlie instructs.

"But Mac told me not to let go," I remind.

The little girl huffs. "We weren't playing then.

That logic is sound enough for me. My pose resembles an airplane as I follow orders. "Like this?"

The little boy nods. "Now zoooooooom like a jet."

"Nah-uh." I wag my finger. "Cheese didn't say, 'Mac and Cheese says' first."

"Oooooooh, he's smart," Kenzie whispers.

Charlie thumps his forehead. "I did a booboo. Mac and Cheese says to zoooooom like a jet."

My lips buzz together with the imitation. "Time for takeoff."

Kenzie's laughter increases in volume. "Mac and Cheese says stand on the saddle!"

My butt stays rooted to the seat. "I think we've lost sight of my skill level."

"Chicken," the little girl teases.

"Cluck, bawk, cluck," I squawk.

"You're sooooo funny." Charlie squints while

contemplating the next directive. "Mac and Cheese says pretend to a lasso a cow."

I spin my wrist overhead before launching a fake loop. "Got 'em!"

"Look at you go," Cassidy shouts. "You'll be running barrel patterns in no time."

Which is what she's doing. My focus tracks her loping Leita in the cloverleaf formation. Their speed isn't extreme, just an effortless stroll to showcase their joined talent. It looks like they're flying across the dirt to the next obstacle. How Cassidy claims they're not meant to be a forever team is unbelievable. The proof is on display in front of me.

I get lost watching them. It's a mesmerizing performance. A connection I can see bonded between them. If I'm only certain of one thing, it's that Leita is meant for Cassidy. She can't sell that horse.

"You looooove my mommy," Kenzie suddenly coos.

I smile at the observation, but don't shift my attention from the destined pair. "Is it that obvious?"

Her head snaps up and down. "There are hearts in your eyeballs."

"That's a cool trick." I widen my peepers for everyone to see.

Charlie slams on the brakes and Fire takes the cue to stop as well. "Mac and Cheese says to go on a date with Mommy."

"Only if you two join us," I amend.

Kenzie wrinkles her nose. "But that's not romantical."

A chuckle shakes my upper half. "What do you know about romance?"

"It's for grownups. They hold hands and get married and live happily ever after." She exhales, a dreamy glint in her eyes. "I'm too young to have a boyfriend."

"Girls are yucky," Charlie adds.

"Romance is for adults," I agree. "You can be our chaperones to make sure we don't get into trouble."

They nod in unison, liking the idea. Kenzie says, "Mommy shouldn't get home too late. She hasta tuck us into bed 'fore it's dark."

"Early dinner. We can eat at my restaurant." Calling Roosters a bar in this situation doesn't feel right.

"You've gotsa restaurant? Coooooool." Charlie gazes at me like I ordered him an unlimited supply of chicken nuggets.

"I'll give you the VIP treatment."

"What's a VIP?"

"Very important person," I inform. "You're my VIPs. Your mom too."

"VIP, VIP, VIP," they chant.

"What are you three plotting over there?" Cassidy's lyrical voice reaches us on the breeze.

"Nothing," we respond in harmony.

I wink at my fellow schemers. "It's a date, Mac and Cheese."

CHAPTER FiFTEEN

Cassidy

"HAVE YOU RECOVERED YET?" DRAKE SQUEEZES my knee that's thankfully quit trembling.

I swipe at the unshed tears dampening my lashes, daring another to fall. "Totally."

But that's a lie. The guarded version of myself that existed prior to Drake Granger barging into my heart is long gone. That protective layer didn't stand a chance. Good riddance. This man is providing a detailed definition of what devotion looks and feels like. Don't even get me started on the fact he's wearing a western shirt with the sleeves rolled up to expose his inked, veiny forearms. Freaking yum. It's safe to admit I'm smitten.

When he showed up at Greener Pastures thirty minutes ago, claiming we had a date to fulfill our Saturday tradition, I stood motionless as the math tried mathing. But the missing pieces couldn't be ignored. It was my weekend with the kids. There wasn't a babysitter in sight. Drake hadn't said a word about hanging out.

The only part that made sense had been the twins urging me to wear a pretty dress for dinner. Although, at the time, I'd questioned their insistence. As far as I knew, we were eating at Auntie June's house, but I decided to play along. There's no harm in looking nice for family.

Except that wasn't the plan, much to my surprise.

Drake and his sidekicks had this night sorted into a very different format. Emotion got the best of me when my boyfriend explained he'd purchased and installed the same booster seats in his truck that I have for the kids. We were going out. Together. I've been a blubbering mess ever since.

Afternoon fades into evening outside the passenger window. I still don't know where he's taking us. Nobody has spilled the beans. The familiar landscape passing by in a blur doesn't offer any clues.

Drake's palm rests on my thigh, staking a permanent residence that I sense in my soul. "Are you happy, beauty?"

I shift my watery gaze in his direction. "Extremely."

"That's my cowgirl. My beautiful sunflower." He snags my hand and kisses my inner wrist, then lowers our clasped fingers to my leg. "You brighten my days. When I bask in your warmth, all is right in the world. Shine on me always, beauty."

"Good grief. My chest might burst." In addition to the fresh wave of heat attacking my eyes as I recall the oversized bouquet he gifted me.

"Can't have that," he rasps. "Allow me to turn those wobbly lips right side up."

Which could involve so many things. I brace for the unexpected. Drake takes a tight turn and punches the accelerator. The engine roars, launching us full speed ahead. Kenzie and Charlie squeal in the backseat. Giddy applause soon follows.

"Wheeeeeeee!" The twins erupt in a chorus of glee when he hits the gas after another curve.

"He got stuck in the mud again," my daughter giggles to her brother.

"It's sooooo fun," Charlie laughs.

My smile is stretched so wide that an ache blooms. It's a welcome twinge, sending my mood even higher. "You bend to them like a willow branch."

Drake flicks on his blinker when we reach Main Street. "Can you blame me? Your kids are perfect angels."

A sting spreads in my nose, reigniting the waterworks. I sniffle while fanning my face. "This is too much for one night."

A dry chuckle rumbles from him. "You'll get used to it."

"Uh-huh, 'cause we're the VIP."

I turn to see Kenzie dancing in her seat. "VIP?"

"Mhmm", Charlie replies. "It means very important peoples."

My makeup is a lost cause at this rate. "Oh, my."

"I've got the dream league." Drake nods to us and parks the truck.

My jaw unhinges when I notice where we've stopped. "You can't be serious."

"What's the problem?"

"My kids can't go into your bar." I fling an arm at the windshield as if there's any question of our destination.

Drake unbuckles himself. "It's a family-friendly restaurant."

My butt remains firmly in place. "Since when?"

"Until about nine o'clock. The crowd gets rowdy after dark."

"Oh, oh, oh! Mommy, look." Kenzie has taken the

liberty of removing herself from the harness. "There's a rooster."

Charlie follows her lead, propping himself on the center console. "Can we climb on it?"

"I don't think—"

"Absolutely," Drake says at the same time. "He's a very sturdy—"

"Don't say it," I warn.

"Statue?" He winks at me. "Dirty girl."

Kenzie sniffs my hair. "Do you need a bath, Mommy?"

"I'll hose her down later," Drake offers.

An outraged squeak rips from me and I thwack his bicep. "Pinkie Pie is just teasing me. Isn't that right, trouble?"

He nods dutifully. "Your mom smells like sunflowers and happiness."

Charlie glances between us, shrugging after his analysis. "Can we ride the rooster now?"

Drake drums on the steering wheel. "What're we waiting for?"

Kenzie purses her lips. "You were talking. It's rude to interrupt."

"Raisin' 'em right, beauty." He blows me a kiss and opens his door.

The incorrigible charmer frees the children, scooping one under each arm. Their legs spin in the air and immediately blast off once touching the concrete. My boyfriend grabs the activity bag before joining them on the sidewalk. He stomps the ground like a bull ready to chase. Kenzie and Charlie squeal in delight, racing around the rooster statue to avoid getting caught. They're no match for Drake. After two spins, he has them lofted and plopped astride the metal mascot.

I'm frozen for a second, caught in a rare moment where I don't need to do anything other than get myself out of the vehicle. It's two parts strange and magical. Drake slides into the role effortlessly, as if he's truly been waiting for the opportunity. The way he interacts with my kids is the most attractive thing I've ever witnessed. He might surrender to their every whim, but that's something we can work on. Or he'll figure it out on his own when they push too far. That's a problem for later. For now, their bond strengthens before my eyes and I'm about to bawl. Instead, I snag my phone to snap a picture.

Drake beckons to me. "C'mon, mama."

The nickname shouldn't be sexy coming from him but I trap a moan while climbing down from the truck. His gaze is hot on me as if he can sense my desire. A sigh breezes from me but it does little to extinguish the flames. I'm about to hump his leg when he tucks me tight against his side. Sandalwood and mutual affection swaddle me. Promises of delayed gratification join in too. My body slumps into his, which he rewards by kissing my forehead.

"Look at us, Mommy!" Kenzie flaps her arms like the rooster she's perched on.

Charlie crows. "Cock-a-doodle-doo!"

"Too cute for words. Let's capture the memory." I grip my phone and turn the camera on us huddled close. "Say cheese!"

The prompt shouts from us and sweeps Main Street.

Our smiles mirror each other as I snap the shot. We get several curious glances from fellow pedestrians. I'm sure it's not a regular occurrence to see two kids riding a rooster.

"Shall we?" Drake motions toward the entrance.

"Are you sure about this?"

"You wound me, woman." He clutches his chest. "My place of business isn't that seedy."

"Except when it's called—"

"Don't say it," he teases.

"The most popular spot in town?" I wink. "Get out of the gutter."

"They're weird," Kenzie mumbles to her brother.

"Okay," I laugh. "Off you go."

Drake swoops them back on solid ground and holds the door open for us. We stride into Roosters as a cohesive unit, which warms my heart to romantic mush. My eyes adjust to the dim lighting to reveal a sparse crowd. There are no sordid activities on open display. But I recognize several familiar faces.

"Hey, honored guests." Harper waves from behind the bar.

"It's the moment we've been anxiously anticipating," Garrett hoots from beside her.

Drake snorts. "Are we in the right place?"

A little girl swivels on a stool, waving wildly. The twins rush forward to join her. They're already acquainted thanks to riding lessons.

"Mama is teaching me how to make a Shirley Temple with extra cherries," Sydney explains.

"See?" My boyfriend hitches a thumb at where she's

proudly sitting. "We're a kid-friendly establishment. Put that on Google." He returns her enthusiastic greeting. "Hot date tonight, Syd?"

She frowns. "Daddy wouldn't like that."

"Mhmm," Harper cuts in. "Don't put ideas in her head. She's leaving shortly for a sleepover."

"Such trouble." I elbow Drake.

"It's my job to stir the pitcher." He mimics the motion.

"Or a pot. Whatever." Harper rolls her eyes but she's grinning. "The others have already arrived."

A question for clarification parts my mouth but firm pressure at the base of my spine sets me in motion. I peek at Drake to find a smirk slanted in secrets aimed at me. Kenzie and Charlie begin weaving patterns around the tables, taking the long way. My stride falters when the others in mention are revealed.

"Auntie June! Paisley!" The kids screech and dash toward them.

The older woman stands to wrap them in a hug. "Welcome to the party."

My cousin gets to her feet as well. "Surprise! The other two are on the road. You know how it is."

My lips work soundlessly for several seconds. "What...?"

"We're having family dinner," Drake fills in the gaps for me.

"It's a date," Kenzie corrects. "Buts don't forget we gotta get home for bed, m'kay?"

Amusement brightens my expression until the room sparkles. "Oh, I see. You were all in on this."

My boyfriend nods and pulls out a chair for me. "Your parents send their regrets. They already had plans."

I snort while sitting down. "Some fancy dinner party no doubt. Their social life is fit for New York City."

Drake folds himself into the neighboring seat. "Sounds like mine."

"You don't talk about them much," I note. "I only met them once when you hosted that homecoming bonfire in eighth grade."

"They're great, if you recall. Wonderful folks." His broad shoulders bounce. "Just busy doing their thing. You'll see them again eventually. Until then, we've got plenty of ties binding us together in town."

My gaze travels from my aunt and cousin loving on the twins to Drake's besties tending the bar. "We're blessed, huh?"

His soulful blue depths sink into mine. "Very much so."

"This is so thoughtful," I breathe. "Thanks for organizing this."

Drake drops a peck to my temple. "Anything for you, beauty."

"You've found yourself a keeper." Aunt June pats my hand. "Keep it that way."

My throat clogs, vision blurry. I lower my gaze before more tears fall. "Wow, so… what looks good to eat?"

"Mini tacos!" Charlie exclaims.

Drake cringes. "Those aren't on the menu, but I'll get them added."

My son pouts but his enthusiasm rebounds instantly. "I want mac and cheese."

Kenzie gasps. "Me too!"

"I'm hearing there are big appetites to feed." Harper appears, balancing a tray of water glasses. "This is my assistant. She's still in training."

Sydney bows before helping her mom distribute the full cups. "I'm gonna work at Roosters when I'm old like Mommy."

"Jeez, thanks." Harper huffs, barely looking a day over twenty-five.

"Want some candy?" Syd wedges herself between Kenzie and Charlie.

"Yes!" The twins lift their cupped palms in eager acceptance.

"It's rainbowed and funny shapes." Sydney opens a metal box, popping a tiny piece into her mouth. "Tastes yummy."

"Holy smokes." Harper is immediately at her daughter's side, horror painting her face. "Where did you get that?"

Syd blinks. "On the counter."

The feisty blonde snatches the tin and whirls on her heel, marching to the bar. "Garrett Foster!"

"Uh-oh, that's her mad voice." Sydney skips off after her mom, completely unperturbed by the outburst.

"Peens are private," Harper hisses to the man responsible. "Don't leave your junk lying out."

"That's definitely what she said," he jokes.

"It's not funny." She presses the container into his chest. "Sydney was munching on these and offered them to her friends."

Garrett shrugs. "Sharing is caring."

The two begin arguing while we return to our gathering. Kenzie and Charlie slouch in their chairs, sullen after the loss of a sweet treat. I shudder at what they almost put in their mouth. Paisley and Drake are on the verge of laughing their pants off. Nothing like penis candy to spark a controversy. My aunt fidgets, more than likely trying to scrounge up a more appropriate topic.

"Oh!" Her expression shines. "Are you getting excited for T-ball, Charlie? Your first practice is next week, right?"

I wince and subtly shake my head. "No, no, no."

My little boy's bottom lip begins to wobble. "It got cancelled."

"What? Why?" June appears stricken at the thought.

"The coach backed out at the last minute," I mutter. "I'm looking for a different activity but kindergarten starts soon."

My optimistic gaze studies Charlie for a shift in mood. The mention of school usually boosts his energy like a plug into a socket. But his posture stays stooped, along with his frown.

"I'll be the coach." Drake announces the suggestion casually as if the option is that simple.

"Trouble," I scold.

But it's too late. The little baseball hopeful heard him. "You gonna be my coach?"

"Sure thing," he drawls. "I happen to know my way around the bases. Not too bad with a ball and bat either."

"You can't just..." My words trail off as I flounder for why this isn't the best idea since I went to Bean Me Up five Saturdays ago.

"I can," he murmurs into my ear. "Let me do this."

"But why would you? You're a professional. This is T-ball we're talking about."

"For starters?" He nods toward Charlie. "Look at your son."

My little boy is beaming like he swallowed pure sunshine. "I get to play! Thanks, Rake."

"You bet, Cheese. We're gonna go undefeated."

The kiddo glances at his sister who appears just as clueless. They share a shrug before refocusing on Drake. "Huh?"

"You'll see." My boyfriend extends an arm for a high-five, which Charlie is fast to slap.

But I'm not convinced this will go well. "Do you have any coaching experience?"

"Beauty." The nickname is paired with a cluck of his tongue. "I've got this."

"My kids might've convinced you that entertaining them is easy but there are only two of them. You're talking about a dozen in an open field."

"It's fine," he insists.

"You don't expect me to accept that answer," I laugh. "Natural instincts only get you so far. Those children are going to eat you alive."

"I'll bring the utensils."

A grin appears, spreading with the warmth in my chest. "I can't believe you'd do this for him."

"For us," he amends. "We're a team, right?"

"You're my MVP," I exhale.

"Love the sound of that, beauty." Drake's palm reclaims its rightful place on my thigh. "Makes me think you're ready to depend on me to be there. Rely on me to be an equal partner. Believe in me to show up. Trust that I'm in this with you."

"Whew," Paisley presses a hand to her forehead. "Marry him or I will."

"Don't let him slip away," my aunt reiterates.

"I wouldn't dare." My stare falls headfirst into the unconditional devotion reflecting at me. "He's stuck with us. Endgame style."

CHAPTER SiXTEEN

Drake

I PACE THE LENGTH OF THE CRAMPED SPACE WHILE waiting for Cassidy. My boots clomp on the scuffed concrete, disrupting the silence. Excitement thrums faster in my veins when I glance at the clock. She should arrive any minute unless her bedtime routine for the kids got derailed. Not that it matters. Her instructions were simple and explicit and I plan to follow along. Even if it takes hours.

Okay, fine. That might be pushing it. But I have every intention of holding out for what's to come.

The scent of leather and wood combined with anticipation creates a concoction that goes straight to my head. A restless energy buzzes in my veins like a caged beast. Hunger snaps its jaws when quiet footfalls approach. The hurried stride drifts along the length of my spine and I groan.

Cassidy appears in the open doorway. A single lightbulb illuminates the tack room and traces her curves in a soft glimmer. The first thing I notice is that her hair is free from the braid I'd been fantasizing about tugging throughout dinner. Glossy waves cascade around her shoulders, the auburn set ablaze from the glow above. My fingers flex as I imagine getting a tight grip.

But then I notice her sly grin is painted in a fresh

coat of red. The color is so shiny, appearing wet. My cock jerks at the sight.

"Hey, trouble." The sultry caress in Cassidy's tone gets me harder than a fence post.

I widen my stance to alleviate the pressure behind my zipper. "Hi, beauty."

She seems to be vibrating with the same barely restrained desire that's thrashing through me. "You stayed put."

"I'm capable of following directions."

"Especially when you get rewarded."

My dick leaks. "Is that what this is about?"

She nods. "I'm gonna make you melt in my mouth."

"Like penis candy," I croak.

The dress I've been admiring all night swishes against her thighs. That gentle noise tickles my ears as she steps forward. Her stride is liquid as she slinks toward me. "Be a good boy and accept it."

"Fuuuuuuuck." My brain misfires, almost sending me to my knees.

Which would be problematic since Cassidy is lowering to hers. I'm granted an ample peek at her cleavage that gets my blood pumping hotter. She undoes my belt and jeans during the descent. A nimble tug exposes me to the cool air. That slight chill pebbles my skin but is instantly sent packing by her hot exhale.

"Damn, you're big." Her fingers try to meet in a loop at my base. "It's crazy to picture you inside of me. I could wear you as a scarf, or a medal if I manage to shove your entire length down my throat."

A visual of me stretching the delicate column is too

much. I blindly reach for the saddle behind me. The stand creaks but manages to support my weight.

Cassidy flicks her tongue against my tip. "Are you happy?"

"Is that a serious question?" My strangled voice should be answer enough.

"I mean in general. With everything." She blinks up at me and repeats, "Are you happy?"

Through the lust, I realize this is what I asked her just hours ago. "I couldn't be happier."

"You're sure?"

"Zero doubt." The conviction in my tone is a gavel delivering an undeniable verdict.

But her gaze still searches mine. "This life is enough for you?"

My palms cradle her upturned face, smoothing at the worry creasing there. "Where is this coming from, beauty?"

"I just want you to be satisfied." Her touch drifts along my length, almost absently.

"Sounds like a trap while I'm in such a vulnerable position." I thrust my hips.

She releases me. "I'm not joking. You're a professional athlete—"

"Was," I correct. "That's history."

"Do you miss it?"

"Of course, but I knew baseball wasn't forever. That's reserved for you and the kids. I can't spend forever in a dugout on the road. The spotlight won't keep me warm at night. Who cares about pitching no-hitters when you don't have anyone waiting for you at home? A real life, a family, a purpose beyond the game, a future. That's what I want. Something to complete me. And that's you." I drag my hand through her hair, tucking a section behind her ear. "Besides, I get to coach."

"Hmm, yes. Solid response. You're very sweet to me. I'm gonna be sweet for you too." Cassidy presses a kiss to my shaft.

I quake from the sensation. My arousal has been steadily building and that soft tease threatens to burst the dam. But then my vision clears to see the mark left behind. The stain doesn't usually smudge when we kiss. Maybe my dick is—

"Different brand," she reveals to burst my bubble. "This doubles as lube. Strawberry flavored."

It takes warrior willpower to remain upright while she drops more sloppy smooches on me. "That's… tasty."

"Very." Another peck on my dick. "I didn't think sucking a cock could hold appeal until I saw yours."

Need strains my muscles until I ache. "Oh?"

She hums and brands me again. "You're going to get blowjobs on the regular, trouble."

"Good Lord, woman." I'm openly trembling. "You're actually turning my penis into a piece of candy."

"Mhmm," she mumbles against my shaft. Her lips smack after a rapid attack to the flared head. "Yummy."

"Not gonna last," I grit out between clenched teeth. "I'll bust the instant your mouth is on me."

"You're giving me too much credit."

Denial is a sharp grunt as she polishes my pole until I'm slick and covered in her affection. "Not nearly enough."

Her laughter puffs against my slippery length. "Allow me to test your theory."

White streaks across my sight when she pushes me straight to the back of her throat. I blink at the stars but the haze turns blinding as she slurps, pulling my cock deeper. My earlier wish is granted when she guides my hand to clutch her neck. She swallows, allowing me to feel where my dick is lodged. I add gentle pressure and her lashes flutter. A curse spews from me as she swirls her tongue on the underside of my length, mapping the protruding ridge there.

My balls tighten and I curse. "Too good, beauty."

Moisture glistens in her eyes while she bobs up and down for a brief reprieve. Pleasure laps at me, keeping pace with her steady rhythm. The onslaught squeezes my desperation into a vise until I almost double over. A tear tracks down her cheek as I strike the limit of her gag reflex. I'm about to protest but the words become a wheeze when she takes me to the root again.

My fingers clench where she's got me wedged in. I use my other hand to stroke her jaw. Cassidy grins, the expression distorted. Her mouth is fully stretched around my length. So. Damn. Snug. The sight is obscene and almost makes me feel guilty, but I can't look away. A pleased sound rumbles from her to scold my concern. Rather than retreat, she takes me deeper. She moans while increasing suction, hollowing her cheeks in the process. Tingles erupt at the base of my spine. Relief begins to flood downward in a rush.

"Gonna come," I rasp.

She nods but doesn't quit. The last of my restraint

is spent on staying still, allowing her to finish me off the way she intends. Euphoric bliss erupts from me with a shout. My cock throbs, spilling every drop down her throat. Cassidy's throat works to drain me dry. Heat surges under my skin as I lose myself to sensation. I jolt from the powerful release, seconds from collapse. It's sheer determination that keeps me standing.

"Holy… shit. Fuck me sideways." Spots dance in my vision. "What was that?"

Her chest rises and falls while she dabs her puffy lips. "Good?"

"That's an understatement," I mumble. "You might've broken me. Nope, scratch that. I'm definitely ruined. Now you have to marry me."

Cassidy laughs. "Very funny."

"I'm not joking." I wipe the drool from her chin. "But next time I ask, it'll be worthy of the intended response."

Her watery eyes roll to the ceiling. "The blowjob wasn't that great."

I tuck myself away and hoist her into my arms, stumbling to our next stop. "You're right. It was better."

She giggles, clinging on tight when I try lowering her onto the nearest saddle. "What're you doing?"

"I owe you several orgasms."

"Definitely not multiple."

My knees greet the floor while I bunch her dress around her waist. "Feed me two while I recuperate and then I'll dick you straight to sleep."

CHAPTER SEVENTEEN

Cassidy

I JERK IN DRAKE'S HOLD WHEN HIS TONGUE SWEEPS along my clit. "Oh my—"

"Better not be anything other than my name about to spill from those lips." This is his second warning. He probably won't offer a third.

The urge to test him squirms my hips. "I'll curse yours, trouble. Give it a rest."

His chuckle is muffled against the most intimate part of me. "Still hungry."

"That was two."

"Gonna deny me?"

"No." I tug on his forearm that's cinched around my thigh. "Get inside me."

"But your pussy—"

"Misses your cock," I insist while yanking on him again.

The saddle wobbles beneath me as a reminder of my precarious position. Drake's gaze locks on mine, nose and mouth still buried. My bared nipples pebble under his shameless attention. The piercings feel electrified, and I arch for his approval. Crinkles appear at the corners of his eyes to reveal he's smiling. I brace myself but a zap shocks me when he gives my slit a farewell lick.

This man. Good grief. I try to give him a no-strings sexual favor and he turns me into a boneless heap for my gracious efforts. His lips are wet from the pleasure he wrung from me. A delayed spasm clenches my empty core, demanding to be filled.

He untangles our knotted limbs and I slump into the unstable seat. My legs twitch while sensation returns, the bent and suspended pose kinking my blood flow. Sweat slicks my skin regardless of the cooling temperature. I try to move but a rough groan stops me.

My heavy lids lower to where his are focused. Denim material gapes wide to expose my breasts. The babydoll dress is a disheveled mess. Buttons missing. Hem gathered at my waist. Sleeves better off as restraints. Laughter shakes my frame and I accept the shambles I'm in.

Meanwhile, Drake is too composed. He stands to his full height, giving me a view that sizzles and slaps. Only his jeans hang open and loose. Black fabric strains over the prize penis he returned to solitary confinement after I sucked him dry. He proceeded to treat himself to a double portion of dessert and left me in this predicament. What a pair we make.

It's only fair I take a play from his book and even the score. My fingers fumble for the bottom of his shirt, grasping the two sides with purpose. The pearl snaps don't stand a chance against my parting motion. A pleased sigh tumbles from me as his chiseled abs are put on explicit display for my ogling.

"That's better."

Drake glances at his bared torso. A smirk praises my efforts. His hand grabs mine, slapping my palm onto him. My nails curl into him as if I could leave a dent. The guy might as well be a slab of rock. A filthy chuckle applauds my attempts, and I melt a bit more.

He leans forward to support himself on the wall, towering over my shaky state. I'm very much trapped between a cock and a hard place. His stare smolders into mine until I'm dizzy. A bent knuckle gently caresses the flush heating my cheek.

"Only my name comes from that dirty mouth," he reminds.

I part my lips. "Yes, Drake."

His eyes burn into molten blue. "Get my dick out."

There's no hesitation. My hand wraps around his steely length and tugs him free. A grunt puffs from him once he's exposed to the bite in the air. His palms scoop under my ass. He uses that grip to lift me until I'm where he wants me. A nudge at my entrance earns a moan. The harsh thrust that follows rips a soundless scream from me.

"Ohhhhhh my—"

Drake's fingers clench on my ass. "Whose dick are you on?"

"Yours," I gasp. "Drake."

"Again."

"Fuck me, Drake." A whimper spills from me as he forces himself deeper. "Only you, Drake."

"That's my good girlfriend," he praises.

My eyes roll back when he slams forward to the hilt. His piercing immediately rubs my clit, hitting the spot that sparks fire to my veins. The stretch in my core aches with painful pleasure but I'm wet enough to take him easily.

Drake seals his mouth over mine, swallowing my next moan. Our tongues glide together to match the pace of him pounding me. I grab onto him while he sets a punishing tempo. The position I'm caged in demands compliance. Any resistance flees, allowing him to fill me to the brim. I'm already on edge, primed from the previous climaxes. Drake's exhales paint my lips as our passion ignites into a feverish blaze.

As his cock strokes in and out, my fuzzy brain decides I'm just along for the fucking. He's using me for both of our pleasure and I very willingly accept my role. The muscles in my inner thighs pinch as I spread wider. Drake is quick to hammer me harder. Our frantic motions shake the saddle stand. It's probably seconds from collapse, much like me. A clench tightens my sex and relief is fast approaching.

A dry chuckle chides me. "Not yet, beauty."

Drake suddenly pulls out and I whimper from the loss. Before I can demand his return, he flips me on the seat. My shoes touch the floor just as he bumps my ankles apart. I scramble for a handhold, fingers curling into leather as he slides in. A hoarse cry shreds my throat.

This angle sends him even deeper, reaching the place that makes me shatter. The slap of our hips connecting gains momentum. He's mounting me into a frenzy. I'm crazed, mindlessly bucking against him.

His hands grip my sides, using the hold as leverage to spear me onto his length. I'm rocked forward and back in even strokes. My nipples rub on the suede seat, the friction going straight to my clit. The metal hoops drag back and forth from the rushed movements. Sensation balloons until I'm about to burst. That's when a change in angle strikes.

"Oh, ohhhhh, what…?" My thoughts cut off as my clit grinds into the saddle, stroking me into submission. "This is… yes, yes! There. Don't stop."

Somehow, his speed increases. "Never."

"Please, please," I chant.

"Come on my cock. I need it, beauty. Now!" Drake shouts.

A demanding thrust pushes me over the edge. Heat rushes over me in an outward ripple. My vision swims while I'm submerged in pleasure. Trophies and awards line the walls but the real victory is building inside of me. Tingles spread until I'm shaking. Drake's steady rhythm becomes disjointed as he follows me into release.

"Fuuuuuuck," he groans while redecorating my vagina.

I feel him flood me with passion. That burst triggers another from me. Trembles rack my limbs as I stumble through a third or fourth wave. I've lost count at this point. The peak of ecstasy explodes between us, thrumming at where we're joined until nothing exists but this moment.

A clamp from my inner walls latches us together while relief flows between us. We float in our shared bliss, labored breaths the only sound in this serenity. His body slumps over mine, but he props himself slightly to avoid crushing me. I'm still quaking when his face nuzzles into the crook of my neck.

"And that"—Drake's exhale smiles against my skin—"is how my tack earns a permanent place in your room."

CHAPTER EiGHTEEN

Drake

My grin spreads as I study the young minds looking to me for knowledge. "We're going to focus on basics today. How does a game of catch sound?"

"Yay!" The team of ten T-ballers shout and stomp their feet.

"That's the spirit. Pick a partner and practice tossing the ball." I mimic the action.

They nod in tandem while glancing at each other, already moving as a cohesive unit. Pride warms my chest. Cassidy thought this would be difficult. I scoff. This will teach her to underestimate me.

"And don't forget you have to earn that aqua shirt," I remind before setting them loose.

"Yes, Rake," they recite.

I chuckle and wag my finger at Charlie. "Didn't we already go over this? That's a special nickname."

"Like Pinkie Pie."

Kenzie pauses her doodles in the dirt to offer that tidbit. The little girl didn't want to play, but she volunteered to be my assistant. So far, she's great at delivering comedic relief. Giggles erupt and the kids begin chanting the fluffy title she's shared.

"Just call me Coach," I tell the team.

But they aren't listening. Two start poking each other. That encourages three of them to roll on the ground, knocking into their neighbors. Another gets distracted by a plane flying overhead. Those remaining are still repeating 'Pinkie Pie' like a mantra.

I clap my palms together. "Settle down or we don't get to play."

That gets their attention. "Yes, Coach."

The strain whooshes from me. Just a minor hiccup. I inhale the scent of freshly cut grass and budding talent. This is going to be a huge success.

My hands get parked on my hips. "Okay, what are you going to do?"

Wide eyes bounce from left to right in search of the answer. Almost every expression turns blank.

"Catch balls," Charlie says.

"That's right." I bend to give him a high-five. "Are we ready?"

The kids jump to their feet in a collective motion. "Yes!"

"Who are we?"

Tiny fists pump in the air. "The Colts!"

"Go, go, go!" I roll my wrists, sending them onto the field.

Excitement squeals from their scattering cluster. My mistake unfolds in front of me almost immediately. The semblance of cooperation evaporates while they race off in different directions. There's no logic to their movements. Screams and laughter combine into shrill noise. Nobody is working together. The balls remain in a pile on the mound.

"Yo, Colts!" I bellow. "Remember to find a partner. Practice throwing and catching."

But my directions are drowned in their ruckus. Kids zoom back and forth, going nowhere. It reminds me of recess in elementary school. One spins in circles until she falls over. Four appear to be having a race. They're just burning energy at this point.

"Oh, come on!" I toss my hands in the air. "At least pretend to throw a ball."

A dash of motion nearby catches my attention. Kenzie leaves her position beside me and dashes into the fray. Her braids whip from the fast pace.

"Mac? Where are you going?"

She doesn't pause. "Gonna play tag!"

I gape at her retreating form. "But that's not what they're doing!"

Except that's exactly what they're doing. Much to my disappointment. Irritation spikes as the nonsense spreads into a chase where everybody is trying to get caught. Bodies collide before bouncing away to find another crash.

I'm not ready to admit defeat, but this is getting out of hand. My lack of experience is exposed like an infected wound. I glance at the parents who don't seem the least bit concerned about their children acting like hellions. Most probably assume this is a strategy from me.

My focus returns to the kids. "Colts! Can I have your attention?" Nope, but I wait in vain. "Listen up, team!"

I get nothing in return other than pitchy giggles

lobbed at each other. A select few take aim for knee-caps, trying to make a tackle.

"That's the wrong sport," I shout.

Five of them gather into a huddle, putting their hands in the middle. They break apart and one takes the role of quarterback. She cocks her arm back and throws an impressively fake pass.

I hang my head at the mockery. "Now you're just being mean."

A boy zips by me in a blur. I'm not sure why he's in such a hurry until a kid behind him throws a handful of dirt. Dust billows and blasts me in the face. Particles lodge in my eyes, which burns like fire.

"Son of a bit—ter beaver." I slap a palm over the wounded area. "All right, that's it. I've had enough of this… silliness. If you can't listen—"

"Hey, trouble." Cassidy's melodic voice cuts into my rant. "You hanging in there?"

"Yup. Couldn't be better," I joke.

My ruffled feathers flap, carrying me to where she's standing behind the fence. The stress melts off my shoulders as I get caught in her gaze. She's dressed to entice me in a Mustangs shirt that has my name on the back. A hat that matches mine shadows her face but there's no shrouding the concern resting there.

Her fingers curl in the chain link, brushing against mine. "Does your eye hurt?"

"This?" I point to the blazing ache. "Just on the inside."

She winces. "It's super red."

"Not surprised," I admit. Grit flakes off my lashes

when I rub at the soreness. "Can you believe this crew of misfits?"

"Um, yeah." Cassidy laughs at my dumbfounded expression. "They're children. You gave them permission to run free."

I frown. "The directions were simple to follow."

"For you," she argues. "Remember they're four and five at this level. Maybe six. This is their first practice."

"Doesn't matter. That"—I hitch a thumb at the frenzy behind me—"isn't how you get in the big leagues."

Her brows leap under the brim of her cap. "They're just kids."

"Who aren't taking this seriously."

"Did you consider the possibility that you're taking this too seriously?"

That gives me pause. I dig through my memories, trying to recall when I started playing at their age. It's fuzzy but there were plenty of occasions when I acted like a little shit. No wonder my coach made me run extra laps.

Cassidy must see understanding dawn in my expression. "They don't necessarily want to go to the big leagues. These kids just want to have fun. There has to be a balance, especially while they're so young. Have patience with them."

"This is normal?"

Her head toggles. "To an extent. I'm not sure what else you were expecting."

"Perfect angels on their best behavior, ready to play ball."

She blinks, and then cracks up like a hyena. "Ohhhh, you sweet man. That's not realistic. Kids are messy and wild. Think of them as rowdy customers during happy hour at your bar. Just less belligerent and more adorable."

I scrub over my jaw, glancing at the tornados of chaos whipping across the field. "That tracks."

"We're outside in an unstructured setting. Lucky for you, they're corralled somewhat. That doesn't mean you should turn them loose and assume they'll do what they're told. They're not capable of following directions that well. Those who are, such are Kenzie and Charlie, will conveniently forget what they've been taught and join the herd." Her chin lifts to where the twins are hopping over others like frogs and logs.

"Pack mentality," I mutter while supervising what's become preschool recess. "I've lost control of the situation."

"Get it back," Cassidy retorts.

My lips slide into a smile at her encouragement. "You make it sound so easy."

"It is. They're testing you right now and you're letting them take advantage. Didn't I warn you about this?"

I avert my gaze, taking a sudden interest in a cloud overhead. "You might've mentioned it."

"And did you listen?"

"Obviously not." My arm thrusts toward the disassembled team that's moving nonstop. "They'll poop themselves out eventually, right?"

"You better be joking," she cracks.

"What if I'm not?"

Cassidy's stare bores into mine, digging at my insecurities until I want to squirm. "Get out there and show them who's in charge. You're the coach. Be firm but fair. Stick to a smaller section of the field. Take control. Give them a reason to respect your authority. Earn their trust. Establish rules and boundaries. After that, you can expand the safe zone. Trial and error. Never give up. These kids need you."

I allow her pep talk to wash over me in a warm wave. "Damn, that's hot. How can I repay you?"

"You're coaching my son's team," she deadpans.

"Not good enough. I'm going to give you a hot beef injection."

Cassidy gags. "Please don't ever repeat that."

"Stun you with my cum gun?"

"Absolutely not."

"Pump you full—"

"How about you focus on building an unbeatable team, stud."

"Or we could ditch this—"

Her glare silences me. "Don't make me fire you, trouble."

"Not possible. It's a volunteer position," I remind her.

"Just do the job then. It makes bragging that you're my boyfriend slap harder. The other moms are already jealous, but if you're good with children?" She kisses her fingers in a chef's kiss style. "Irresistible."

I tip my ball cap at her. "Yes, ma'am."

"Nope," she laughs. "That's not sexy either."

"Striking out left and right. Maybe I should quit while I'm already down."

"You've got this, champ. Use that carrot in your back pocket."

I pat my gym shorts. "What?"

She rolls her eyes. "The shirts. They want one. Use that to reel them in."

"Great advice. What would I do without you?"

"At this rate? Be used for batting practice. Swing and a hit." Cassidy's gaze lowers to my groin.

I wince. "Wicked woman."

"Good luck." She wiggles her fingers while backing toward the bleachers.

My cleats eat dirt as I jog to midfield. A loud whistle rips from me, halting the mayhem I allowed for too long. I cross my arms and widen my stance.

"Gather 'round, Colts. First person in front of me gets to be the leader." I point to the spot without removing my gaze from them.

The group rushes at me in a stampede. Charlie arrives a second faster than anyone else. There are a few grumbles but nobody puts up a fuss. Kenzie parks herself next to me as the second in command. All eyes are on me for what comes next.

"You've had your fun. It's time to listen." My tone demands silence. "There are only fifteen minutes left. We're going to practice throwing and catching as planned. After we're done, I'll pass out the team shirts."

Several kids whoop and begin going off the rails but others are quick to shush them.

"Hey, look at that. You're learning. Let's try this

process again. Pick a partner." I pause as they pair up. "Looks awesome. Now follow the leader to the fence. That's Charlie. Don't cut ahead of him."

He waves, the powerful position straightening his posture. "I go first."

"Yep, that's right." I motion him forward before continuing the instructions. "We're going to form two lines. One against the fence. The other facing it. You should be looking at your partner."

The kids do as they're told. My victorious grin shifts to Cassidy. I'm hoping to find her smiling back at me but she's talking to someone. The other woman is leaning close, her bleached hair shining in the sun. Even wearing a hat as a shield, I can see my girlfriend's emotions on display. Cassidy's expression crumples at whatever the blonde says. The anguish wipes away in the next second, firming into a neutral mask. I would've missed it had I not been paying attention. A protective surge flexes my legs, prepared to defend her against the unknown.

The clang of metal realigns my concentration to where the kids wait on me. This isn't the moment to get distracted. Whatever is bothering her will have to wait.

"All right, Colts," I say while striding to the mound. "I'll bring you a ball. Practice tossing it back and forth. Gently."

Kenzie skips along beside me, assisting in the distribution task. "You're like the best coach ever."

I chuckle. "Not sure about that, but thanks."

"Baseball is sooooo fun," she gushes.

"What's your favorite part?"

Her features scrunch. "Chasing boys. They tried to give me germs. Yuck."

"Did you win?"

Kenzie stares at me like I've sprouted horns. "Um, no. That's not the rules."

"My mistake." More laughter rumbles from me but a glance at the stands cuts the amusement short. The blonde is still next to Cassidy, her hands moving in animated gestures. "Do you know that lady your mom is talking to?"

The little girl barely gives her a peek. "Nope."

"Figures," I mumble.

But that's probably for the best. Serves me right too. I need to keep my head in the game. Or practice. Either way, the kids are actually listening. An internal fist pumps at the accomplishment.

"Great teamwork, Colts. Let's change things up a bit. Instead of throwing, roll the ball to each other. This is good practice for catching grounders." I model the action of scooping and returning.

The kids are quick to comply. They do well and remain on task. That makes the rest of practice run smoothly but I can't get Cassidy's reaction out of my mind.

When the clock strikes six, I rush to pass out the shirts. The team erupts in cheers, no complaints about my hurried methods. Everyone is smiling as they show off their earned uniform.

I'm racing to the gap in the fence when Cassidy

approaches. My stomach plummets at her forced smile. "What's wrong, beauty?"

Her lips wobble but she tries to stay strong. "I have a buyer for Leita."

CHAPTER NiNETEEN

Cassidy

BRENDA JABS HER HEELS INTO LEITA'S SIDES again. The roan jolts forward, trying to fulfill her rider's request. A harsh yank on the reins suggests she did the opposite. Frustration bubbles as I watch my horse fight to understand what this woman wants.

"I think she needs a bit in her mouth." Brenda rattles the hackamore shanks as if useless.

I swallow a scream, reminding myself this is a business. "That's not necessary. She responds very well."

"Not to me," the blonde retorts.

A sour gurgle twists my gut when her mixed signals almost steer Leita into the fence. "She only needs gentle pressure from your legs. Just take it easy. Try being softer with your hands too."

"We'll reach an understanding," Brenda insists.

The tight circle she forces Leita into suggests that point will be met with the mare sour and ruined. The wind whips to stir the upset on my horse's behalf. She's trying her best to please and adapt to these unfamiliar cues but she only receives more backlash.

Paisley cringes, done being the silent bystander. "Cass—"

A painful ache cramps my chest. "Not yet."

"It's obvious they're not a good fit."

"She just got in the saddle," I argue. "We need to give her more than three minutes."

"Why bother?"

"This is business," I state. It's a reminder I've had to repeat to myself too often when it comes to the roan mare.

"But there's a limit."

I follow my cousin's gaze to where Brenda flops in the saddle like a rag doll while sending Leita mixed signals. "She's supposed to be an experienced rider."

My cousin snorts. "According to her?"

"Not just anybody looks for a barrel prospect in this price range."

"If they want to win. She probably has a money tree in her backyard." Paisley mimics plucking bills from branches.

Which would explain why she didn't blink at the amount I'm asking for Leita. I even upped it to top dollar, in no rush to sell her. When that had no impact, I tried to hold off setting a date to avoid this disaster. The eager beaver's patience only lasted a week.

The sentimental value I've tried to ignore is mocking me. *Not attached, huh?* Brenda treating Leita this roughly turns my stomach and proves I'll have to find a different buyer. But letting her go is going to hurt no matter what.

"She'll live her best life at Greener Pastures," my cousin cuts into my thoughts.

"I refuse to let her go to waste," I mumble absently.

"You should call the whole thing off." Her chin lifts to my phone.

"That doesn't make any sense." Yet I palm the device.

The loud roar of an engine slices into our country quiet. An unmistakable black truck barrels up my driveway as if there's an emergency. Dust plumes in thick clouds from the speed. Brenda pauses her attempts to ride Leita, bringing the horse to a stop near us. We watch the interruption approach and slam to a halt next to the arena.

Drake flings open his door, waving erratically while stomping our way. "Stop the sale!"

My mouth drops. "What...? How did you know when she was coming?"

I hadn't told him, especially after his reaction at the baseball field. As if I needed another voice of reason against selling. But the days have passed without mention. Drake seemed to have forgotten, or he didn't care. A huff escapes me. I'm clearly missing something.

Paisley's smile is too smug. "I texted him."

My gaze rips off Drake to glare at my cousin. "When did you get his number?"

"Easy there, death stare. I used your phone." Her grin tips higher.

"No, I would've—" But a glance at my screen confirms her method of deception.

"I can't let you do this, beauty." Drake is beside me, cradling my cheek in his hand. "That horse is meant for you."

A sharp refusal shakes my head. "We've been over this. Please don't make me repeat myself."

"Fine." He straightens. "I want to buy her."

"Gonna have to get in line." The saddle creaks as

Brenda leans forward, most likely offering a juicy shot of her boob job. "Unless you'd like to make a deal."

The sultry purr in Brenda's voice solidifies my newfound dislike for her. Whatever delusions she's under must be potent for her to believe this situation is hers to control. My shoulders tremble with silent laughter.

"There's nothing to negotiate." My statement is meant for both of them.

"I beg to differ," Drake tells me before flicking a dismissive glance at the woman still astride my horse. "Listen, Barbie—"

The blonde giggles while curling a lock of hair around her fingers. "It's actually Brenda."

"Doesn't matter," he drawls. "This horse is very special to my girlfriend, which makes her important to me. I'm going to need you to step aside and let me have her."

"What's in it for me?" Her coy tone makes me want to gag.

Drake doesn't miss a beat. "You get to find your next barrel racing champion elsewhere."

"That's not going to satisfy me," she deadpans.

"Want to play high stakes? I can spin that roulette wheel."

The blonde's expression goes blank. "Don't you mean hardball?"

"Whatever blows your boots off. I'm willing to pay..." He dangles the pretense of an offer until I'm ready to jump out of my skin. "Ten thousand dollars."

Silence thick enough to suffocate greets the amount. His smile is triumphant, thinking he's shocked us. Brenda's cackle bursts his bubble.

She wags a finger. "You'll need to do better than that, pretty boy. The asking price is twenty."

"Grand?" His eyes bulge, swinging to me. "Does that horse poop golden apples or what?"

"She has fantastic breeding and incentives," I tell him, fully aware he doesn't have a clue what that means.

But the cocky haggler nods. "In that case, let's make it thirty."

Brenda's eyebrows disappear into her bleached bangs. "You're not very subtle, huh?"

"Like a noisy fart in the library," he boasts.

"I can't even with you," I mumble.

"Does that mean I win?" He rubs his palms together.

The blonde clucks her tongue while dismounting, the conflicting signals a final farewell to Leita. "Too rich for my blood."

Drake snatches the mare's reins when Brenda carelessly discards them. Leita is quick to sniff his pockets, nuzzling the left side. A collective sigh comes from his adoring audience—me very much included—when he whips out several carrot pieces for her.

"Such a good girl," he croons.

"You packed treats?" Tears spring to my eyes and I fan at the burn. "What are you doing to me, trouble?"

"I could ask you the same question, beauty." His smirk slides my way. "All I did was bring a snack in case someone got nosy at my britches. You made me buy a horse."

My hands lift. "Oh, no. I had nothing to do with this."

Drake chuckles. "You have everything to do with every decision I make. I'm always thinking about you."

"Damn, that's a great line," Brenda breathes. Why she hasn't left yet is beyond me. "If you need riding lessons—"

"My cowgirl has me covered," he interrupts her potentially crude suggestion.

But I stiffen at what she's implying. The urge to claim my man has me lunging forward. A grip on my arm stops me from getting far.

"Remember this is business." Paisley echoes my earlier thought. "There's no need for a pissin' match."

"But there's a line, right?" I can repeat phrases too.

"Not in this case. Drake hasn't taken his eyes off you."

And he hasn't. His stare blazes into a smolder that strikes a match to my arousal. I squirm at the heat flooding me. Our chemistry doesn't go unnoticed.

"Gotta get me one of them." Brenda grumbles about a former sugar daddy under her breath. Gravel spits at us as she storms to her car in a huff.

"Bye!" I wiggle my fingers. "Thanks for stopping by. Better luck next time."

She returns my wave while driving away. It's only then I realize she didn't bring a trailer. That's a universal sign in this industry. Maybe she wasn't that interested after all. But somebody else swooped in regardless, which reminds me…

"Drake," I exhale. Exasperation heaves my chest. "Why did you do that?"

"Grand gesture, beauty."

"Not this again." But my belly flutters to spite me. "You can't be serious about buying her."

"I'd never joke about that."

"What're you gonna do with this very expensive horse?"

His baby blues twinkle. "Give her to you as a pre-engagement gift."

"That's not…" My brain stumbles. "I'm not even sure how to respond, but… you can't just say that as a reason."

"Just did," he grumbles. "But fine, she's a regular present then."

"I don't accept. She's yours."

"How convenient." His wink is paired with a flash from his dimples. "What's mine is yours."

I flail my arms between us. "We aren't married."

"Yet," he amends.

My laughter borders on hysterical. "You're very presumptuous."

Drake dips to kiss me. "Thank you."

"That wasn't meant as…" The fight abandons me, and I sag into him. "Oh, forget it."

"You'll keep her?" Hope brightens his tone.

"But she deserves to be more than a pasture ornament," I mutter.

"What if she's like Pago? You won't know unless you try."

There's a lurch in my belly. "But they're nothing alike."

"Their connection to you," he murmurs.

"You're reaching."

"Am I?" His fingers tug on my beltloop, pulling me against him. "Don't deny your passion."

"I have a simple solution," Paisley interjects. "Leita can join my rotation. I won't mind winning every competition we enter."

My eyes roll. "Of course you won't."

"Somebody has to ride her for you to be satisfied. Might as well be me in the saddle. Unless you have a better idea." My cousin stares at me, waiting for the reaction she's aiming for.

I gulp as a familiar pang spreads in my chest. The pain accompanies a flood of memories. It hurts to imagine Pago as my past. He's gone but never forgotten. Much like my competitive spirit.

But then I look at Leita. The mare catches me staring and whinnies. My heart melts like it did the day I first saw her. The ache fades. Guilt doesn't slam into me. Instead, a lightness fills my entire body as if the weights holding me down suddenly vanish.

She can't replace him. That's never been her purpose. I've just been too stubborn to consider other options.

Drake saved me from making a huge mistake. I snuggle into his side while stroking Leita's velvety nose. My very thoughtful boyfriend feeds her another carrot, which she happily crunches on.

"She's a reminder of how sacred a bond between horse and rider can be," I whisper. "Thank you for buying her, but I won't take your money."

He tucks me flush against him, bending to press his lips to my forehead. "How about a compromise?"

I lift my face to study his expression. "Such as?"

"You take her to a show. Just to see how it feels." His thumb brushes along my cheek. "But no pressure. I'll gladly pay thirty thousand to make sure she's yours."

My mind wanders to the steady thump of his pulse. Paisley takes Leita's reins from Drake and walks her to the barn, already anticipating my response. The persistent pressure rooted deep inside of me loosens as a possibility appears. Maybe returning to this path is the right direction.

"I'll consider a trial run."

CHAPTER TWENTY

Drake

WARMTH FROM CASSIDY'S GRIN SPEARS straight into me, spreading her joy through my veins. "I think we should celebrate."

She laughs. "I haven't decided yet. It's a maybe more than anything."

"That's just a delayed yes. The smile on your face says it all." I trace her upturned lips with a curved knuckle.

"Does it matter that much if I compete?"

"No, not to me." When her features crumple, I rush to explain. "But it does to you. I can tell how much it bothers you. This has been holding you back. I also see how much Leita means to you. If she's destined to be a great champion, only you can ride her to victory. But again, no pressure. Whatever makes you happy."

The green in her eyes shines, turning glassy. Wildflowers and devotion float on the breeze. "You're such a sweet man. Perfect, really. How do I deserve you?"

I tuck stray stands behind her ear, fresh from escaping her ponytail. "If you believe me to be perfect, it's only for you. But for the record, I'm far from it."

She leans into my touch. "You make me so incredibly happy."

A rumble sounds from deep within my chest to announce my pleasure. "That's definitely worth celebrating."

"We'll have to wait. My hay delivery is arriving." Cassidy's gaze flicks over my shoulder.

"Your what...?" The question trails off as I track where she's looking. A massive tractor is puttering down the road, pulling two gated wagons stacked with bales. "That's a wide load."

"Sure is."

"Is the delivery going to make the turn into your driveway?" Seems impossible from this angle.

"Don't worry about him. It's not his first rodeo." The familiarity in her voice sits in my gut like a rock.

Kenzie races from the barn, arms and legs a blur. "He's here!"

"Yayyyyyyy! Gonna be sooooo fun." Charlie zooms behind his sister, equally as excited.

My mind struggles to focus. "Who is this guy? Why are your kids acting like he's Santa? And where have they been hiding?"

"A lot to process, huh?" She bumps me with her hip. "The twins were probably chasing the dogs or goats. Maybe both. They're free range farm kids. Crop up when they're ready and make themselves scarce otherwise. It's a smooth system."

I cross my arms and study the glint in her gaze. "You skipped over the dude and his big rig."

Cassidy squints, examining my expression in return. "Wait. Are you... jealous?"

"Just protective. I've never met him."

"Uh-huh." A snarky brow quirks. "Ease off the trigger, trouble. He's harmless."

"Like when Barbie offered to give me very private

riding lessons?" I didn't miss my girlfriend's rabid reaction to the blonde. It pumped my junk a bit, not going to lie.

"That's different." She sniffs.

"Or exactly the same."

The slap of her eye roll is diluted by a coy grin. "Scott is just a nice guy who lets the kids climb in the hay while he unloads it."

"How cute," I mutter.

Her attention slides to where Mr. Nice Guy is chugging up her driveway. "You don't need to stick around. This will take an hour or so. I can text you when he's done."

As if she can get rid of me that easily. "Nah, I want to see what all the fuss is about."

"Maybe he'll let you slip into his tall stacks," she coos.

"One can only hope." A vibration from my back pocket gives me an excuse to unclench my jaw.

Unknown Number: Hello, Mr. Granger. This is Alan from Sutherland Homes. It was great meeting you in person several weeks ago. Your contribution and assistance to the Knox Creek project has been extremely valuable. We're hoping to connect with you about another investment opportunity. Unfortunately, our calls and emails have gone unanswered. Is this a better method to contact you? It would be extremely beneficial for both parties. Please get back to me at your earliest convenience. Call or text. Thank you.

Aggravation distracts the potential rivalry on the tractor. I delete the message, similar to what I've done to their previous attempts to communicate with me. These leeches are sucking on a dry teat.

"Hey." The angelic tune of my beautiful sunflower soothes the upset. "Are you okay?"

I roll my shoulders. "Why wouldn't I be?"

"That's an evasive response." Cassidy's gaze lowers to where I'm clutching my phone. "You're about to crack your screen."

She had a similar reaction to them and their persistent methods. Now I understand her frustration. But this is what I volunteered for. They can harass me until they quit. That's the only option.

"It's nothing." Which is the truth. "Just an annoyance."

Her lips press into a firm line. "Sutherland?"

I consider avoiding again, but nod instead. "They're just trying to squeeze more money out of me."

"Since when?"

"It's just been a couple calls recently. I didn't think much of it."

"You won't—"

"No, I made you a promise. One I won't break." I brush my lips against her forehead.

"Even if they come after me again?"

Plastic creaks in my fist. "They wouldn't dare."

"But they're ruthless," she reminds.

"The situation is under control. You can trust me."

She smiles and wraps me in a hug. "I do."

The pressure whooshes out of me as I soak in the comfort she provides. I bury my nose in her hair and inhale. Peace and sweet dreams flow to my lungs. All is well in this moment.

But then my gaze shifts to where Kenzie and Charlie are greeting Mr. Nice Guy. I bristle at their interaction. The twins are leaping at him in an attempt to get the candy in his grip. He grins at them, but doesn't relent. His jaw works like he's chewing, which only gets the kids more riled. They're practically begging when he finally tosses a few gummy bears into their hands.

"He's teasing them. Real nice," I grumble.

Cassidy steals a glance at what's reinstated my attitude. "Oh, stop. He's like family. Think of him as their uncle."

Scott's gaze moves to where Cassidy is flush against me. He narrows his eyes on me before taking a meaningful dip to her ass. My palms roam from her back to cover what's mine from his view.

"That's not how a brother should look at this sister," I remark.

"Harmless," she reminds.

"We'll see about that." I loop an arm around her waist and lead us toward the action.

Kenzie spots me first. Her expression goes bright, chasing off any hint of gloom. The little girl doesn't hesitate to lunge at me and quickly attaches herself to my leg.

"Pinkie Pie!" Her hold could cut off circulation. "I've missed you."

"Hi, Rake!" Charlie cinches himself to my other side. "Where you been?"

"Right here, Cheese. You've been busy playing with Mac." I ruffle their hair.

The twins share a glance before shouting, "Horsey ride!"

And I'm off as if spurred. My stride is stiff and wide to keep them latched on. Their giggles could flip the stiffest frown right side up. We take several laps along the path, their glee tickling my ears. Cassidy sighs. The sound is pure bliss.

"What about me?" The candy hog dumps more pieces in his mouth.

The kids don't react to his petulance. They're too busy padding my ego. At least until their short attention spans shift to hunting cats in the grass. Charlie scrambles off me and kneels in the dirt. His sister is more practical with her dismount, folding into a silent crouch.

"Good luck," I whisper.

That earns me double the thumbs-ups. Soft laughter escapes me as I amble back to Cassidy and the dude who still hasn't started doing what he's here for. Nope, he's preoccupied himself with my woman. *Such a nice guy.* His beady leer ogles her curves in the cowgirl uniform I've already thoroughly admired.

Confidence widens my stance, putting my six and a half feet frame on display. "Who are you?"

"Took the words outta my mouth," he chuckles. "The name's Scott. I'm the hay guy 'round here."

The intro matches with what I've already heard. Not that I'd admit we were talking about him.

I extend a hand, squeezing hard on purpose. "Cassidy refers to me as the best sex of her life, but you can call me Drake. You've probably heard about me."

My girlfriend's freckled cheeks burst into flames, but she doesn't dispute the title. I wink at her while keeping Mr. Nice Guy in a firm vise.

Scott smirks. "Tight grip. Use it for jerking Jill up the hill?"

"That's clever." My fingers clamp down until he winces. "Gotta show dominance, right? This is my house."

Cassidy exhales roughly. "If you two are done flirting, there's work to do."

Paisley chooses that moment to join us. "Did somebody say two for the price of one?"

A disgruntled scoff rejects her discounted rate. My biceps clench in preparation for heavy lifting. "I've got this. Just tell me where to put the bales."

"Whoa there, buckaroo." Scott blocks me from the nearest wagon. "Are you trying to do my job?"

"Thought that was obvious." But I do a few more stretches to prove my point.

"I'm used to handling Cassidy's hay by myself," he boasts.

"That was before she had me. I can do it."

"Trouble, let him stack the bales. He knows what he's doing," Cassidy presses.

"And I don't?"

She cringes. "No offense, but—"

"Gonna stop you right there," I interrupt. "It can't be that difficult. I'm built like an ox from Oregon Trail."

Scott grunts. "You got those muscles in the gym. True grit isn't sculpted by a monthly membership at Planet Fitness. That strength is given to those who earn it the old-fashioned way. But let's see what you've got."

He strips off his shirt as if that's a requirement for manual labor. The dude is ripped, almost making me feel inadequate. Cassidy appears unaffected, discussing evening chores with Paisley. If interest sparks in her gaze, I want that desire solely aimed at me. I reach back for my collar and yank the cotton over my head. We stand bare chested, flaunting our toned worth. This scene is beginning to have a Gladiator vibe and I'm hyped to beat him at his own game.

As if entering the gauntlet of my thoughts, Scott's grin curves to a vicious angle. "How about we make this interesting?"

"I highly doubt you have anything interesting to say but I'm willing to listen."

His glare threatens to flay me open. "You do that wagon. I'll take this one. It's an even one hundred fifty bales each. Whoever empties theirs first is the winner."

"Deal," I agree.

We don't need to state a prize. There's not a price on bragging rights. Cassidy catches wind of our plans as we approach our designated trailers.

"This isn't the competition we were going to celebrate," she says.

"Consider it extra credit. When I come out on top, I'll buy dinner."

She parks her hands on her hips. "Shouldn't I pay? You're stacking my hay."

"Snappy rhyme, but now isn't the time." I blow her a kiss.

"When I win," Scott barges into our conversation like a drunk relative. "I'll let you buy me dinner, Cass."

"Pathetic," I sneer. "I'm going to enjoy beating you."

"Bold claim coming from a guy who doesn't know the weight of a bale. Too bad I didn't bring my elevator for you. Could've offered you a head start." He makes an 'awww shucks' motion but it's faker than his charm.

"Don't need it." Not that I have a damn clue what equipment he's referring to. I lower the rear grate on my wagon and then, with a fluid motion that feels practiced, hop on. "Ready when you are."

Scott gets to copy my lead for a change, which morphs his scowl into fierce determination. "May the best man eat."

That sounds like something I would say, but his rushed movements don't allow me to appreciate the phrase. A strategy for success forms and a loophole presents itself. I'm ready to execute.

My fingers grip twine and heave. The square is probably pushing fifty pounds. I toss the bale off the trailer and grab another. Throw, bend, lift, repeat. A somewhat smooth cycle directs my motions.

Scott slams to a halt after exiting the barn, his glare pinned on the pile I'm creating. "What're you doing?"

"Emptying my wagon," I breathe. "As we wagered."

His eyes widen. "That's... fuck!"

A chuckle scolds his assumption that I'm cheating. These are the rules he set. Mr. Nice Guy didn't read the fine print. Bummer. Now he's racing to imitate my methods. There's not a chance he can beat me. But just in case, I increase my pace.

It doesn't take long for my back to start cursing me. Sweat slicks my skin and hay particles stick to me like glitter. The sun is cranking up the heat to a punishing extreme. There's a burning sensation streaking through my muscles. This specific task isn't my norm but I don't falter. I've trained my body and mind to push harder. Quitting isn't an option.

Cassidy appears in my peripheral, clutching onto the trailer's metal cage. "What're you trying to prove, trouble? You're going to hurt yourself."

"Beauty," I exhale gruffly. "There's something you should know about a man's ego. It's fragile and needs to be pampered. Give me a stroke, not a shove."

"What?"

"Praise my reckless decisions and then coddle me once I get injured," I rephrase.

"No," she huffs.

"Just this once?" I pause to wipe my damp forehead, seeing that half the stack is gone.

Cassidy's shoulders slump. "Fine."

My steady but rapid pace resumes. "You're the best girlfriend ever."

"I feel like we're back in middle school."

"Now you'll know how it could've been."

Her laughter slices through the pounding in my ears. "Mhmm, a real thrill so far. Very mature."

"Almost done." The reassurance is for me more than her.

Paisley sidles up beside Cassidy to watch the demonstration of male stupidity. We'll do just about anything to prove a point. It seems that gender trait isn't a trade secret. While I'm busting my ass, parts of the women's conversation reaches me.

"They're acting like boys," Cassidy complains.

"Hush. Let 'em swing their cocks around."

My girlfriend gasps. "Don't suggest that. My children are home!"

"Um, wow. I didn't mean literally. Get your mind out of the gutter. It's like peacocking. Sword fighting."

"A dick measuring contest," Cassidy adds.

"Exactly. Fun for us, right?" Amusement is thick in Paisley's voice.

"Until they need medical attention."

"Not our problem," her cousin chirps.

"Just mine." Cassidy doesn't sound too upset to be hitched to my wagon.

"You claimed him. It's your responsibility to spank him upright after he collapses."

Which happens the instant I pitch the final bale. My knees crash into the wooden floorboards before buckling completely. I flop flat on my back, staring at the cloudless sky. Every nerve is pinched. The numbness from running on autopilot cuts off and allows pain to flood me. Spots dance in my vision. I'm panting, fighting for oxygen.

The only consolation is that Scott must be in a similar state.

Cassidy's beautiful face appears above me, blocking out the sun. "Hey, trouble. Still ticking?"

My heart thumps triple its regular rate but going strong. I try to lift my arm to pump the air but fail. "Victory is mine."

"Worth it?"

"That depends," I rasp. "Are you proud of me?"

"Sure." Her tone lacks a convincing edge.

"Am I doing better than the other guy?"

She peers over to the left, humor immediately curling her lips. "Yup."

"Home run, beauty."

Cassidy extends an arm and wiggles her fingers in invitation. "Need a hand?"

"Nope, change of plans. How about you eat dinner off me?" I wince when a spasm attacks my calves. "Not sure I can move."

CHAPTER TWENTY-ONE

Cassidy

I PROP AN ELBOW ON THE KITCHEN ISLAND, MY FOCUS riveted on Drake and his adoring fans in the living room. He's sprawled on the couch while Scott occupies the loveseat. The twins sit on the floor beside my boyfriend, gazing at him in awe.

A sigh buzzes my lips. "What're they doing in there?"

Paisley shrugs. "Bonding."

"Didn't the men hate each other this afternoon?"

"Guys are weird." My cousin states that comment as a fact. "They're probably regaling each other with tales of the great hay battle. At least they stacked the bales afterward. Great teamwork in the end. Kenzie and Charlie are hanging on every word."

"I still can't believe those two nincompoops did that." My back hurts just thinking about it.

Paisley scoffs. "Seriously? Drake will do anything to win you over. Even if that involves aches and pains. You better rub him the right way later."

"Stop it." But the heat collecting in my lower belly confirms our thoughts are following the same path. I grab my drink to cool the rising flush. "He doesn't have anything to prove."

My heart melts into the consistency of mush as the twins begin doodling on Drake's arms. They're coloring in his tattoos while adding their own designs. The big softie reclines deeper into the cushions and lets them have their way with him. Scott mumbles something about lacking discipline.

"Just jealous," Drake retorts. "Mac and Cheese can do no wrong."

"Wow. He's incredible," Paisley breathes.

"The whole package," I agree. "And mine."

She laughs. "If we weren't besties, I'd hate you a little bit. That guy is going to worship the ground you walk on for the rest of your life. He'll never dull your shine."

"Only enhance it." My lips curl as I watch him treat my kids like his own.

Paisley's attention shifts to me. "You're different."

I straighten my spine. "Is that bad?"

"Relax." She swats me. "He's bringing out a calm side of you that I haven't seen in too long."

It's a change I've sensed in myself. I allow my smile to spread, that lightness giving me renewed energy. The man responsible definitely deserves to be rubbed down the right way.

"Is this real?" It's been almost two months at this point and the whirlwind romance vibe continues to gain momentum.

Her brows dip. "Are you still questioning him?"

"No, not at all. It just feels too good to be true." And I've told Drake that much.

"That's how love is, or so I've heard." Paisley exhales a lungful of impatience.

Meanwhile, my breath hitches on the concept. "We're not there yet."

Her nod is just for show. "Has he met Shawn?"

"Not yet."

"On purpose?"

"No, it just hasn't happened naturally. There aren't requirements for that sort of thing. I didn't meet Pam for months after they started dating and that was just fine. Shawn trusts my judgment in return. We invited him to Charlie's T-ball game in two weeks. His schedule hasn't allowed him to attend any of the others." I glance at the calendar packed with tasks to complete in the meantime.

"Is the team ready for that? I went to one practice and... yikes."

My eyes roll. "There was a game yesterday."

She cringes. "How did that go?"

"Better than expected. They're young children," I laugh. "You can't assume they'll become professional athletes overnight. It's a miracle the sport holds their concentration for thirty minutes."

Kenzie and Charlie complete their artwork, racing off to find the next project. Drake rises from the couch. The hem of his shirt is askew, but not bunched enough. As if listening to my silent demand, he stretches and exposes a mouthwatering slice of sculpted abs. I swallow a sip of iced tea, suddenly parched. Paisley fans my face before doing the same to hers.

"Their coach, though." She hums when he turns in our direction, which earns her a harsh jab to the ribs.

"I'm gonna have to ask you to leave soon," I snark.

"It's just innocent ogling. He should be on the cover of romance novels. I'd like to display him on my shelf."

"No way," I blurt. "Not unless I own the only copy for my private collection."

She sticks out her tongue. "It's fair to share."

"Get your own book boyfriend brought to life."

"Trying and failing, thanks for the reminder." Paisley flips a section of hair over her shoulder.

"If a certain someone would just forget about the grump." I pat her head. "The grass is much nicer on this side of the fence."

"Yeah, yeah. Here's comes your paradise in the flesh."

Drake struts toward us, his skin freshly decorated with nonsense scribbles. His hair is mussed to match the heavy droop of his eyelids. Thick stubble coats his jaw but those devastating dimples pop as he smirks. I grip the counter to resist launching at him.

"Are you talking about me?"

"Maybe." I wink.

"Thought so. My nose was itchy."

"Did you scratch and sniff?" I inhale the scent of woodsy spice and artificial fruit, which must be from...

"Oh! Speaking of markers, check this out." Drake angles his chin to expose sloppy words scrawled on the side of his neck. "Mac and Cheese branded me. Gonna make it permanent."

"Don't you dare." My ovaries won't survive and I'll end up pregnant with triplets.

The blue ocean in his gaze pulls me under. "You can come to the appointment. Maybe get ink of your own."

I've actually been considering it, especially after recent events. "Okay."

"Really? That was easy."

"It's not a big deal. I already have one."

"No sh—oot?" His wide gaze latches onto the twins sitting at the table, very much within listening distance. "Where?"

I fold my right ear to expose the spot. "Got this after Mimi passed."

His thumb drifts over the infinity heart. "This is the symbol from the post that's hanging over your driveway's entrance."

I nod, fondness wrapping me in a hug. "We adopted it as Greener Pasture's logo. Mimi made that wood sign ages ago. More sentimental than anything."

"Very special. I love it." He bends to kiss the token I always carry with me. "Maybe I'll get one added to my Mac and Cheese tattoo."

"You're messing with me," I breathe.

"Nope, I wouldn't joke about something so personal. I'll have the kids keep their design fresh until we can get an appointment."

"Why would you permanently mark your skin with their random doodles?"

"What you consider a random doodle will soon be my most treasured piece." Drake winks. "At least until you draw on me."

"Gladly." I hook an arm around the back of his neck and pull him into a kiss.

"Get a room." The complaint comes from Scott as he shuffles into the kitchen, a noticeable limp in his stride.

"We had one." I gesture to the suddenly crowded space. "You intruded."

His gaze roams to my cousin. "Still single, Paisley?"

"Not if you're asking."

"Ouch." But he chuckles. "I'll take that as my cue to exit gracefully."

"Like that's possible for you." Drake laughs and claps him on the back.

Scott winces. "Thanks for letting me crash after your boyfriend railroaded me."

"Two peas in a very strange pod," Paisley muses.

Kenzie and Charlie wedge themselves into the small gap separating me from Drake. My little girl blinks up at him. I brace myself for the slew of possibilities she might spill.

"Are you staying for dinner, Pinkie Pie?"

He smiles. "It's my treat."

Charlie gasps. "Like cupcakes?"

"Ah, not quite." My boyfriend looks at me, desperation pinching his brow. Such a softie.

"Maybe after supper," I concede.

The twins whoop, cinching us together in an unbreakable embrace. Drake's gaze collides with mine. Waves crash, spilling between our stares. There's a tugging sensation like we're drowning in each other. We fight the tide to deliver us ashore. Together.

Paisley glances at us, huddled in a quad formation. Her posture deflates. "Ah, crap, I better make myself scarce too."

"How convenient. I'll walk you out." Scott gestures to the entryway.

"Have fun," I croon. "Thanks for the delivery and extra help today."

"Our pleasure." His eyebrows wiggle at my cousin. "After you, blondie."

Her skeptical awareness skewers him. "Don't get any ideas. This doesn't mean anything, Scottie."

"Yeah, yeah. Benson would unalive me if I actually tried anything."

Her sharp cackle echoes down the hall. "He couldn't care less."

"That's what you think," Scott drawls.

The front door closes, shutting out the rest of their conversation before we can say goodbye. Charlie and Kenzie struggle to free themselves of our pretzel. Their feet skid on the floor as they race from the room. Chester and Cheeto appear from who knows where to chase after them.

"Don't go too far. We're going to eat soon," I call after them.

They send me a backward wave. "M'kay!"

Drake slides a palm into my back pocket, giving me a firm squeeze. "What's on the menu, mama?"

My chin rests on his sternum while I flutter my lashes up at him. "I thought you were buying?"

"Should we go to my place and see what cobwebs are available in the fridge?"

I falter. "You're inviting us to your house?"

"Why do you sound so surprised? It's not the first time."

"Just might be," I reply.

"You're not missing much. Been thinking about putting it on the market."

My heart stutters. "Are you moving?"

His fingers dig into my ass, pulling me flush against him. "Once you're ready for that."

"Wait." Static crackles in my ears. "You want to move in together?"

"It's the next logical step. I'm over here constantly as it is. My bed is the only thing I use."

"You'd just pack up and leave your home behind?"

"That bachelor pad isn't much of a home. Lacks personality. Too quiet. No history. But this place?" Drake motions to the personal knickknacks and decorations I've purposely arranged. "Love grows here. There are memories embedded in the walls. Deep roots. Positive energy. Welcoming atmosphere. Greener Pastures is where you find comfort after a hard day. Where you raise a family. Build a life. Stay put."

I glance around, seeing the space through his description. Emotion clogs my throat and I gulp. "Yeah, it's really special."

He swoops low, pressing his mouth to mine. "Just like you."

I smile into another kiss, gliding my tongue along his bottom lip. "Impossible to resist."

"And don't forget I'm good at doing laundry."

Our conversation from Bean Me Up floats to the surface. "You were coming onto me. Vigorously."

Drake smirks, a naughty gleam entering the equation. "I'll be your Dixon. Permanently. Just let me in, beauty."

My nod bumps his chin. "But this is a huge decision. It's not just me. I have to think about what's best for the kids."

"That's more than fair. Whenever you're ready," he repeats.

"You'll be the one I tell."

"Until then, I'll keep my humble abode for our sex dungeon."

"That's definitely something I want to see." My grin reflects his.

Drake studies my features for a moment. "You're happy."

Laughter bubbles from me. "What was your first clue?"

His gaze bores into mine. "I can read you, beauty. This is your happy face."

I trace the crinkles at the corners of his eyes. "And this is yours."

"Thanks to you." He kisses my inner wrist.

I hum. "Such trouble."

"For your panties." His rasp curls my toes, and threatens to send my mind to the gutter.

"On a less serious note," I tease. "When was the last time you ate dino nuggets?"

"As in chicken shaped like dinosaurs?"

"Those are the ones."

Drake strokes his jaw. "Can't recall."

"Well then." I begin backing to the freezer. "Hope you brought your appetite."

CHAPTER TWENTY-TWO

Drake

"DAMN, I'VE MISSED THIS." GARRETT TIPS HIS head to the sky, the sun showering him with rays.

I sip on my beer. "How long has it been since you two came aboard Shipfaced?"

"Start of summer," Ridge grunts.

The boat rocks on a wave and I sway in the captain's chair. "We've been too busy."

"Which reminds me," Garrett drawls. "Is your lady love occupied elsewhere? Or how did we make the cut for this outing?"

The mention of Cassidy sends a rush of heat in my veins. We parted ways last night but she won't have the twins this weekend. Her filthy promise strokes me in a tight grip. The seductive pace is quick to get me on edge. My eyes slide shut behind my shaded lenses, giving me a moment to imagine her lowering to her knees. A groan threatens to release when she peeks up from under lowered lids. Pouty lips stretch around my cock while she sucks me to the back of her throat. Arousal pumps me and my dick twitches.

Cold droplets splash on my rigid position, knocking me from the fantasy. The gleaming surfaces on Shipfaced welcome me back to boating. Garrett and Ridge are waiting for me to answer.

Fuck, I can't pop wood in front of my friends.

A subtle adjustment hides the evidence as I picture Billy and Gruff mounting me. I shudder. That deflates my desire real quick. "I figured it was time to get on the lake, just us guys. Like the good old days."

"Uh-huh." Ridge's aviators block the glare I'm certain he's aiming at me. "You could just admit we're the alternates."

My frown can't compete with his grump face. "You're my starting lineup."

"More like a sure thing. You know we don't have plans when the bar is closed."

I shrug and scratch at the stubble collecting sweat. "For the record, Cassidy has yet to grace Shipfaced with her presence."

"She's got her priorities straight." The former defenseman fights a grin.

Garrett chuckles, tipping his can to his lips. "Look who's flinging shit. As if you'd choose us over Callie."

"How about that," I hoot. "Foster is the voice of reason."

He brushes off his bare shoulders. "I'm maturing."

"That's one term for it," Ridge mutters.

"What's wrong, Crusher?" I stand and my legs wobble as the water turns choppy. "Do you need a hug? Have I been neglectful? C'mere, you big lug."

He smacks my open arms. "Save the shmooze for your girlfriend."

An exaggerated sigh escapes me as I reclaim my seat. "If you insist."

"Speaking of, has Cassidy been to your house yet? Or are you still afraid she'll think it's a dump?" Garrett rolls his eyes as if the idea is ridiculous.

My gaze lowers to picture her reaction. "I'm ready when she is."

"She's gonna flip her shit."

"Here's hoping," I laugh.

Ridge's scowl cracks slightly and he lifts his Coors Light. "Cheers to finding your baby mama, Granger."

"And minus the drama. Winning!"

"Glad to see you settled," he adds.

"I'll drink to that." I tap my beer to his.

Garrett leans in, joining the toast. "And to kinky sex that never gets boring."

"I'll be sure to add that in my speech at your wedding." Cool relief soothes my throat as I chug the rest of my beer.

Ridge almost smirks. "That'll go over well with the missus."

"Grace is worse than me. Insatiable. Just the way I like her," Garrett chuckles.

"Well, damn. Cassidy only unleashes the freak every other weekend." Not that I'm complaining. Those three kid-free days are real bangers.

Laughter folds Garrett in half. "Don't act deprived. You'll take what you can get."

"Got that right." I would've waited for marriage if she wanted to. That would've given me an excuse to rush her down the aisle faster.

Ridge scrubs over his face, most likely thinking about his own vixen. "Shouldn't we be talking about fishin' or some shit?"

"We'll get to rigging your pole in a bit, Crusher." Garrett blows him a kiss before his affection swerves onto me. "Is it true you bought a horse?"

"For Cassidy," I chuckle. "To be fair, she already owned her and isn't going to make me pay the thirty thousand."

Ridge chokes on his sip of Coors. "The fuck?"

"Grand gesture," I explain.

They share a knowing nod when my phone rattles on the dash. A glance at the screen has me immediately silencing the call. Almost as quickly, the buzzing begins again. My humor fades into a pile of ash. I spit a curse and send them straight to voicemail. Another attempt soon follows.

Garrett's brows lift. "Problem?"

"I'm choosing to ignore them." My phone skitters across the surface, disrupting our peace.

Ridge snorts. "Not sure they're getting the message."

Nope, but I'm getting theirs. My glare matches the one cutting across the text. Irritation brews into a cloud as I check their latest lines of bullshit.

Unknown Number: *Hello, Mr. Granger. We're still having difficulty getting ahold of you. Are you getting these texts? How about the voicemails? We've left several. I just need a few minutes of your time to discuss the next investment opportunity. If I'm unable to reach you, I could stop by your place of business. Roosters, right? Or I could try* *contacting Ms. Brooks. Perhaps she would be more willing to talk to us. If I recall, she's the reason you approached us to begin with. Remember that, Mr. Granger. You came to us. We look forward to hearing from you. Have a wonderful day.*

Fumes stream from my flared nostrils. If this is their strategy for getting a response from me, they can sit and spin. I dare them to try using Cassidy to get what they want. Fuckers have no boundaries.

Ridge is about to take a sip of beer but his can pauses midair. "Who the fuck pissed you off?"

I crack open a fresh Coors and guzzle a mouthful. "Remember when I told you about Sutherland Homes?"

Garrett scrunches his forehead. "That construction company you wanted us to invest in?"

"Be glad you didn't." I toss my phone to Ridge since he's closest to me. "They're worse than I thought."

The former hockey pro whips off his sunglasses, menace burning in his eyes. "Who the fuck do they think they are?"

"A huge pain in my ass. Might as well be a thorn bush to the balls."

Garrett whistles after reading the text. "Just block them."

I bang my head on the steering wheel. "Why didn't I think of that?"

Ridge scoffs. "Your fanbase never crossed into harassment territory?"

The memories are a bit crispy on the edges. "Not that I'm aware of."

"Consider yourself lucky," Garrett says. "But yeah, cut off their access to you. Easy as pressing a button."

"Huh." I toggle over to the options and strike them out. "Done."

Garrett stretches to slap my back. "Feel better?"

The throb at my temples pounds harder than my hips slapping into Cassidy's ass. "Not really."

"Dude, let it go. They can't touch you."

My nod flows with the waves. "You're right. They're grasping at dingleberries."

Ridge crosses his arms. "And if they so much as step foot in our bar, they'll be dealing with me."

"Aww, thanks." I pretend to swipe at a shed tear. "See? This is what I wanted. Brotherly love."

His stony expression doesn't appear convinced. "We're still the lowest rung on the ladder."

"Last resort." Garrett's dejected sigh is laughable.

"Nah, don't be butt hurt." I lift my beer in the air. "Bottoms are always up on Shipfaced."

CHAPTER TWENTY-THREE

Cassidy

Sweat prickles my palms and I wipe them on the front of my shorts. It's unseasonably warm for late August but the weather can't take credit for the nerves somersaulting in my stomach. I'm jittery for no reason. This is just another date.

Tell that to my finger that shakes on its way to ringing the bell. These butterflies are probably fluttering from shock. I wasn't expecting to arrive at a suburban paradise when Drake gave me his address. His house is located in a cozy neighborhood not far from the park. The lawn is perfectly manicured, along with the flowerbeds framing the path to the porch. There's even a white picket fence to polish off the picturesque landscape.

Drake suddenly appears, leaning against the open doorway. His smirk greets my parted lips. The naughty gleam in his eyes jolts the tension from my system, allowing me to breathe easy.

"Hello, beauty."

My mouth lifts into a grin. "Hi, trouble."

"Thanks for coming." That gruff tone licks my arousal.

We've let too many days drag on without being

intimate. Need claws at me, desperate for an outlet. A soft whimper slips free and my gaze lowers.

Laughter bursts from me in a wheeze when I notice the unforgettable apron hanging from his neck. "Wow, that's a relic."

Drake turns slowly, revealing the boxers underneath. "Play your cards right and I'll strip for you later."

My knees quake and I slump against one of the rocking chairs arranged around a stained-glass table. A mason jar full of sunflowers sits on top. Of course he has an adorable setup out here. That reverts my focus to the sleepy street and peaceful environment.

"This is a great area," I exhale.

"It's why I chose to live here. Best part of Knox Creek." His gaze is molten, so hot that the flames are blue. "Do you want to see inside?"

I can't imagine it's better than the exterior, but I brush past where he's holding the door for me. My stride slams to a halt just beyond the threshold. The open floor plan spread in front of me doesn't match the description he provided. Not even close.

"Ummm..." That's about all I can say.

Drake scrubs the back of his neck. "I tried to warn you. It's lacking."

I whirl to face his sheepish expression. It's odd to catch his confidence slip. A blush colors his cheeks as he avoids my gaze. The only explanation is that he misinterpreted my reaction. Can't have that.

My fingers thread into his. "Trouble, I'm in awe. This is way nicer than my house."

"Absolutely not. There's no character or depth here." He swats at the interior design as if it offends him.

I admire the rustic style that's fit for a country living magazine. "Who decorated?"

His gaze skips across a distressed wooden chest that pairs with the coffee table. "Me."

"Shut up." I slap a palm over my mouth. "What I meant was you have incredible taste."

Drake tugs me into his side. "You like it?"

"A lot. We should spend more time at your place from now on."

The smile he flashes is steeped in his regular glory. "Whatever makes you happy."

"That'd be you. All. You."

His arm circles my waist and he dips me low. Our lips crash together in a shared gasp. My tongue finds his, gliding in a languid caress. He groans into me and I feel that sound deep in my soul.

Drake sets me upright, dropping another kiss on my mouth. "Thank you, beauty."

It takes me a second to regain my bearings. "For what?"

"The reassurance." His thumb traces the shape of my chin. "Along with everything else."

"You don't need it, but I'll gladly applaud your effort. What you've created with this space is spectacular." My feet spin me to get the full picture. Large windows allow natural light to flood in. It's bright and spacious and brilliant. "I'm appalled you called your beautiful home a bachelor pad."

"It's never felt like anything else." Drake's swallow is audible. "Until now."

"Oh, you sweet man. I'm glad you're mine." My hand grips his apron, yanking until my lips press to his.

He smiles into the kiss. "Fuck, I love hearing you claim me."

I cup his face in my palms. "You're mine, Drake Granger."

A tremble shakes his entire body. "Want to see the rest, or should we go straight to my bed?"

My hips bump his, nudging the hardness that's begging for attention. "How about a quick tour?"

He encircles my wrist, sliding our hands together. "Right this way."

I follow him further into the house, becoming more mesmerized with each step. Each section reveals a new layer of splendor. The kitchen is massive and puts mine to shame. My fingers drift along the butcher block island as Drake steers me into the dining area. Another bouquet of sunflowers is displayed in a turquoise pitcher. It looks like he entertains company often as an accomplished host.

"Wow." I pause when we arrive at the wide space that's purposed as a living room.

"You approve?" Pride shines in his voice.

The entire view is somehow more impressive from this angle. "Uh-huh."

My toes dig into the fuzziest rug. The couch is plush and oversized. I want to collapse into the cushions and cuddle Drake to sleep. He deserves it. Taking care of him in this haven he created sounds better than sex. Well, almost.

But these pillows are calling my name. I pull in a deep breath and a very distinct scent hits me. It instantly fills me with a sense of calm.

"Is that... apple pie?"

Drake inhales. "I lit a candle."

"You lit... a candle?" The pause is necessary for my processing.

"Smells real, right?" His attention snags on my dumbfounded expression. "What? Is that weird?"

I smooth the shock from my features. "No, just unexpected. Like most of your traits and talents."

He tucks his hands behind his back. "I wanted you to feel at home."

"You're full of surprises, huh? That's so thoughtful. Talk about setting the mood." I take a meaningful glance at his creative genius. "Have you lived here ever since moving to Knox Creek?"

Drake nods slowly. His stare moves across the furniture and chill vibe surrounding us. There's wonder in every piece but it doesn't seem like he's seeing any of it.

"I tried to prepare a home to prove I'd make a good husband. It's just been me and my wishful thinking for years. But then you showed up and changed the game."

Tears well in my eyes. His voice is soft, and vulnerable. How he could think any woman would deny him, with or without this palace, boggles my brain.

I launch myself at him. Drake catches me before we collide, but I've stunned him. Not to fret. An urgency pushes me into action.

It's a savage need that rips off his apron. The elastic of his boxers doesn't stand a chance against my desperation to show him how worthy he is. How attractive I find his dedication. How fast and hard I'm falling. How I want to share my life with him. How endearing it is when he asks my kids to retrace their names on his neck, and will continue to do so until I'm ready to get another tattoo.

Just how beyond words amazing he is.

This man has nothing to prove. But just in case he doubts me, I'll remind him at every available opportunity.

Hormones propel through my veins at lightning speed. I'm backing toward the sofa and bringing his nakedness along for the ride.

"You're going to shag me rotten on this gorgeous sectional." The husky edge in my tone is sliced from seduction.

Drake's cock jerks against me. "Fuuuuuck."

"Yep, that's the idea. Give me that prize penis, trouble."

I flop onto the couch and spread my legs. Just as predicted, the luxurious softness swaddles me until I'm drowning in comfort. Drake follows me down and drapes his body over mine. My knees lift to bracket his hips. The skirt of my dress pools around my waist, exposing me for his taking.

He props an arm over my head to hold his weight off me. The other hand dives between my thighs to find me wet and wanting. I arch into his touch, but it's not enough. My restless movements guide him and there's a harsh yank at the crotch of my panties. Cool air tickles my slick flesh but the fever in my blood chases that bite away. The lust wafting off Drake does the rest.

He's better than a blanket, heating me from the inside out. We're pressed close, almost there. I tilt my hips and his dick teases my entrance. He swoops to kiss me just as a solid thrust shoves him to the base. My gasp is swallowed by his groan, our mutual pleasure exhaling between us.

"Always ready for me," Drake breathes against my parted lips. "My good cowgirl."

"Just for you." I mewl while my pussy stretches to accommodate his girth. That slight ache adds to the pleasure. "This house was the best foreplay too."

He slides in and out at a frenzied rate to satisfy our hunger. "Should've brought you here sooner."

My legs shift higher on his sides to send him deeper. "I would've come running."

"Better late than never, hmm?" His piercing grinds into my clit and tingles burst free.

"Ohhhhhh, yes. There."

Primal gratification rumbles from him. "That's right, beauty. I know what you like. Only I do this to you."

I'm already nodding. "Only you."

Drake palms my ass and uses the grip as leverage to strike harder. I widen my thighs, desperate to be stuffed to the brim. His girth forces my resistance to concede. My hips buck against his, the slapping obscene. At least the cushions are large enough to accommodate our position.

His breath is hot on my throat while he travels lower. I spear my fingers into his hair, shoving my concealed breasts into his face. The grumble he expels is muffled by the fabric. My neckline is modest, restricting his access. A loud rip announces how he feels about being denied. I glance down to see my dress torn down the middle. His gaze leaps to mine, searching for a reaction but he doesn't stop fucking me. My wardrobe malfunction is a problem for later. The thrum under my skin is addictive, gaining momentum with each stroke.

"Harder," I whimper.

He complies, his cock spearing me at a punishing rhythm while he yanks my bra down. A smirk slants his mouth before he dips to latch onto my nipple. His teeth tug at the loop hooked in the pebbled point. The friction sends shocks straight to my clit.

I jolt while sensation spreads. A hoarse cry explodes from my lungs. There's a clench in my core, clamping onto him as he sends me over the edge. A final strike from his piercing gets me there. Warmth flows from my center, the relief instant. I feel Drake grow thicker as spasms control me.

His motions become jerky when he pushes into me and stills. He bellows, the guttural sound bursting through me. I grip onto him as we ride the current. Heavy exhales rise and fall from his chest to mirror mine. There's no beginning or end to where we're connected.

As the pleasure ebbs and subsides, our frantic demands rest. My palm drifts along Drake's back. The lazy caress sprouts goosebumps and his smile stamps my skin. Our sweat begins to cool. He lifts his bulk off me but doesn't pull out. An aftershock zips up my spine. His eyes roll back while he trembles.

"I'll never get enough," he groans.

"That'll save me the trouble of hunting you down. Not gonna lie, moving isn't high on the list right now." This sofa might as well be a throne. "We're definitely keeping the sex dungeon."

Drake's smirk is drowsy. "There's more to it than that. You didn't see the bedrooms yet."

"Plural?" I lift my brows. "More of a castle, huh?"

"Two are reserved for the twins."

"What?" My voice is barely a whisper.

He goes still above me, wildly searching for answers in my expression. "Is that too much?"

"Did you decorate them?"

He cringes. "No, I thought we could do that together."

Emotion rushes through me, bubbling until I can't contain it. "I love you."

His mouth swoops down to crash against mine. Drake smiles into the kiss before pulling away. "About time you admit it. I've loved you since the seventh grade."

"Really? That's a tad excessive."

"Which is one of my best qualities."

"Confidence too," I quip.

"When it comes to you and our relationship? I'm certain we belong together. Nothing can convince me otherwise."

"Well," I purr against his lips. "I'm positively in love with you."

He groans when his cock jerks inside of me. "Since when?"

I squint, pretending to count. "My crush felt like love at thirteen. The doodles in my notebook margins agree. But the knowledge that this is forever? When you showed up at Greener Pastures and wouldn't take no for an answer."

"Can't get rid of me."

"Thank goodness." A breeze sweeps across my bared chest, reminding me of the destruction. "Well, there goes a night out on the town to celebrate us."

The twinkle in Drake's gaze is suspicious. "I've got you covered, beauty."

CHAPTER TWENTY-FOUR

Drake

CASSIDY SMOOTHS A WRINKLE FROM HER NEW shirt. "We're really going into public like this?"

My dick is half-cocked just staring at her in clothes I bought. After she drained my balls on the couch, we cleaned ourselves up and got dressed. I happily provided her with stuff to wear after I ruined her dress. A custom tee is one thing. The shorts and underwear I had in her size were hard to explain without making me sound unhinged.

Luckily, she thinks my brand of crazy is romantic.

"Are you embarrassed to be seen with me?" Our clasped palms steer us to the front door regardless of her answer.

"Not even a little bit. Have you looked in the mirror?" She gets distracted ogling me but shakes her head. "It's just the implication."

I chuckle as she gestures to the bold words printed on the front of her tee. The blush darkening her freckled cheeks captivates me. My knuckles trace the heat.

"I'd Ride That," I recite.

"How silly of me to assume the meaning was horse related." Her gaze shifts to my shirt. "Until you put yours on."

Mine is simply stated, marking me as *That*. Obviously. "I'm your favorite mount."

"It's true," she murmurs.

"But how's your second favorite steed doing?"

She toys with a lock of her hair, twirling the red silk around her finger. "Leita is horribly spoiled and still working her way through the last bag of carrots you brought."

"As she should be." I gesture her outside. "And on that high note, let's tell the town we're madly in love."

Her body very purposefully brushes against mine. "I'm sure they already know."

"Visual proof never hurt anyone."

She tugs the collar to her nose and sniffs. "Smells like you."

"Might be on purpose," I rumble.

"Not surprised." Cassidy laughs as we hop down the porch stairs. "Should we take my truck?"

The gleaming paint sparkles under the setting sun. "I'll drive."

"You'll let me be a passenger princess in my own vehicle?" Her hand flutters to her chest. "Oh, my."

I open her door, hoist her onto the seat, buckle her in, and snatch the fob from her loose grip. In that order. She blinks at me. I kiss the shock on her parted lips.

"Sit tight, babe."

Rubber soles skid on cement in my rush around the hood. Cassidy's smile greets me as I slide behind the wheel and jab the key into the ignition. My gaze bounces between her and our surroundings while I reverse onto the street.

There's no sound from the radio until something seems to connect. A raspy voice picks up wherever it left off. My eyes bulge when the context becomes clear.

I give myself an anticipatory stroke.

She immediately advances a step in response.

I cock an eyebrow. "No, pretty girl. Get on your knees for me and crawl."

Whitney lowers herself, holding my stare. She leans forward, palms flat on my floor, and my cock jerks—

Cassidy smacks the knob, cutting off the scene. "That's enough of that."

"I don't think so." My finger jabs the button and the story continues.

—at her willing compliance. Her breasts point down, those red tips tight, and that little bit of stomach she's so worried about looks like an enticing handful, creating a delicious crease where it meets her curved hip. If only she knew how badly I want to lick her there, to trace her insecurities with my tongue.

"Slowly," I demand as she starts to crawl.

"Is this good?" Her voice is breathless yet strong. She knows exactly what she's doing to me.

"You look like a fucking goddess."

My foot slips off the gas pedal and I swerve. "Holy shit, this might be kinkier than the last book."

"I can't believe this is happening again," she grumbles.

A sideways glance exposes her hurried methods to end the audio on her phone. My palm glides across the steering wheel, imagining her soft skin rather than leather. It's no wonder she reads these novels. I'm harder than steel and ready for the climax.

"Beauty, beauty, beauty," I chide. "My naughty cowgirl. Have you no restraint?"

"Says the man who gave me a shirt broadcasting that I want to ride him." She snorts, aiming for nonchalance but the flush racing up her neck betrays her.

"That's straight facts. You were the one listening to an erotic scene on the way to my house. No wonder you were soaked." The road curves as we approach Main Street.

"Oh, puh-lease. Spicy romance helps me—"

"Unwind," I finish for her. "It's a guilty pleasure."

She blinks. "Your ability to remember the tiniest details is uncanny."

"Mhmm, are you surprised? The subject matter is very… titillating." My brows waggle. "What's the title?"

Cassidy points to the display where it's listed on pause. "Surrender by A.M. Wilson."

"Do you want a copy in print? I could read to you." My cock is ready to punch through denim at the thought.

"I wouldn't survive that." Her complexion resembles a tomato. "You're already too much for me. I'm constantly on edge because of you, not a steamy scene. Accept the credit you deserve, trouble."

After taking a sharp right, I rest my palm on her thigh. My thumb drifts along a freckle. "But it's suggestive inspiration. What happens next?"

Cassidy gulps, eyes lowered to where I'm touching her bare skin. "I'm not sure."

"Should we take it from here and create our own ending?"

Her plump bottom lip is tortured by her teeth. "What did you have in mind?"

"I could find an abandoned lot," I hint.

"Oh," she breathes. "You want to do it in the truck?"

"Very much so. Haven't broken it in yet. Not with me," I mutter as an afterthought.

Cassidy's hand covers mine. "Jealous?"

"Of your past lovers? Always."

The green in her gaze sparks with heat, slinking out from behind the flush. Her lids lower as she turns slightly toward me. This is the sultry side of her that I like to assume didn't exist until me. That honor is mine along with reaping the rewards. Especially when she glides our joined hands upward, roaming beneath her athletic shorts to reach between her thighs.

"Find somewhere private to park." Her throaty voice fondles my balls. "I'll bang the worries from your mind. It's just you and me and our future together."

The wheel jerks in my grip when she presses my fingers against her panties. All traces of envy flee my brain. I'm thinking with my dick as if I wasn't drained dry an hour ago. My hazy eyes scan for potential options. A strip of industrial developments might as well be beckoning to me. The lots are empty for the weekend. My shaky grasp steers us to a section behind the buildings that's hidden from the street.

We lurch forward when I smash on the brakes too hard. Cassidy smacks a hand on the dash, a gasp tripping from her. A stampede thunders in my pulse. I whip off my seatbelt to escape the suffocating restraint. She stares at me, an expectant lift to her brow.

My chest is rising and falling as if I chased her through a pasture. "Fuck, you make me crazed."

She licks her bottom lip in a languid caress I feel along my shaft. "What're you gonna do about it?"

"Crawl to me, beauty."

A soft whimper spills free from her before she scrambles to unbuckle herself and do what she's told. I blindly search for the button to push my seat as far back as possible. My stare tracks Cassidy's fluid movements as she kneels and rests her palms on the center console. The t-shirt hides her cleavage but I imagine her breasts almost spilling free. She crawls across the short distance between us, pausing when an inch separates our mouths. I inhale her hitched breaths like my survival depends on it. Our gazes collide and lock, green wading through blue. We're suspended in this heated moment where the next one to move gains control.

Neither of does for several strained seconds.

Cassidy snatches the reins, pressing her lips to mine in a gentle kiss. The chasteness tips the scales in the opposite direction and I'm practically vibrating to deepen the exchange. That's my only excuse for startling when her fingers begin undoing my jeans.

I straighten with a groan as my cock is released, immediately met by her tight grip. She sighs while giving me an introductory tug that shoots lightning up my spine. Her expression turns sultry and I brace myself to get tortured. The vixen doesn't disappoint. My shaft throbs as she strokes all the way up to the flared head, swiping her thumb in the pre-cum forming at my tip. She uses the droplet to lube her downward sweep. I buck into her hand, which gets me nowhere. The pace she sets is maddening. Pressure builds but there's no outlet. Her smile spreads in the face of my struggle. When the next glide resembles a feather taunting my desperation, the threads of tolerance snap.

"My turn," I growl.

She squeaks as I make my move. In an impressive maneuver, I grasp her waist and spread her astride my lap. She hovers in the straddled position while I tug her shorts and thong to the side. I chose these bottoms well—the leg hole loose enough to accommodate a quick fuck. To demonstrate, my dick threads through the opening and slides along her slit.

My fingers flex for a steady hold while my composure slips. "Let's fog up the windows."

Her lashes flutter shut when I bump her clit. "Not sure that's possible in the summer, trouble."

"Challenge accepted." I huff on the glass until it fogs and draw an infinity heart.

"Good grief," she mewls. "I'll do whatever you want. Just have mercy on me."

"Ride this cock," I rasp into her throat.

"Don't you mean that?" Cassidy shoves her tits—and the message stamped there—forward.

"Yeah, beauty. Accept the whole package." I guide her onto my length.

She grips my shoulders and lowers slowly. With each inch she takes, her mouth drops wider. The urge to thrust shakes me to my core but I fight the need. We exhale once she's seated fully, stretched around my girth. That's when I press us tighter together and grind her into my piercing. Her pussy clamps me in an unforgiving squeeze to return the favor.

Our mutual groans fill the cab with thick lust. I'm already intoxicated when she starts to roll her hips. Cassidy pushes up and plunges down, ripping a grunt from me. The slap of our union is muffled by clothes but there's no disguising her slick arousal coating mine.

That warmth floods my veins but I need more. My palms drift under her shirt, the contact thrumming through me. She's soft and pliant and taking me deep. I cinch my arms around her waist to hug us close. Lilacs and fulfilled desires strum my senses. Her breathy gasps increase in volume when I punch my hips into her downward strokes. My smirk kisses her grin while we get lost in the motions.

Cassidy rests her forehead on mine, our bodies joining in a steady tempo. "Are you happy?"

"Fuck, I'm delirious with joy."

Her hum paints my lips. "Same."

The pace rises and falls, taking our pleasure to the peak. It doesn't take long before we're both trembling. Cassidy cries out when my barbell nudges her clit. My composure falters as her spasms clench me in an unforgiving fist. Flames lash across my lower back, spreading until I'm ready to explode. She shatters first and triggers my release.

I flood her with warmth while she swims in relief. We tread through the depths of bliss, our labored efforts doing little to steam the glass. But that doesn't impact the success of our smutty scene.

Cassidy snuggles against me. Her features are relaxed

and sated. Pride expands in my chest while I reinforce our embrace, bringing us impossibly closer. An exaggerated sigh wheezes from her.

"That was..."

My fingers skip along the notches of her spine. "A climatic ending of our own making."

"Definitely deserves going on a shirt. Oh, wait." Her laughter jostles our angle and we groan.

"Still in the mood for me to show you off as mine?"

That seductive glint hasn't left her stare. "Always."

CHAPTER TWENTY-FIVE

Cassidy

GIGGLES PULL ME FROM THE DAZE I accidentally stumbled in. The warmth in my belly cools as the grocery store returns to focus. Charlie and Kenzie are whispering, their grins stretched wide. I pull the cart to a stop and give them my full attention.

"What's so funny, moo-boo?" A smile pops on my lips when they don't fuss about the combined nickname that's apparently not cool anymore.

"We passed the snacks, Mommy!" My daughter thumps her forehead. "See?"

My gaze slides to where she's pointing, at the aisle very much behind us. "How did that happen?"

But the question is rhetorical. Not that my kids know that. Thoughts of Drake have been distracting me since the beginning of July. The obsession is worse than normal after the sexcapades marathon we banged out last weekend. It's becoming quite inconvenient, especially when my kids notice.

Charlie laughs loud enough to startle me. "You're thinking about Rake."

My cheeks burn. "How do you know?"

Kenzie joins in and the chorus of their amusement

attracts several stares. "You got hearts in your eyeballs. Pinkie Pie gets 'em too."

"But only when he's lookin' at Mommy," Charlie chimes in.

A dreamy exhale precedes the trick flips in my belly. As if I need encouragement to fantasize about Drake. His unique blends of romance and grand gestures are my kryptonite. He's a tug in my gut stronger than basic instincts. I shake off the temptation to text him and whip the cart in reverse.

"Okay, we need chips and cookies. Your game starts soon, monkey moo."

"And Daddy is gonna be there," Kenzie squeals.

My little boy punches the air. "The Colts are gonna win!"

I'm reaching for a bag of Ruffles when a man appears at the end of the aisle. He looks familiar, but I can't place him. His face is one of those that blends into a crowd. It's strange and unsettling.

"Hello, Ms. Brooks. I thought that was you. What a pleasant surprise."

The coaxing edge in his tone is creepier than a tarantula crawling toward me. Ice fills my veins as recognition slams into me. It's a shock I don't immediately curse his name. Kenzie and Charlie scurry behind my back, sensing the threat. Our reactions probably fill him with satisfaction.

Without taking my gaze off him, I grab treats for the team and turn to get us out of this situation. The enemy doesn't get the hint. He jogs to get ahead, cutting off our retreat. I slam to a halt to avoid a collision but he could benefit from a strike of common sense. My pulse hammers as I realize we're caught in a trap.

"Let us pass," I demand.

"Mommy," Kenzie murmurs and yanks on my dress. "Who's that man?"

"Nobody, bunny. Just ignore him."

"Shhh," Charlie whispers to his sister. "He's a stranger."

"Don't you remember me? I'm Alan from Sutherland Homes." His toothy smile raises the hair on the back of my neck.

An ache blooms in my jaw as I clench down. "Move."

Alan crouches on the floor, putting himself level with the twins. I widen my stance to block them from his view. His chuckle lacks any trace of humor as he rises to his full height.

"Just wanted to say hello."

"How dare you corner me while I'm out with my children." It's a challenge to keep my voice even.

Especially when his eyes flash. "Would you prefer I speak to you in private?"

Bile climbs up my throat and I gag. "This is a new low, even for you. I'm going to call the police."

"There's no need for that. This is a polite conversation." Alan holds out his palms as if that will placate me.

"I strongly disagree. Get out of my way." I grip onto the cart until my knuckles bleed white.

He taps on the metal buggy acting as a barrier between us. "Just a quick message."

"Spit it out." A tremor rolls through me when his friendly mask slips into a sneer.

"Your rich boyfriend is ignoring our calls and texts. We don't appreciate that. What you're going to is—"

"Not listen to a word you say," I snap.

His glare turns mean. "Don't interrupt me."

"You started it, but I'll end it." I grab onto the twins and prepare to crush Alan like the pest he is.

His manic laughter freezes me on the spot. "Ah, Ms. Brooks. I'm going to thoroughly enjoy leveling that precious farm of yours." He slaps his palms together to mimic the destruction. "Such a shame we couldn't reach an understanding."

I square my shoulders, staring Alan down as if intense eye contact will send him running. "Stay away from me and my family. If I ever see you again, I'm getting a restraining order."

He snorts. "On what grounds?"

My focus doesn't waver. "This is harassment. I should've reported you months ago, but that's no longer necessary. It's obvious your business is in trouble. You're pathetic and karma is a bitch."

The cart screeches as I swerve around his threatening leer. I pay and shove us out of that store like we're being hunted. Might as well be. That sense of being followed sears into my back. Kenzie and Charlie exchange a glance, worry creasing their foreheads. My fingers tremble while I get them situated in the backseat.

I'm shaking as I drive to the game. It's too quiet, allowing the altercation with Alan to repeat on a loop. Heat burns my eyes and I fight the urge to scream. I need to stay strong for the kids and prove bullies don't win. Those bastards deserve to go bankrupt.

"Mommy's mad," my little girl murmurs.

Leather creaks in my unforgiving grip. "I'm fine, moo-boo."

"Bleh," Charlie scoffs. "That's for babies."

I should've known twice was pushing it. My bottom lip trembles. "Right. I forgot. Can I still call you monkey moo?"

He must hear the hitch in my voice. "Why are you sad?"

"I'm not." But there's no disguising the warble in my reply.

Kenzie gasps. "You can say moo-boo. Don't cry, m'kay?"

I avoid glancing at them in the rearview mirror. "No promises."

A thick exhale does little to dislodge the lump in my throat. It's a miracle we arrive without me shedding a single drop. The instant I shift into park, the twins are racing for the field. My approach is much slower as I try to regain composure.

I lose the battle when the scene comes into view. Charlie and Kenzie are hanging off Drake's arms, trying to reach his neck where their names require a retrace. He lifts them like sacks of flour while talking to none other than Shawn. The two men laugh as if they've already bonded as besties. I can't fully appreciate that right now, which needles me. It's just too much and I release a muffled sob.

Drake's concentration follows the noise to find me standing there. I'm momentarily distracted by his backward hat and coaching gear. That is until the humor twinkling in his baby blues fades. A storm rolls over his expression while he gently puts Kenzie and Charlie on their feet. My hurried steps carry me straight into his embrace. Safety and comfort hug me tight as I give myself permission to fall apart.

He rubs a palm along my broken spirit as I dampen his shirt. "What happened?"

"It's… nothing," I blubber.

"I call bullshit, beauty," he mumbles into my ear. "Tell me."

But my throat is raw and coated in shards of glass. I roll my head back and forth on his chest. There's a pressure sitting on my stomach that spreads until I can't move. I clench my eyes shut, begging the emotion to recede. The opposite happens as more tears stream down my cheeks.

"There was a bad man talkin' to Mommy," Kenzie reveals. "He was suuuuper mean and didn't listen to our words. Oh! I think he knows you, Pinkie Pie. You're Mommy's boyfriend. Are you rich? That's what he said. We left but Mommy was still mad. And then we almost made her cry 'cause we don't like moo-boo anymore, but she can use it for today."

Drake becomes rigid against me, his body taut and armored. "Give me a name."

I gulp and draw in a deep breath, but the emotional turbulence rattles me again. "Al-Al-Alan."

He pries me off him, forcing my gaze to meet his. "Alan?"

My nod releases a fresh trickle of tears. "From Sutherland."

His thumbs swipe away the droplets before lowering to my shoulders. There's thunder in his eyes, preparing to strike a specific target. Drake doesn't look away from me when he says, "Hey, Shawn?"

The children's father is beside us in a second, or maybe he was already there. "Yeah, man?"

"Can you coach this game for me? Somebody made a big mistake, and I need to fix it."

"No," I blurt.

"Yes," Drake argues. "He made you cry. That deserves a swift punishment."

A moan nearly spills from my lips, which is ridiculous. But Drake in protective mode is next-level sexy. The appeal makes me squirm. I can't appreciate that in this moment either. That doesn't mean I want him to hurt Alan. Well, maybe a little. But now isn't the time for violence.

I grip onto his wrists. "Don't leave. He's not worth it."

"Beauty," he sighs. "You're not happy and it's his fault. Today was meant to be great, but he ruined it. There's not a chance he's getting away with that."

My gaze slides to Shawn for a moment before returning to Drake. "I'm sad I missed the beginning of this bromance."

"Do you want us to reenact our meet-cute?" Shawn's smile suggests he's willing if I'm interested.

Meanwhile, Drake looks ready to snap a certain sales consultant in half. "I'm not in the mood."

"That's a first," I mumble.

His exhale is rough, fluttering my hair like a breeze.

"This is just something I have to do. It won't take long. I'll be back before the game is over."

My frown is stooped low to deny his request. "It's fine."

"You know I'm not accepting that as a proper response."

An ache blooms at my temples. "I don't know why I'm so bothered. They can't hurt me."

"Tell me what happened." Drake motions for me to spill the beans.

"You have a team to coach."

"I'm not going on the field until you tell me what he did." His firm stance reinforces the message.

That earns him an eye roll. He doesn't budge, only lifting his chin at me to get on with it. The story blabs from me in a sloppy replay. With each detail, his muscles flex tighter. I watch him grow into an imposing force when I expose Alan's plans for my farm. Even Shawn notices the change in my typically carefree boyfriend, giving me a thumbs-up before ushering the twins to the bleachers.

That allows me to use a variety of colorful terms to describe the bane of my existence. Once I'm done, Drake's expression resembles a stone wall. He's practically frothing at the mouth. I almost feel guilty for aiming his fury on Alan, but then I remember the bully's threats. Sutherland Homes will probably give him a bonus for accosting me. The entire company deserves Drake's wrath.

"So, yeah," I breathe. "He's a menace along with the shady business that employs him."

"I can't believe he came at you." My boyfriend cracks his knuckles. "He's officially made an enemy out of me."

"It's just a tactic. I don't think he's dangerous. Not that I'm excusing his awful behavior," I add.

"Doesn't matter what reason led him to you. It's messed up and can't continue. That's why I need to handle this."

My palms drift across his Colts shirt. "Let's focus on winning the game."

His heart hammers beneath my hand. "Like it's that simple."

"It's for the kids."

A conflict sparks in his gaze. "That's not fair. Shawn can take my place."

"But he's not their coach. Please stay," I urge. "For me? Sutherland can wait."

His stubborn streak remains fixed on my gaze. "But they're going to pay."

"Tomorrow, trouble." I rise onto the balls of my feet to kiss him. "Honor is defended best after breakfast."

"That doesn't sound right."

Laughter bursts from me, bringing a smile along for the ride. "You're questioning my phrasing?"

"Ah, there she is." Drake's focus dips to my mouth. "I've missed your happiness."

My grin spreads into pure bliss. "It belongs to you, just like the rest of me."

"Jeez, woman. Fine. I'll wait to defend your honor until dawn."

"That's all I ask. Love you." A loud smooch gets planted on his cheek.

He twists to kiss me properly. "I love you, beauty. More than anything."

"Which is why you're here." I check our surroundings for children before patting him on the butt. "Get out there, big guy. They're depending on you."

He winks and jogs backward to the field. "What happens when we win?"

I don't overlook his optimistic choice in verbiage. "You know that drawer in my bedroom I don't let you touch?"

Drake stumbles but catches himself. "Uh-huh."

My eyebrows wiggle to the throbbing beat between my thighs. "Make me proud and I'll let you slide in there."

CHAPTER TWENTY-SIX

Drake

The tires squeal as I take the last turn too tight. I can almost hear Kenzie giggling about me getting stuck in the mud, but there's no humorous tone in my truck on this drive. Not when the headquarters for Sutherland Homes is straight ahead.

I speed through the enormous parking lot that's far too large for their measly business. It doesn't surprise me that the assholes insist on occupying more real estate than needed. The reflection shining off the mirrored building is blinding. Go figure. These dipshits want me to be disoriented when I stumble inside. Rather than risk giving them an advantage, I crank the wheel and slam to a halt in the center of four spaces.

My trusty bat beckons me from the backseat. I consider slinging it over my shoulder as added insurance, but Cassidy's logic stops me. As I stomp toward the entrance empty-handed, the promise I made to her pounds into my skull.

She insists that I don't use physical violence or cause bodily harm. Not sure how one happens without the other but that would've been another argument entirely. Besides, what I have planned is much worse.

But it was in my best interest to agree with Cassidy last night, especially once she whipped open that secret drawer. My ass clenches at the reminder and I smirk. That sexual exploration wouldn't have been possible if it weren't for Shawn swooping in like Gary Poppins and taking the twins home with him. If Cassidy had to procreate with someone other than me, he was a solid choice.

Those thoughts vanish in a bubble of lube when I nearly rip the front door off its hinges. Time to get my main brain in the game. Unfortunately, normal functioning hits snooze as I step into the lobby. A sterile scent burns my nose to the point of frying circuits. The stench matches the stark white appearance. I almost shield my eyes against the offensive glare bouncing off every surface. There's no trapping a gag while I wade into enemy territory.

The receptionist is on the phone, but she smiles at my approach. That coy tilt to her lips falls flat as I storm past her. She scrambles to stand and gets yanked backward by her headset. Should've gone wireless. Cheap bastards.

"Excuse me, sir?" She calls after me. "Do you have an appointment? You can't just walk in—"

"Watch me," I bellow in return.

The layout is a standard maze and I follow my gut to the rear wall. A section of oversized offices reward my assumption. I search for the boss, not bothering to knock. Several people are gawking at me from their cubicles and I offer them a gracious wave. Unless Alan is in the audience. Fuck that guy.

As luck would have it, Mr. Sutherland himself is available when I stride into his corner fortress. The view is superb and steals my breath for a moment. Ken whirls around, putting an end to his putting practice. Alarm registers on his wrinkly features but quickly melts off once he recognizes me.

"Hello, Mr. Granger. This is a surprise. Tracey didn't inform me that you were stopping by." He glares at his phone as if scolding the woman remotely.

"I didn't have an appointment." My arm swings in an aww-shucks motion.

"Oh, that's quite all right. My schedule is always open for you. Take a seat." He motions to a leather monstrosity that probably moonlights as a sticky trap.

"I'd rather stand. This won't take long."

Mr. Sutherland rounds his desk and takes a load off. "I must admit that I'm a bit starstruck. The Mustangs are my favorite sports team. I'm a major fan of yours in particular."

"How nice," I deadpan. "I'd give you an autograph but that would be too kind."

Ken recoils at my harsh rebuttal but he recovers like the professional he's pretending to be. "We've been waiting to hear from you. A personal visit is more than I anticipated." A wide grin flaunts his porcelain veneers. "Alan deserves a raise."

I cough into my fist. "That's fucking rich."

"Precisely."

"Are you responsible for his actions yesterday?"

"Can you be more specific?" Slippery fucker, this one.

"You're aware Alan spoke to the mother of my future stepchildren."

"I'm not sure who you're referring to, Mr. Granger."

"Cassidy Brooks." I snap my fingers, demanding

he keep up. "They had somewhat of an altercation last night."

His loose flesh jiggles when he nods. "Ah, yes. The interaction didn't sound successful, but here you are."

Anger rushes to the surface but I choke down the slew of expletives desperate to slap him. This is meant to be dragged out entirely for my benefit. "Agree to disagree on that one, Ken. We'll circle back in a moment. As Cassidy was recalling the monumental error your dear Alan decided to make, I began to wonder if you sent him to intimidate her. Do you know why that is?"

"Are you suggesting that my employees are engaging in unethical practices to obtain information?"

"No, not at all. That's none of my business." I chuckle when Mr. Sutherland has the audacity to look proud. That won't do. "What's really piqued my interest is if you understand the clusterfuck you've created for yourself."

Ken straightens in his chair. "I beg your pardon?"

My boots scuff his polished floor as I take a lap of his luxury to delay the inevitable a bit longer. "My lawyer strongly advised me to not get involved and allow him to do his job. In most cases, I'm not even aware when Frank is handling legal matters for me. But this is personal."

"How so?"

"Let's not beat around the beaver bush, Ken. You know why I'm here."

His eyes gleam. "To invest in our next project."

Laughter folds me in half. I smack the wall on my way down for extra impact. My upper half shakes from the effort of really nailing this performance. There might even be fake tears on my cheeks that I make a point to wipe away.

Ken's saggy jowls remain unflappable. "I missed the joke, Mr. Granger."

"There wasn't one. Your incompetence is hilarious."

"I've had enough with the insults," he gripes.

My lips pucker at his attitude. Such a fun sponge. "How close did you inspect the contract my lawyer drafted before signing it?"

Mr. Sutherland sighs, reaching his limit of the game I'm playing. "I assure you that we're very diligent."

"Is that right?" I scrub my chin. "Do you recall section four on page three?"

"Afraid not, Mr. Granger. What're you getting at?"

"I believe it was item B that clearly states Sutherland Homes hereby agrees to terminate all communication with Ms. Cassidy Brooks upon entering this partnership with Mr. Drake Granger. Failure to do so will result in a breach of contract. Don't quote me for accuracy but that's the gist." My smile stretches to the stars as he sputters. "Now, let's return to the topic of Alan's successful discussion with Cassidy. It went pretty well for you, hmm?"

His complexion is blistering red, ready to pop. "You're lying."

"Nah, Ken. That's not one of my specialties. But I do cover my bases. Something told me you couldn't be trusted, but I gave you the benefit of the doubt. Did you really think I wouldn't include an escape clause? All you had to do was abide. Unfortunately for you, I'm smarter than you expected. You saw me as an easy payday." I cluck my tongue, heaving a loud sigh for good measure.

"What are you—?"

"Don't worry," I cut him off. "I'm not done. You've underestimated me and my devotion to Ms. Brooks. To your detriment. And now your business will pay for it."

Mr. Sutherland rises to his feet, stabbing a finger into his desk. "Listen here, Mr. Granger. I'd never sign such a document."

"You did and there's proof." I offer a lame shrug. "This is the point where my dramatic display steps aside to allow my lawyer to do his thing and take you for all your worth. It's been a real delight passing along the news. I can't wait to watch your ivory tower collapse."

Ken's eyes widen as I begin backing away. "You can't do this."

"There you go, underestimating me again. We'll see how well that works out for you, yeah? Enjoy your demise." I salute him with my middle finger. "Tootle-fucking-loo."

CHAPTER TWENTY-SEVEN

Cassidy

I PROP MY ELBOW ON THE BAR, LEANING FORWARD TO get the best view. "Nice ass, trouble."

"This old thing?" Drake smacks his denim-clad butt. "It's yours."

"Mhmm, come to mama." My tongue glides across my bottom lip to collect drool.

"Keep ogling me like that and you'll never get your cocktail."

"Ditch the tail. You can quench my thirst." I pop my mouth for emphasis.

He glances at me over his shoulder. Ice rattles in the shaker as he vigorously mixes the contents of my mystery beverage. "What's gotten into you?"

The warm fuzzies in my belly are served with a sigh of blissful contentment. "Happiness."

"My penis?"

"That too," I laugh.

"Irresistible combo."

My brows bounce. "Quite addictive."

Drake turns and grabs a mason jar. I watch as he slicks sugar on the rim before setting it on the counter. His steady hand pours in a yellow concoction until the liquid almost spills over. A striped straw and lemon are the final touches.

"How fancy," I croon.

He lowers onto his forearms, putting us at eye level. "Only the best for you."

My mouth waters but I resist for a moment longer. "I've heard about similar specialty drinks from Grace and Callie. Is this mine?"

"Beautiful Sunflower." Drake gestures to the pretty blend he created. "Just like you."

"I feel like this makes me an official cock den groupie." A giggly snort escapes me when he rolls his eyes.

"Taste it." His low demand tickles my desire and I squirm while reaching for the jar.

"Oh!" A burst of crisp flavor bathes my tongue. It's tart but sweet, which fits the inspiration. I eagerly treat myself to another sip. "Super delicious."

Drake's gaze is fastened on me biting the straw. "Worthy of touching your lips?"

I nod and pucker purposefully for my next suckle. "Might be the best thing I've put in my mouth."

He scowls. "Now you're exaggerating."

"You're one to talk." I wink.

There's no argument from the pro. "I suppose it's appropriate. We're celebrating."

"That's the spirit." I pause but can't connect the dots. "Wait, the first day of kindergarten gets me a yummy for the tummy that's uniquely handcrafted by none other than Drake Granger?"

The man responsible blinks at me. "How much booze did I put in there?"

"Plenty, but you'll have to try harder to get me tipsy." I blow him a kiss.

"That wasn't part of the plan, but the evening is young." His gaze scans the thin crowd, which leads him to where Kenzie and Charlie are playing with Sydney in the game area. "Maybe we can get Harper to babysit."

"What am I doing for you, boss?" The blonde's ears must've been burning.

"A great job tending this bar." He knocks on the wood.

She crosses her arms. "You want something."

"Maybe like thirty minutes of private, uninterrupted adult time in the office." Drake glances at me. A naughty smirk reveals his dimples. "An hour would be better."

"Ewww, no. I recognize that smile. Please don't do unmentionable stuff to yourself again. My vision hasn't fully recovered from the last time." She slaps a palm over her eyes as if suddenly traumatized.

I choke on my recent swallow. "What happened?"

Drake hangs his head. "I was doing inventory."

"Nobody is buying that bucket of bologna," she jests. "Besides, I'm already on child duty while you two get inked."

"Thanks again for doing that," I tell her.

"No problem. It's a breeze now that there's a designated kid section. I should be thanking you for convincing him to add a space for them."

"Totally his idea." Which has my heart skipping several beats.

Drake shrugs, a rare blush staining his cheeks. "I thought they'd appreciate it."

"Us more than them," Harper states. Her gaze catches on a couple who need a refill. "Don't talk about me while I'm gone."

"We're not actually sneaking off, right?" Although the heat rushing through my veins demands relief.

My boyfriend regains his confident composure. "No, but we're celebrating."

"Ah, right. The twins went to school. Major milestone. Kenzie calls the school bus a banana limo, which is adorable and deserves a toast." I raise my jar and clink against his nonexistent beverage.

"Not that," he chuckles.

"Then what's the occasion? It's not Saturday."

"Doesn't have to be. Every moment we're together deserves to be cherished."

"Oh, my," I breathe.

"And there's this." He pushes his phone across the counter.

The screen displays an article. My eyes bulge after reading the bold headline. "Is this real?"

Drake's smug expression is answer enough. "News broke this morning."

"Sutherland Homes filed for bankruptcy," I repeat. "How did this happen?"

"I took care of it."

My lashes sweep upward to study his prideful stance. "Bodily harm?"

"Nope."

"Physical violence?"

"Not even a scratch."

"This is legit?" I wave his phone.

He nods. "You'll never have to worry about them again."

A hot sting blurs my sight but I see him standing in front of me like an invincible pillar of strength. Affection spreads through me in a comforting wave. I rise off my stool and scramble onto the counter. Drake grabs my arms, refusing to let me fall. His encouragement will always catch me.

My palms clasp his neck and use the grip to pull him toward me. "I love you."

"Love you," he mumbles into the kiss.

"Grosssssss," Charlie cries. "Rake is getting Mommy's germs."

Kenzie pretends to vomit, which could earn her a spot on Broadway. "Nooooo, Pinkie Pie! You're giving Mommy cooties. That's disgusting."

Sydney stares at the twins as if ten years separates her from them rather than two. "They're just kissing."

"Yeah, Mac and Cheese." Drake gives me a chaste peck before I return to my seat. "Don't yuck my yum."

The twins exchange a blank stare. Charlie's nose wrinkles when he refocuses on the man who was recently attached to my mouth. "I don't like yucky yum. Too slobbery. Bleh."

"More for me," he responds. "Your mom's slobber is my favorite."

I nudge him. "Hush."

Kenzie has her fists parked on her hips. "You're gonna get a baby in your belly."

My wince scolds her lacking knowledge of the birds and the bees. "That's not how it works."

"Yes-huh," she demands. "Pinkie Pie is gonna give you his seed when you do the kissing. You plant his seed in your tummy and drink lotsa water until the baby grows."

I make the mistake of taking a sip during her explanation. Beautiful Sunflower spews over the floor as I register the words. "No, bunny. Just... no."

"Maybe we should put in more effort," Drake mumbles.

My lips roll between my teeth to trap a laugh. "Stop it."

Charlie's expression is full of wonder. "Wow."

"What's that face for, boo?" I don't mention the awe in his voice.

"You've got a garden in there." He points at my torso.

My arm slides across my midsection as if that will make him forget the subject. "Nope, just food. No seeds or plants or gardens."

"Just wait until I become a farmer," Drake mumbles under his breath.

My cheeks burst into flames. "Oh. My. Gosh. You're in so much—"

"We're hungry," Charlie whines.

"My tummy is mad." Kenzie squishes her stomach as if it's complaining.

"Can I please have a snack?" Sydney bats her eyelashes. This girl gets it.

"Don't let Garrett feed them," Harper yells from the opposite side of the room.

I giggle at the reminder of rainbow peen candy, along with my upgraded version. "Definitely not. They need something more substantial."

"I've got just the thing." Drake taps on the register to send an order to the kitchen staff. "Shouldn't take long, VIPs."

"Let's keep shooting each other!" Charlie whips around, taking aim at the two girls.

Before I can interject, Kenzie points at her leg. "I'm gonna finger blast myself."

"Me too!" My little boy repeats his sister's actions.

Sydney huffs. "But I don't wanna blast myself."

"We'll do it together as a team," Kenzie offers and yanks on her arm.

Drake whistles as the kids race off to their play space. "That's a shocker."

"I can't believe you." But there's no upset in my tone. On the contrary, I'm once again melting into mush over how good he is with them. "My children are thoroughly distracted by the craft corner you arranged for them. Could you be more perfect?"

"Probably."

"You're right." I tap my lips. "Something is missing."

He clutches at his chest. "Ouch."

"Maybe this will help." I fetch the wrapped package in my purse.

Drake rubs his palms together. "You got me a present?"

"Consider it mutually beneficial."

His eyes heat. "Is this like the goodies in your drawer?"

"Gosh, no. This is appropriate for public."

He rips open the paper. A dramatic *ooooooh* streams from him as he reveals the orange fabric. The shirt is tugged over his head before he notices what's written on the front.

"Fits great." He yanks on the hem to see the bold script. "I'll do whatever the cowgirl says."

"We match." I unbutton my western shirt to reveal mine.

"The cowgirl," he reads.

"Your one and only."

"Damn straight." Drake claps and gestures at me. He succeeds in gathering everyone's attention. "Hey, guess what? She totally gets me!"

"We know," Harper replies while exiting the kitchen. "Get that tattoo done and make it permanent."

My boyfriend glances at the clock. "Still good to go at seven?"

"Absolutely. I'm looking forward to it."

Harper pauses beside me and drops off a basket of mini tacos. "What're you getting again?"

I'm momentarily distracted by one of my favorite foods. "Um, a tattoo."

"Obviously," she scoffs. "But what's the design?"

"Oh!" I thump my forehead. "A sunflower with a horseshoe blended into the petals."

"And what in the middle?" Drake prods.

The aroma of fried goodness is going straight to my brain. "A baseball."

Harper exhales a groan. "You two are the cutest. I better be invited to the wedding."

The taco in my fingers pauses halfway to my mouth. "Umm...?"

But she's already walking away to serve the kids. A chorus of joy erupts when they discover what Drake ordered. I couldn't agree more as I crunch down on a savory bite. This is another win for the troublemaker.

"Mini tacos!" Charlie whoops, pumping a fist into the air. "You're the bestest, Rake."

"Right back at you, Cheese." He waves as if my son isn't already fawning over him. "Same goes for you, Mac."

My daughter is too busy munching on a taco, which I realize is poor phrasing far too late. Luckily, nobody can hear my thoughts. She gives Drake a thumbs-up and rubs her belly in glee.

"When did Roosters get these things?" Sydney holds one up like it's a foreign object.

"I asked for them," Charlie beams. "Put it in your mouth and swallow."

A sharp edge of the shell gets stuck in my throat, or maybe it's just my son's provocative advice. Drake vaults over the bar and begins patting my back. The obstruction clears after another thwack.

"Good grief," I croak.

"Careful how much you shove in there at once. Go slow, beauty." His concern is betrayed by a dry chuckle.

"It's been too long." My hungry grasp already has another plucked from the basket. "I've missed you, mini tacos."

Drake's laughter booms louder. "That's what I told yours this morning."

"And she thanks you for the cream filling."

His inhale morphs into a cough. "Damn, that's rough."

"Sure was," I croon.

He hooks an arm around me, hauling me flush against him. "Hey, beauty?"

My chin rests on his sternum as I admire him. "Yes, trouble?"

His hands gather mine. "I have a very important question to ask you."

Between the tender timbre of his voice and the fact he's stroking my left ring finger, assumptions rush to the surface.

"Will you," he pauses to gulp and my answer prepares itself on the tip of my tongue. "Dance with me?"

"Yes!" I blurt. Then I blink. "Oh, what?"

But Drake is already taking the lead on this foul play. His wolfish grin greets my parted lips before he spins me. Our arms fold when he brings my back to his front, skipping us forward. We're quickly facing each other again while gliding into formation.

I recognize the style immediately. "You know how to two-step?"

"Taught myself when we first started dating."

"Of course you did," I laugh. "Good grief. How is this my life?"

Drake twirls me again before we stride ahead. "You fell in love with me."

My heart sings to the beat of riding off into the sunset. "Best. Decision. Ever."

CHAPTER TWENTY-EiGHT

Drake

Beauty: Heyyyyyy. Bad news.

Me: Uh-oh. You have hemorrhoids?

Beauty: ...

Beauty: I'm not going to entertain that with a response. Anyway, I need to cancel tonight.

Me: Why?

Beauty: Just because...

Me: If you don't give me a real reason I'll assume it's hemorrhoids.

Beauty: Omg. You're ridiculous. Shawn needs to swap weekends so I have the kids. We're going for a ride and having a lowkey night. I'll make it up to you.

Me: I'm on my way.

Beauty: What?

Me: What?

Beauty: Why are you coming over?

Me: For our date…

Beauty: But my kids are home.

Me: And?

Beauty: That changes our plans. It's Friday. I'm sure there's somewhere else you'd rather be.

Me: Babe. If I've ever given you that impression, I owe you a grand gesture. Should I clean your gutters? Power wash the house and barn? Restack the hay? Mow the lawn? Vacuum and dust?

Beauty: You're not my maid, trouble. But I should probably do all of those things.

Me: We can do them together.

Beauty: As a team. :)

Me: Which is why I'm coming over to enjoy quality time with you and the twins.

Beauty: You'd trade a night out for one at the farm?

Me: Sounds like an upgrade. This is what I've been missing. A real life. A family to head home to.

Beauty: A future.

Me: See? You remember my big speech. I want to be present always. This is just the beginning for us, beauty.

Beauty: You're right. Of course. Not sure what I was thinking. You should be here with us.

Me: Glad to hear you admit it. Those kids are practically mine at this point. Their names are tattooed into my neck. I love it when they're around. Believe in me, yeah? Depend on me too. I want the whole package. Forever.

Beauty: Good grief. You're making me cry from a text message. Not sure what's gotten into me lately.

Me: Happiness. And trust. You're comfortable to let it all out around me. I can share the burdens and I think you feel that.

Beauty: Or I'm a sappy romantic. Either way, I love you so very much.

Me: Love you! <3

Beauty: Did you leave yet?

Me: Just about.

Beauty: Pack some extra clothes.

Me: Yeah?

Beauty: Yeah.

Cassidy is saddling Leita at a hitching post when I arrive twenty minutes later. Fire is already tacked, and the twins are perched on his back. Kenzie is in the front, weaving the Appaloosa between a row of troughs. Chester and Cheeto circle the horse as if keeping him on track. The scene raises my brows but their mom doesn't give them more than a watchful glance.

I reach into the backseat for a couple things before strutting toward my cowgirl. Cassidy peeks over Leita's neck as I approach, quickly doing a double take. Her gaze slides over me in a heated caress that strokes my cock. This woman gets me harder than wood from a single look.

"Nice hat," she purrs.

I tip the wide brim at her. "Matches my boots."

The seductive redhead bites her bottom lip while I close the distance between us. "You look ready to ride."

"Are you offering?"

The green in her eyes smolders. "Mhmm."

My head tilts as I swoop in for a kiss. "There are children present."

"They'll go to bed eventually." Her smile promises that she's going to do very dirty things to me.

My throat works audibly and I force myself to straighten away from temptation. "These are for you."

Cassidy gasps when I whip two sunflowers from behind my back. "How beautiful."

"Just like you." I wink. "Can Mac and Cheese have candy?"

"Yes!" Kenzie is already steering Fire in our direction.

Charlie pokes out from behind her. "I want candy!"

"Shouldn't have bothered asking," Cassidy laughs. "Better give it to them or you'll start a riot."

The twins make grabby-hands at the gummy worm packages. Fire obediently stops next to me as if Kenzie's grip is still on the reins. He's very well trained. I open the bags and pass them up, one for each.

"Thank you," they chirp.

"Welcome," I return as Fire resumes their stroll. My wariness studies them for a moment as they begin shoveling the sugary treats down their throats. "Is that safe?"

"They're not going to choke. It's okay." Cassidy finishes tightening the cinch and grabs the bridle off the horn.

"I meant for both of them to be on him like that."

"Yeah, for sure. That's going double."

"Ah, right. I knew that."

Her hip bumps mine. "It's sexy when you pretend to be a cowboy."

"Hey," I scoff. "I'm a work in progress."

She tugs on my straw hat. "You'll be herding cattle before you know it."

"That's better." I shift around her to improve my skills in real time. "There's the best investment I've ever made. Hi, Lele Loo. Did you miss me?"

The roan sniffs my pockets, her nose wiggling across the denim.

"What did you find?" I dig out a chunk of carrot. "There you go."

She munches happily while Cassidy clucks her tongue. "You're spoiling her."

"So? She's such a good girl. Yes, you are." I glide my palm down the mare's long face.

"I'm getting jealous," Cassidy mutters.

"Need me to feed you? Open wide." I dangle a carrot in front of her mouth.

She does and I glide the piece in, only to drag it out slowly. Her teeth bite down and I wince. Amusement gleams in her gaze while she chomps on the treat.

"Yummy," she mumbles.

I cough into my fist. "You're way too good at that."

"Shouldn't tease me."

"Lesson learned," I chuckle.

"Okay, buckaroo." She swats my ass. "I thought we could go for a ride through the back forty. Maybe watch a movie afterward."

My boots kick across the gravel as I return to her

side. "Can't think of anything I'd rather do. But who am I riding?"

Cassidy pats the space behind her saddle. "Right here, trouble."

I freeze. "We're going double?"

"Double trouble," she croons. "Why didn't I think of that sooner?"

"I don't love the sound of that when it comes to me and horses."

"You'll be safe. We're just going to walk." Cassidy puts the hackamore on Leita and tosses the reins over her neck.

A noisy exhale sputters from me while I prepare for this challenge. "What if I fall off?"

She shrugs. "Tuck and roll."

My eyes bulge. "What?"

Her laughter isn't reassuring. "Drake, I won't let anything happen to you. I'm pretty attached, if you couldn't tell."

"Doesn't hurt to hear it," I grumble.

"Just put your foot in the stirrup and swing your leg over. Like every other time you've done this." Cassidy holds onto the mare while I fumble through the motions.

"Okay. Now what?"

"Hold on."

"Got it." I lift my arms and wait for further instructions.

She hangs her head, shoulders shaking. "I meant literally. Grab the back of the seat."

"Just testing you." My fingers grip the raised

portion she gestures at, leather creaking from my efforts.

Cassidy hoists herself into the saddle without kicking me in the face, which seems very considerate. "You good, trouble?"

"So far." But we haven't started moving.

"Ready?"

My heart kicks. "Sure."

Her palm rests on my thigh, giving me a gentle squeeze. "Just relax."

"I've heard that before." My dick twitches at the reminder.

She drifts her hand along my leg. "And how did that go for you?"

"Blew me away."

"This won't be quite as explosive," she muses. "But still enjoyable. Just sit back and take it all in."

"That sounds familiar too," I chuckle.

Cassidy urges Leita forward and we're off. My stomach lurches, but settles into the horse's smooth gait. Kenzie and Charlie ride ahead of us, following the dirt path around the barn. Chester and Cheeto race beside us to guide the way. The goats wail as we leave them behind. Serves them right for taking advantage of me.

We reach the pastures and the rest of the herd. Several horses perk up at our approach, but they don't cause a ruckus. I breathe a bit easier after that. There's a section between the two fenced areas that creates a grassy trail. My accelerated pulse slows to a trot. A deep inhale grants me a burst of fresh air. The smell is clean and comforting, allowing a calm energy to find me. I rock into Leita's steady motions while appreciating the scenery.

"This is incredible," I voice aloud.

The view of Cassidy's land stretches in front of us. Green prairies lift into rolling hills. Sections of leafy trees offer spots of shade. Sunshine dapples the earth, highlighting the natural wonders. It could almost make me emotional.

Cassidy's right palm still rests on me while the left steers us through paradise. "Nothing like being on the back of a horse."

"Especially with you," I exhale. "And the kids along for the ride. I could get used to this."

She twists slightly to catch my stare. "Good thing I plan to keep you around."

The twins start singing a familiar song and my ears strain on a certain word. "Is it just me or does it sound like they're saying fucks?"

"Funny you should mention that." Her hum matches the tune. "That's how their version used to go."

"No shit?"

"It was 'ducking' hilarious." She nudges me. "Get it? I didn't tell them but they figured it out on their own."

"They're such amazing kids."

"Yeah, I got lucky."

I grow bold, removing a hand from the saddle to grasp her hip. "Thanks for sharing this life with me."

She nods, a grin curving her mouth. "I've made a decision. A few, actually."

My patience waits for her to say more, but she

dangles that tidbit like bait. "Okay, I'll bite. Put me out of my misery and tell me, woman."

Her laugh carries on the breeze. "First, how would you like to move in with us? Make Greener Pastures your home."

I jolt and almost slide off Leita's ass. "Fuck yes. I'm in. Where do I sign?"

Cassidy drops her head back against my shoulder and taps her lips. "Right here."

I give her a fast peck but she isn't satisfied, staying reclined against me. "Watch the road, beauty!"

Instead of listening, she releases the reins. "Oh, look. No hands."

"You're getting a spanking later," I warn.

"Don't threaten me with an orgasmic time," she fires in return.

"About to call you trouble for a change." The strain in my chest loosens when she reclaims the reins. "What else have you decided?"

"There's a competition of sorts next weekend." Her tone is nonchalant, but I can feel her squirm. "I'm thinking about entering."

My grip on her tightens. "Really?"

Cassidy fidgets, her thoughts churning loudly. "Would you come with me?"

"Wild horses couldn't keep me corralled."

"That's not quite right," she giggles.

I scoff and take a risk, looping both arms around her waist. The tattoo on her forearm glows like a beacon. My thumb traces the new ink while unconditional love pumps into me. "Everything is the way it's meant to be so long as we're headed for home together."

CHAPTER TWENTY-NiNE

Cassidy

THERE'S A TIGHTNESS IN MY CHEST THAT WON'T quit throbbing. I rub at the ache, bumping over my necklace. My fingers tremble as I tug the pendant from under my shirt. The picture of Pago blurs as my eyes fill with tears. He's with us. That knowledge allows me to breathe.

But then the next exhibitor is called and my pulse spikes. This has been a vicious cycle. At least my nerves aren't bothering Leita. She's calm beneath me while I continue to fret. Her chill disposition anchors me and my stiff posture sags with a thick exhale.

"Doing okay?" Drake's hand rubs soothing circles into my thigh.

I rip my focus off the competition and concentrate on his concerned baby blues. "This is more stressful than I remember."

"Is it because you're running barrels on a baseball field? I gotta tell you, beauty." His whistle is low and exaggerated. "This is a sight I never thought I'd ever see."

"The arena is a bit unconventional," I agree.

"That's putting it mildly." His dry tone cracks through the static in my ears.

"Race for the Fences is a charity fundraiser," I explain.

"Ah, yes. They received a very generous—and

anonymous—donation thanks to a certain construction company meeting their end. I bet Mr. Sutherland would be proud to know his fortune is supporting a worthy cause."

The reminder chases off my nerves for a second. "The fight to stop hunger and homelessness thanks them. I chose this event for another reason as well. There's no pressure. It's just for fun to raise money and awareness."

His brows lift. "Repeat that to yourself until you believe it."

I try but the words scramble. "Leita hasn't experienced a competition. Plenty can go wrong."

"She's solid as a pine tree." He pats her neck while grabbing an apple from his pocket. Drake's smile restores mine as he feeds her. "You're a great team. Trust her judgment."

"This is just for fun," I mumble.

"Next up is number thirteen," the gate attendant booms.

The saddle creaks under my restlessness. "That's us."

"Hey," Drake murmurs. "Just relax. You're gonna do great."

"Uh-huh."

"Cassidy."

"Yep."

"Look at me."

I do. The knots in my stomach quit twisting at the sincerity in his gaze. He hasn't left our side since I finished warming up. I didn't ask him to hang out in the on-deck pen with us. This perfect man just knew I needed his presence beside me.

"Hi, trouble."

"I love you." His voice stomps with conviction. "Go out there and give it your best. That's all you can do."

"Right." I nod too briskly, shifting my hat. As if I need another thing to worry about. The gate person waves me forward and I grab onto the reins. "That's my cue. Oh, and I love you too."

He gives my leg a final rub. "Knock 'em sideways!"

My shoulders hike skyward as I steer Leita into the makeshift alley. This is the worst moment for him to screw up a phrase. I choose to see it as a good luck charm. Those barrels are going to stick.

The speakers crackle as my name is announced. I tune out the applause and concentrate on the field coming into view. Leita's ears perk forward, assessing the task ahead. One right turn and two left. We've done this in practice but never with a crowd cheering. My horse doesn't seem bothered by the noise. She begins to prance and bobble her head, giving me the signal to turn her loose.

I haven't pushed her through a pattern and don't plan to start now. That's not what this is about. We're just taking a trial run. She's only four. There's still next year to enter the futurity races. But I'm getting ahead of myself.

My grip goes slack on the reins and Leita takes off at a gallop. I decide to let her run, trusting her instincts to set the pace. Wind smacks my face as we approach the first barrel. Leita's stride digs into the dirt, entering at an angle for the pocket. I grip onto the horn and lean into her motions. We whip around in a tight circle that makes this look easy.

Her fluid momentum flies us to the second can. I barely notice the hitch of her changing leads, just a smooth glide in the process. She lunges forward and gains ground quickly. The distance between us and the next turn seems far but her speed is practically eating the sand. My horse sets herself up and curves around the barrel like a seasoned pro. I don't even need to guide her.

We're off to the third in a rush of speed and adrenaline. The pattern is large, but she's making the size seem miniature. Her body wraps the can like a label and I sit deep in the saddle. I'm lurched upright to hover over the seat as we head for home. Leita's hooves pound the turf to the beat of my rapid pulse. Tears leak from my eyes from her swift sprint, along with the memories chasing us. The clock stops when we cross the line and disappear into the alley.

I fold myself over her neck, showering her in appreciation and affection. A thrum fills my veins as I realize what we accomplished. My mare slams on the brakes before hitting the gate. Our job is done.

My body slides off the saddle like a bale of hay. I go limp before my knees crash into the dirt. Emotion floods me in a torrential downpour. Leita stands beside me as a loyal companion. Maybe she understands how important this moment is.

Drake is there is the next second, scooping me into his arms. "Holy shit! That was unbelievable, beauty. Like faster than I could track. You're gonna be the barrel racing champion of the baseball field."

I laugh, but it resembles a sob. "That's not a thing."

"Should be." He tips my face to his with a knuckle

tucked under my chin. "You two are meant to be partners. Totally called it. She ran so hard for you."

My nod is jerky. "I'm so proud of her."

"Good thing you let me swoop in and buy her for you."

A garbled snort dribbles through my emotional turmoil. "To think I almost sold her. We would've missed out."

"But you didn't." His whistle is tinged in awe. "Damn, that was incredible to watch."

"I couldn't have done this without you."

"You could have," he whispers. "But I'm glad you didn't."

"Yeah, trouble. "We're a team."

He squeezes my hip. "Always."

"Mommy!" Kenzie and Charlie crash into my legs. They grip onto me while shouting, "You did it!"

I crouch to cuddle them close. "Were you there watching?"

"Uh-huh," Charlie answers. "You went zipping there and then zapped, zinged, flash, dodge, and zoooooooom!"

"Wow," I breathe.

"That was sooooo super cool. I wanna be you when I grow up." Kenzie hops on the balls of her feet.

"Maybe Leita can be yours someday." I snag a carrot from Drake's pocket and feed the piece to my horse. "She's going to be a champion for many years to come."

My little girl squeals. "Yes! I wanna be a cowgirl and run faaaaaast."

"I'm gonna ride bulls with big balls," my son states proudly.

Drake clears his throat, gaze cast on the ground. "I might've made a poorly timed observation about a certain animal's anatomy."

Paisley is suddenly beside us, passing Leita's reins to my boyfriend. "How about you take her for a walk. She needs to cool off."

"Oh, I don't think—"

But Drake ignores my voice of reason, leading the roan away. The softie sneaks her another carrot before slinging his arm around her neck. If I didn't know better, I'd assume he's been around horses his entire life. Charlie and Kenzie trot to catch up with them. The picture they create burns my nose with too many feels.

"You picked a good one," Paisley comments.

I swipe at my mouth, making sure there's no drool. "Sure did."

"How did it feel?"

I place a hand on my racing heart, a grin stretching wide. "Amazing. Like a new chapter shooting from the gate."

"Great choice of venue." She hitches her thumb at the field.

"Crazy coincidence, right? I saw an advertisement and figured it was meant to be." The shock on the former Mustangs' face sealed the deal on my giddiness. "If I could choose anywhere to start my comeback, this is the place."

"Totally tracks."

"Cassidy Brooks," the announcer cuts in. "Please report to the arena."

I glance at my fellow contestants, noticing nobody else is moving. "Is there an award ceremony?"

Paisley squints at the sky. "Beats me. Better get in there."

"Umm… okay?" My steps falter almost immediately. "Where's my horse?"

"How should I know?" And she doesn't plan to help based on her backtrack to the bleachers. Her elbow clips a man and she's about to apologize until he turns. "What the hell are you doing here?"

"None of your concern," the recognizable grump rasps.

Paisley pokes his chest. "You better not be trying to sell her again."

He knocks her hand off him. "It's not your business, twinkles."

"Don't even go there." She huffs and pushes past him. "If I find out you're trying to get rid of her, you'll have hell to pay."

I'm caught in a stupor from their drama and almost forget I've been summoned. My stride is wary as I creep toward the fence. What I see at the center of the field freezes me on the spot. Drake is standing with Leita as if this is totally normal. My kids are busy sprinkling sunflower petals on the ground.

"What are you doing?" I whisper-shout.

He spreads his arms wide. "Making a scene."

Kenzie and Charlie rush toward me in a fit of giggles. They shove at my back at hurry me along. My boots drag along the ground, kicking up dust. The silence from the stands is deafening.

Drake releases my mare, trusting her to stay. I'm beginning to believe she can do no wrong as her hooves remain firmly planted where requested. Satisfied, my boyfriend's outstretched hand beckons for mine to hold.

"Hey, beauty," he croons while our fingers interlock.

"Trouble," I mumble. "What's going on?"

His sigh is over the top, similar to this strange situation. "This event doesn't give trophies, but I wanted to get you something for crushing such a huge accomplishment."

"You're really sweet and thoughtful, but this isn't necessary."

"Our parents and brothers are here. They're sitting near Auntie June and Paisley." He points to a section in the front row. "The Roosters crew is there too."

"Oh, my." I wave at our friends and family. "The whole gang."

Drake toys with my fingers, tugging lightly. "I wanted them to see your run."

"It's not that big of a deal."

His scoff calls bullshit. "This is huge. A major win. I'm proud of you. Besides, I figured it was time we gathered everyone together to get officially acquainted."

My mouth pinches to one side. "That makes sense, I guess."

"Do you need a better reason to celebrate?"

"Not really."

"Well, I'll give you one anyway." When he gets down on one knee, I just about tip over. "This one is real. I hope you're ready."

My head is bobbing faster than my heart. "Yes."

"Okay, remember you said that." He chuckles. "My beautiful sunflower. Not sure what I did to deserve the way you're smiling at me right now but I'm not gonna question it. How quickly you've become vital to me. Not just as my girlfriend and lover. You're my best friend. The one I want to share everything with. You're the highlight of my day. The last thought of every night and the first each morning. You were my unfinished story but I'm hoping to write the rest together. I'd love nothing more than to spend forever beside you." Drake reveals a velvet box and pops open the lid. "Cassidy Brooks, will you marry me?"

I clap a palm over my mouth to trap a shout. Tears trickle over my hand while I'm nodding wildly again. There are no words while I stare at the brilliant canary diamond that's haloed by aquamarine gemstones.

His eyes sparkle brighter than the yellow solitaire. "Gonna need you to use that answer from earlier."

"Yes!" I squeak. "Yes, yes, yes."

Drake slides the platinum ring on my finger and rises to his feet, gathering me in a hug along the way. "You're gonna be my wife."

I fling my arms around his neck, smiling into our first kiss as an engaged couple. "Love you, fiancé."

He groans, yanking me tighter against him. "Say it again."

"My fiancé," I purr.

"Mommy and Pinkie Pie are in looooooove." Kenzie's hushed voice reminds me of their presence.

Her brother makes smoochy noises. "We get to live in the happiness too. Rake can be our other daddy."

"Uh-huh, and they're gonna put a garden in Mommy's belly."

"I bet there's a baby seed in there already," Charlie squeaks.

I detach myself from Drake, a fire blazing my cheeks. Leita walks toward us and doesn't hesitate to sniff Drake's pockets. Her mane is decorated with flower petals, which explains what distracted the twins. She definitely deserves extra treats tonight.

My concentration sweeps back to the twins. "We're getting married. Isn't that exciting?"

Charlie grins. "I want a brother."

"And a sister," Kenzie adds.

"Both?" I sputter.

Drake scratches at the thick stubble on his jaw. "Might as well aim high and swing for the fences."

"Is that how you get a home run?"

"You tell me."

I plop my cowboy hat on his head, stifling a moan at the fulfillment he represents. "Yep, that'll do."

"Forever?"

"And then some, trouble."

EPiLOGUE

Drake

CASSIDY BRACES HER PALMS ON MY CHEST WHILE *increasing the tempo. I'm mesmerized as her breasts sway from the faster pace. My palms cup her pierced tits, thumbing at the metal stabbed through her nipples. She whimpers when I tug too roughly but shoves herself into my grasp for more.*

Heat builds at the base of my spine when she clenches on the next downward glide. She grinds herself into my imbedded barbell and shudders at the impact. I plunge upward, giving her every inch she's already taking. Cassidy's hips begin to snap forward and back in a measured loop. A spasm clamps her pussy around my dick and I groan at the friction. Warmth rushes through me as she seats herself deep.

"You have the biggest cock. Ohhhhh, Drake. I might split in half from this thick girth. Give me more," she pleads.

"You get everything from me, beauty. Always."

Her eyes sparkle while she bites her lip. "Fuck me like you never want to stop."

A hungry growl rumbles from me. My shaft feels like steel as I hammer into her. But it's not enough. I drift a hand to her ass, using my grip to swerve us closer to the peak. My balls tighten and pressure squeezes me in desperation for release. The harsh slap of our skin joining echoes in the silence. Her nails dig into me, gaining balance and leverage when our mutual desire becomes frenzied.

"Just like that, beauty." Lust clutches me in an unforgiving fist. "Use me for your pleasure."

"Gladly," she purrs.

Cassidy's thighs flex against mine as she bounces astride me. She rises and falls along my length in smooth strokes. I watch my shaft disappear inside of her, slick with arousal. It's a sight burned into memory. This woman is mine. That's my prize penis stretching her wide.

"I didn't enjoy sex until you," she wheezes. "This is incredible. You're the only one who can get me off. Yes, right there! Stuff me to the brim, Drake."

Her command spurs me into action. I buck into her like a champion stallion. Sweat clings to my skin as I race to the finish line. Cassidy's motions become frantic. She thrashes her head, red hair fanning our flames. My cock throbs to the gallop of my pulse. Her lashes flutter shut while she begins to tremble. Mewls spill free from her parted lips and I grunt in return. Just as she's about to tip over the edge, her hooded gaze lowers to captivate mine.

"Pinkie Pie," she whispers.

My brow furrows at the nickname. I frown and pause my manic thrusting. That's not right. I stare at Cassidy but she's beginning to blur around the edges.

"Wake up, Pinkie Pie!"

I gasp and jolt upright. Kenzie is perched on the bed beside me, beaming bright when my startled gaze swings toward her. The dream bleeds away as reality rushes to the surface.

My cock deflates faster than a popped balloon.

Damn, I should've known. Cassidy is vocal but she's still a bit shy when it comes to fondling my ego to the extreme. A hefty exhale releases the strain in my muscles.

"Hey, Mac." I flop backward onto the mattress, flinging an arm over my face. "What time is it?"

Kenzie tugs on my wrist, forcing me to accept the early hour. "The sun is outside. See?"

A glance at the dull light peeking through the curtains suggests it's barely six o'clock. "Huh."

"It's time to open your eyeballs." She bulges hers to comical proportions.

As if rejecting any attempts of refusal, stomping comes from the hallway. The heavy footfalls are paired with banging that's slightly musical. The chimes grow louder and my lingering drowsiness flies out the window.

"Gooooood morning, Rake!" Charlie appears in the doorway with a xylophone.

The plastic mallet strikes the rainbow keys in rapid succession like we're gearing up for a climax. Nope, wrong choice. More like a big event that's family-friendly.

The little boy leaps onto the bed to join us. His notes don't skip a beat. I chuckle and prop myself upright on the stack of pillows. This ritual has become somewhat of a regular occurrence since I moved in months ago. If I'm not in the barn doing chores, these two take it upon themselves to rouse me. Some methods just happen to be more abrupt than others.

"What's on the daily agenda, Mac and Cheese?"

They share a look that I've come to expect. A silent conversation decides my fate. Their giggles might as well be a warning bell.

"Can I give you a makeover?" Kenzie folds her palms beneath her chin, giving me a pleading stare. Her bottom lip even wobbles. "Puh-leeeeease?"

Charlie copies her irresistible dramatics. "And I wanna put stuff on your fingernails."

My gaze slides to Cassidy's empty spot. I can already hear her calling me a softie. "Don't make me regret this."

The little girl scrunches her freckled nose. "Is that a yes?"

I nod and spread my arms. "Do your worst, Mac and Cheese. Maybe I'll get another tattoo out of the deal."

"Yay!"

They scramble as if I'll change my mind, which is impossible. Their delighted squeals follow them into the bathroom while they gather supplies. That's when Chester and Cheeto race into the room. The dogs propel themselves onto the mattress, hitting me straight in the junk. I muffle a shout but my baby making operation is wounded. Maybe the twins will fetch me an ice pack. Better yet, maybe the pair responsible will do the honors.

"Are you good boys?" I croon, which is more of a croak thanks to the damage to my balls.

Chester cocks his head while Cheeto whines. Their tails thump on the blankets.

"Yes, you're listening. Can you go downstairs and open the freezer?" I wait for movement but they stay put. "Use your paws. Go get it!"

That command does the trick. The Australian Shepherds leap off the bed and disappear to fill my request.

"Maybe they do know how to fetch. I never got that confirmed," I mumble absently.

"Who are you talking to, Pinkie Pie?" Kenzie has a large bag in her grip as she reclaims her position next to me.

"The dogs," I reply. But they're nowhere to be seen, which makes too much sense. "They're getting me ice."

"Oh, no!" Charlie's concern scours over me. "Do you have a boo-boo?"

"Yep, it hurts."

"Where?"

"Uhhh, well..." I trail off and tuck the sheet tighter to my hips. "It's difficult to explain. I'll be fine."

The crease between his brows doesn't appear convinced. "Want a band-aid?"

"That probably won't help. The damage is mostly to my... kumquats. They're very sensitive."

He blinks at me. "What's that?"

"A type of fruit. Kinda strange and fuzzy, but high in protein. Serves a purpose."

"You're eating breakfast?"

I scrub at the back of my neck. "No, it's just what I call a certain part of my body."

"Do I have kumquats?"

"Sure do, buddy. Two of them."

Charlie's smile stretches wide. "Wow, that's sooooo cool. Where are they?"

"Ummm..." The consequences of my own actions are mocking me. I've really stepped into a pile of doo-doo. "Next to your banana."

"A banana? I have one of those too?" His voice goes up several octaves.

"Yep, it's a bit of a bundle."

Kenzie stops rummaging in the makeup kit. "Do I have a banana and kumsquats bundle?"

"Kumquats," I laugh. "Nope, Mac. You have more of a… breadbasket situation going on down there."

She frowns. "Why do I have a breadbasket?"

"Where else do the banana loaves go?" I wince and try to rewind this conversation. The hole I'm digging for myself is quite impressive. "I thought you were giving me a makeover?"

Kenzie nods and whips out a small brush. The end is covered in glitter. "Close your eyes."

I gulp. "Are you sure about this?"

She kneels on the mattress, scooting closer. The sparkly demise of my masculinity is aloft in her grip. "Hold still, Pinkie Pie."

Which reminds me of the face painting. This can't be worse than that. I slide my lids shut on a silent wish. A gentle dusting begins the process. Sprinkles rain onto my cheeks. It almost tickles and I chuckle.

"You can't move," she chides. "I don't wanna make a mistake."

When my thumb goes up to confirm my compliance, Charlie immediately yanks the digit down. "Whatcha doing, Cheese?"

"Your nails are colorful," he says.

"Gonna be sooooo prettyful," Kenzie chirps. Her gentle sweeps are arching toward my eyebrows. "Mommy will be surprised."

"Do you think she'll love me extra hard after this?" I regret my choice in phrasing as fragments of Cassidy riding me resurface.

"Yep, this will make her happy."

"Phew," I exhale. "That's my goal in life."

Kenzie's dedication to the task follows the slope of nose. "You're a really good dad."

Charlie hum and lifts my index finger. "Uh-huh, like super cool."

My eyes fling wide, scanning the two kids pampering me. I'm stunned motionless for several seconds. "Are you calling me your dad?"

"Duh, we gots two now. You and Daddy." The little girl smears something on my lips. She doesn't notice that I've gone unnaturally still. "I really like it when you make us laugh. You let me do fun stuff like jump on the bed and eat lotsa candy. I'm happy you're marrying Mommy. Grow me a little sister in the baby garden, m'kay?"

"And a brother," Charlie interjects.

"I'm a good dad." Awe is thick in my voice.

"That's what I said," Kenzie huffs. "Aren't you listening?"

Heat burns in my unblinking stare, too afraid to miss a second. "Every word. Tell me more."

The little boy plops a sticker on my pinky. "I think I love you. Is that otay?"

My throat clogs and I struggle to swallow. Affection wraps me in a suffocating hug. I'm too choked up, seconds from ruining Kenzie's paint job. A jerky nod is what I manage.

"I love you both very much," I whisper eventually.

"Loves you, Daddy Number Two." Kenzie boops my forehead with a glitter bomb.

Charlie snuggles into me while the beautician finishes her task. I glance at the ceiling, allowing this moment to wash over me. There's a comfort spreading through my chest that I've never experienced. Like a bond solidifying. This is home.

The smell of coffee teases my nostrils and I groan. Cassidy's angelic form comes into view. She's carrying two mugs, which momentarily steals my focus. That's the reason I don't realize she's stopped short.

"Ohhhhh, how cute. I might swoon. My knees are actually buckling." She whips out her phone and takes a picture. "You were wrong."

"About what?"

"You *are* trouble for my heart. It's going to burst." She blinks quickly as if fighting her own tears.

"That sounds serious, but let's focus on the caffeine." I beckon her forward.

Cassidy slides onto the edge of the bed, passing me a cup. "Just how you like it."

I inhale the mouthwatering aroma. "My fiancée loves me."

"Extra hard," Kenzie says while coloring my cheeks.

Cassidy chokes on a sip. "What's that now?"

"Nothing." I swallow a mouthful of dark roast and sigh. "Why does coffee taste better when someone else makes it?"

"It's the devotion mixed into the blend."

I tip the mug to my lips. "Delicious."

Her attention lingers on my face. "Very adorable, trouble."

"I'm a good dad," I explain.

She holds her coffee in midair. "They finally told you, huh?"

"We love Rake," Charlie answers.

Kenzie nods. "He's our Daddy Number Two."

Cassidy fans her face, making my emotional outburst look tame. "You accomplished a lot in thirty minutes."

Charlie sits upright. "Guess what? My body's got two kumsquats and a banana."

"And I have a breadbasket," his sister shares.

Their mother squints at me. "Do I want to know?"

My shoulders slump. "You have a breadbasket. I've been holding out on telling you but they dragged the truth out of me."

"Bananas go in baskets," the little boy continues.

"Now we're getting too technical," I chuckle. "Hey, do Australian Shepherds fetch?"

"That's random," Cassidy deadpans.

"Just something I've been wondering."

She gives me a quizzical glance. "Yes, they'll chase balls for hours."

"Squish them too," I mutter.

"His kumsquats are sensitive," Kenzie whispers.

I laugh when my fiancée blanches. "Don't worry. You'll still get protein from those bad boys."

"Yeahhhhh," she utters. "Maybe I should leave you three alone."

"Nope, you're stuck with us." I lunge sideways, cinching an arm around her waist. "This is what you get."

Cassidy laughs and rests her head on my shoulder. "What did I do?"

"You took pity on a lonely man and gave him a family."

"Best. Decision. Ever."

That's technically the end, but are you curious about what's in the secret drawer? I have a bonus scene for you. Maybe there's one or two more as well.

Get them here!

Want more of the Knox Creek crew? Callie and Ridge have their own story to tell in *Score on You*. Enjoy this excerpt from Ridge's point of view.

As it turns out, silence from Calliope Porter is what tests my limits. This timid woman snatches every ounce of composure I possess just by giving me her attention.

The quiet yawns and stretches, then demands a snack after such a lengthy nap. My jaw itches and I scrub at the stubble there. I need to say something. She just stumbled upon me painting her front door. This was her idea. Kind of. But that's not the point. As the trespasser, it's my responsibility to explain myself.

My tongue swells to the point where speech is impossible. Only a muffled grunt is audible from me. *Real fucking eloquent.* I clear my throat and try again.

"Hey, Callie." My palm lifts to wave at her as if that small gesture will ease the tension. "As you can see, I went ahead and took care of the update you suggested. Now you don't have to get your hands dirty. Not that it would be a bad thing if you did. It wasn't my intention to cross a line. I just wanted to handle the project for you. Consider it a housewarming gift. A personal touch from me to you."

That's not grounds for calling the cops or anything. I tuck my chin and fire off a round of foul expletives aimed directly at my mouth. The fact I'm stumbling over my words like a toddler in ice skates isn't doing me any favors. As if agreeing, Callie's lips twitch in what I trick myself into believing is amusement. At least I'm useful for something.

The affirmation—self-proclaimed or not—loosens the strain in my lungs, allowing me to breathe freely. "I meant to have this done before you got home."

A crease appears between her brows. She still doesn't speak, which is a stark contrast to the girl who has been rambling to me over text messages longer than my dick. This timid version can barely look me in the eye. It seems her fondness for conversation is reserved for our text thread. That's just fine. I'm the one who sprung this unannounced visit on her.

"This isn't how I planned for us to officially meet," I rush to explain. "But here we are. I saw you leave and figured the time was right. It was meant to be a surprise. Guess I took longer than necessary to finish."

Callie peers around me to inspect my artistic ability. The hint of a smile from earlier expands into a full grin.

I follow her line of sight to stop myself from gawking. The effort is commendable, but worthless. My focus returns to her within seconds. "Do you like it?"

A soft hum is paired with a nod.

"If the shade isn't right—"

"No!" She startles at her own voice. "It's perfect."

And just like that, I feel ten feet tall and capable of anything. "Good. That's, uh... really good." I scrub at the prickles spreading across the back of my neck. "I'm glad."

"Thank you," Callie murmurs. She dips her face, but there's no hiding the smile that's likely to spark a heatwave. Or the way she bites her bottom lip.

It's no wonder that I find myself staring at her.

Shamelessly. But I quickly recall how our exchange began. Those handful of utterances she gave me are a big step. I won't test my luck.

"Um. Is there anything else I can do for you? While I'm here, I mean?" The initial deed is done, but I'll gladly stick around for more.

Red splotches appear on her cheeks. Before my mind can take a dirty turn trying to picture what's causing that blush, she shakes her head.

I shove my hands in my pockets and prepare to leave. "Well, I did what I came to do. I'll be next door if you need me."

Callie peeks at me from beneath her lowered lashes. "Bye, Ridge."

My foot catches in the grass and I barely keep myself upright. Damn, I've been waiting a long time to hear that. What I've been imagining doesn't come close to the real deal. My name from her lips is a burst of sweetness wrapped in sinful delight. I'm already addicted and thinking of ways to have her call out to me on repeat.

But first, I need to regain control of myself.

Score on You is available now on Amazon.

Be sure to read Garrett and Grace's book—*Yours to Catch*—as well as Harper and Jake's enemies to lovers romance—*Wrong for You*.

And Paisley's book is coming next to start a new series of standalones.

Want more country romance? *Leave Him Loved* is a friends to lovers, small town romance that you'll love. Here's an excerpt from Reeve and Audria to get you in the mood.

"Whoa, easy there."

I spin on my heel at the gritty timbre, feeling like a spooked horse. *Is he trying to soothe me? Make sure I don't trigger a stampede?* Those thoughts vanish as I take my first decent glance at the man.

When I picture a hunk of farm-raised hotness, Scott Eastwood from *The Longest Ride* pops into my brain. This guy couldn't be farther from that stereotype. He's dark and broody without leather chaps or a Western shirt in sight. Broad shoulders, toned muscles, and a trim waist fill my vision. His white T-shirt is tight enough to hint at a set of defined abs. It's no wonder my arm is still vibrating from the impact. Without shame, I admit my mouth waters at the idea of tracing those washboard lines. I would gladly volunteer to scale him faster than a hayloft ladder.

The logo on his hat is familiar. Carhartt has a recognizable enough stamp, even to someone detached from country style. I'm pretty sure their apparel is made with heavy-duty labor in mind. Back home, the brand is popular with the hipster crowd. I have a feeling this guy didn't choose the label to be trendy. Maybe he's more purposeful about his fashion statements than I'm giving him credit for. He makes a ball cap look ultra-sexy, regardless of his purpose. As if hearing my thoughts, his stare bores into me from the shadows under the curled brim.

The chance to offer a polite apology and salvage my manners is vanishing with each stilted breath. I nearly choke on the buckets of sand lodged in my throat. "Shit... I mean, shoot. I'm really sorry. Are you okay?"

Painful silence is all that greets me. It seems the stranger is too busy giving my body a full scan. I shift my weight from the blatant perusal. The need to fidget needles at me. *Is he sizing me up because I'm seriously lacking in the height department?* A tiny nudge from me certainly wouldn't result in serious damage—to his flexing physique or otherwise. To be fair, anyone over six feet makes me look like a shrimp. I wait several seconds for a response, but he remains disturbingly quiet.

Taking the hint, I creep toward a stack of small baskets and prepare to sulk off without causing further injury. "Um, okay then. I'll just be moving along."

He blinks at me, drawing attention to his alluring gaze.

"Wow, are you wearing contacts?" I squint at him like some sort of stage-five creeper.

If possible, his frown dips lower. "No."

"I'm aware that it's super weird for a stranger to randomly ask. Your eyes are just really blue."

"And yours are brown," he deadpans.

Speaking of, I'm not scoring any brownie points with this guy. "Solid observation. Isn't it rare to have light eyes with dark hair?"

"Can I question the same for your blond hair and dark eyes? Unless you use dye."

I gasp, twirling a loose strand around my finger, holding it out for inspection. "This color is natural, thank you very much. And I'm really leaving now. Sorry again for the bang."

There goes the remainder of my dignity. I press my lips together to trap more nonsense from spewing out, futile as it might seem. The damage is already wreaking havoc on my pride.

The man's harsh mask cracks, a slice of amusement twitching his lips. I catch a twinkle in his eyes while that slight humor grows into a crooked grin. My earlier assessment is no longer valid. He isn't the hardcore, surly sort, other than his resting dick face—also known as RDF, for future reference. It's almost a relief to see the expression I came across so often in high school and college. Without having to mutter a word, these guys would receive a wide berth from most. That skill is essential in chasing off unwanted attention, for themselves and others.

A dimple dents his cheek as he graces me with a full smile. The oxygen meant for my brain fizzles into a puff of smoke. As if this fella needs more ammunition to reel in the ladies.

"You're not from here."

I slap on a grin of my own to cover the undeniable scent of lust wafting off me. "Why is that so obvious?"

"Any lifer could sniff you out in an instant," he drawls. "We don't get a lot of visitors in our small section of paradise."

"No?"

"Not that look like you."

I almost recoil. "That's not very gentlemanly. Do you

make a habit of being rude to women in the entryway of the supermarket?"

My word vomit erases any progress I managed to make, not that he doesn't deserve it. But the stranger surprises me with a raspy chuckle.

"Nah, you're proving to be a special case."

"Should I be offended?"

"Not in the slightest, darling. I meant that as a compliment. You're so… shiny."

I glance down at my outfit, noticing an obvious lack of sparkle. "Like a new toy?"

He scrubs a hand over his mouth, hiding a smirk. "Not sure I'm bold enough to cross that line just yet."

"I'm not following."

He smooths a thumb over the bill of his hat. "You have a certain something that we don't see too often. We usually get truckers, farmers, and the occasional business suit eager to make deals. Crops of ladies looking to let loose pass through every now and then, but that's fairly rare."

I drop my gaze, taking a sudden interest in the checkered floor. "Well, all right."

"So, what brings you to Bam?"

"Bam?"

He motions around us. "The great Bampton Valley."

I track his gesture, still regaining my footing after receiving the heat of his focus aiming at me. "It definitely has some luster to enjoy."

"Only some? You wound me, woman." He clutches his chest, showing off the outline of an impressive pec.

"I take it you're a lifer?"

"Born and raised."

"Well." I offer him an outstretched hand. "It's nice to meet you. I'm Audria."

His loud whistle turns more than a few heads. "I should've known the fancy lady has a name to match. Reeve Colton, at your service."

I raise a brow at that. "It's a pleasure."

A low sound rumbles from the depths of him. "I would hope so after you rammed into me."

"Oh, please. It was a light tap at worst."

THANKS SO MUCH!

I'm sending you endless gratitude for choosing to read *Headed for Home*. There are so many incredible books available and the fact you picked mine from the bunch means more than I can describe. You're awesome and I greatly appreciate your support. I'm able to continue following this crazy author dream because of you.

Headed for Home is a book I've been wanting to write for years. I've had horses my whole life and it seems logical that I would include them in my books. It's never been far from my mind, but I struggled with how to tell my first cowgirl story. The grief and challenges Cassidy experienced after losing Pago is from my real life. He was my horse growing up. My champion. My best friend. My everything. Talking about him all these years later still gets me emotional. Leita helps—she's such a good girl and definitely loves her treats. It was also very therapeutic to put a piece of our past in this book. I hope that came across on the pages. There are more cowgirl romances coming soon as well. I've officially entered my cowgirl era. There are more coming soon—beginning with Paisley.

And that's possible thanks to my family. I have such a patient and understanding husband. He's supported me from the start and always encourages me to follow my dreams. My kiddos give me the best inspiration. They provided so much goodness for Kenzie and Charlie. It's the best when I get to include parts of them in my stories.

Major love to Heather, Shain, Renee, Jodie, Allison,

Jackie, and Kate for being there to support me through the thick and thin. To Stacey for the stunning interior formatting. Candi and her team make promo look easy. Alex with Infinite Well is the best editor ever. Keri, Leticia, Bobbie, and Kayla for being such a huge part of my publishing process. To Harloe's Hotties for being the best group ever. To the readers, reviewers, influencers, BookTokers, and Bookstagrammers for everything they do to support us. There are many more who deserve endless gratitude. You know who you are. I'm forever thankful.

And one more thing. If you loved *Headed for Home*—which I'm really hoping you did—I would greatly appreciate it if you could take a moment to leave a review. These are vital and help new readers find my books, which allows me to keep following my passion. You're fabulous!

Cheers to romance, books, and happily ever after.

xx

Harloe

ABOUT THE AUTHOR

Harloe Rae is a *USA Today* & Amazon Top 5 best-selling author. Her passion for writing and reading has taken on a whole new meaning. Each day is an unforgettable adventure.

She's a Minnesota gal with a serious addiction to romance. There's nothing quite like an epic happily ever after. When she's not buried in the writing cave, Harloe can be found hanging with her hubby and kiddos. If the weather permits, she loves being lakeside or out in the country with her horses.

Broody heroes are Harloe's favorite to write. Her romances are swoony and emotional with plenty of heat. All of her books are available on Amazon and Kindle Unlimited.

Stay in the know by subscribing to her newsletter at;
bit.ly/HarloesList

Join her reader group, Harloe's Hotties, at
www.facebook.com/groups/harloehotties

Check out her site at www.harloerae.com

Made in the USA
Columbia, SC
30 November 2024

48036497R00231